Keith Fisher was born in Birmingham in 1940 during the bombing. In 1952, he passed the eleven-plus examination, allowing him to go to a grammar school in Smethwick. Leaving school, he worked in chemical laboratories and did his degree part-time. He has lived in several countries and finally settled in Australia. Many of these stories, although fictitious, come from his childhood memories and stories told by his uncle.

Brummie Lads and Lasses

Keith Fisher

Brummie Lads and Lasses

Vanguard Press

VANGUARD PAPERBACK

© Copyright 2023
Keith Fisher

A CIP catalogue record for this title is
available from the British Library.

ISBN 978 1 83794 001 1

*Vanguard Press is an imprint of
Pegasus Elliot Mackenzie Publishers Ltd.*
www.pegasuspublishers.com

First Published in 2023

**Vanguard Press
Sheraton House Castle Park
Cambridge England**

Printed & Bound in Great Britain

I dedicate this book to my late Uncle Percy who gave me a love of stories and who features in some of the stories.

I wish to acknowledge three friends who have given me support and help with my writings. David Lawrence (England), Midge Dean (Canada) and Tony Homer (US).

Three Ha'Penny Kippers

"Percy, Mom wants you, now!"

Percy kicked the ball towards the opposition goal and ran to the lamp post where his blond-haired sister was standing.

"What does she want?"

"I don't know, she only told me to fetch you, you had better hurry or you will get into trouble."

Percy ran a few yards down the street, ignoring the calls from his mates and turned right into an entry. The entry was a passage way about twenty feet long, wide enough for two people or a pram or a cart, between houses. It entered a cobble stone court yard. In the courtyard, there were six small houses and one outhouse, this was the brew-house containing two toilets and two washrooms. All the houses shared this brew house. Families were not small and each of the houses had large families. These houses were built in Victorian times, none of the occupants owned these houses, they were all rented.

Percy ran past the brew house to the second house, he opened the door and adjusted his eyes to the gloom. He passed through the room into the kitchen. His mother was standing at the sink washing some clothes. She was quite petite and slim but looked much older than her thirty-five years. Percy was the middle child of seven, and although his father had a good job, life was still a struggle. Life was going to get a lot harder soon when Percy's father was called up into the army. Peel Street was a tough street; most houses were rented, and in most households, there was difficulty in paying the rent. These houses had been built because the area had plenty of industry within walking distance. Working men had to find a place to live and the landlords were getting a good living from these houses.

Percy's mother, along with other mothers, had a struggle to keep the children decently clothed and fed. One of the biggest problems was the boys and their ever need for footwear. Most clothes could be handed down but the boys' boots never lasted that long as they were in the habit of kicking anything kickable. Percy's mom supplemented the family income by cleaning two of the 'big' houses in a posh area called City Road. The work was not tiring but the long walk and her own housework was; it was wearing her out. She enlisted the two eldest daughters to help her but Vi, the eldest, was thirteen and would soon be leaving school. Vi would have to try to find a job when she left school and then her help around the house would be much less. Washing clothes and bed sheets for seven children was a monumental task.

Percy thought about how tired his mom looked as he approached her, but of course, he would never make a comment about an adult, particularly his mom. His mother turned and looked down at Percy, who was small for his seven years.

"On the table you'll find three ha'pence, run up to Swindlers on the Dudley Road and get your father a couple of kippers for his tea, don't be long, he will be home soon. Do not take Dot with you; I do not like her going out of this street, now go."

Percy picked up the penny and the half-penny without a word and left the house. He was used to running errands but he regretted missing the football in the street with the lads. He couldn't complain, all his brothers and sisters had jobs to do except the youngest, Dot. She was still watching the football when Percy emerged from the entry. Dot was only four-years-old, and being the baby, everyone loved and protected her, especially Mom. Percy sometimes wished he was the baby but he was not really jealous, after all, she was a girl. Actually, all the girls in his family were good to Percy, he was their favourite.

"Where are you going?" shouted one of his mates.

"I have to get some kippers for mi dad's tea. So, you will have to win without me."

"Can I come?" squealed Dot.

"No, you know that Mom does not let you near the main road or even out of the street. You stay and watch the football, I wish I was playing but I have to run this errand. I will be back as soon as I can but you stay here."

Percy was jogging down his street, Peel Street, towards Winson Green Road. This was the main road from Handsworth to Dudley Road. Peel Street was one of the side streets built before 1900. These streets were populated with back-to-back houses and housed working-class families.

Percy was in a hurry to get back to the game before they decided they had had enough. When he got to the end of the street, he started walking as his boots were pinching his toes. He had no problem while playing football but he had realised that his boots were too small and had stopped wearing socks some time ago. Mom would be terribly upset when he let her know he needed new boots, Percy thought to himself as he turned the corner. The boots were not worn out and could be handed down to Fred, his younger brother, so Percy felt a little bit less guilty. He dreamed of going into a shoe shop and picking out a pair of new shoes but that was an impossible dream. In later life, Percy would suffer the consequences of badly-fitting shoes as he always had corns. Reality was that the tallyman would get an order for 'Daily Mail' shoes that were two sizes too big for Percy's feet and he would "grow into them." These shoes were not free as they would be later; they were cheap as some charities subsidised the cost. All his friends had these shoes and they all grew in and out of them. If in not bad condition, they would be handed down to younger brothers or even sisters.

Percy found that he could run in short bursts but he had to get his breath back on a longer run. Percy finally reached the junction of Winson Green Road and Dudley Road, and on the corner, was Swindlers. He stopped to watch the policeman directing traffic and then turned to face Swindlers's window. Immediately, his eyes settled on the display of sweets. In the middle of the display were gobstoppers and they made Percy's mouth water. The shop had a very good display but the sweets and the gobstoppers, in particular, were the most tempting. Percy could almost feel one in his mouth.

Percy entered the shop and joined a small queue and found himself next to the fish counter. As he looked at the fish, he saw there were some kippers for a penny and some for three ha'pence. The ones for a penny did not look much smaller than the others and Percy started to think he could spend a ha'penny on the gobstoppers. Finally, it was his turn.

"A pair of them penny kippers and a ha'penny worth of them rocks, the gobstoppers, please."

The shop assistant wrapped the kippers in newspaper and put the gobstoppers in a brown bag and handed them to Percy without speaking. Percy turned, opened the door, and once outside, reached into the brown bag and popped a sweet into his mouth. It was delicious and Percy started to jog towards home. He soon finished the first sweet and popped a second one into his mouth; he was in a hurry to enjoy them. Turning the corner into Peel Street, he only had two sweets left, his friend, Sam, joined him and noticed he had something in his mouth. Percy realised he had to share his last sweets with his mate, after all, that is what he would have expected of Sam. They shared the last two sweets on the corner of the street but then Sam put his arm out to stop Percy from walking towards his house.

Sam said, "Do you see any coppers?"

"No, I don't see a copper, why?"

"You should have been with us about ten minutes ago, it was great fun but we were all scared. We was playin' footy and Jeavons, the copper, come around the corner on 'is bike; you should have seen us run. Richards jumped over the fence and caught 'is trousers on the pailins' and ripped a big hole in the leg. Towner fell into the gutter and cut 'is leg open. I smashed mi elbow against the entry wall and the rest of the mob just disappeared. Apparently, old Jeavons just rode down the street ringing 'is bell and laughin'. Richards 'as gone to find 'is sister to sew 'is trousers before 'is mom sees 'em. I decided to get out of the street just in case Jeavons comes back. He could double back from Aberdeen Street so keep an eye out for him."

They looked suspiciously down the street and slowly walked towards their home. "If Jeavons or any copper asks, I went to Swindlers with you, all right?"

"Ye, we go everywhere together, don't we?"

With no sign of the policeman, they were soon joined by friends excitedly talking about their recent excitement. They all agreed that it was fun and luckily someone had picked up the ball and Jeavons was too slow to catch them. There was no traffic in their street and why would the police pinch them if they were caught?

Percy turned into the entry, and without a care, entered his house. He had thrown away the brown paper bag and had devoured the last gobstopper so all was as it should be. As he entered the kitchen, he saw his mom talking to his dad who was seated at the table. His father was not a tall man but he was broad-shouldered and rather stocky. His arms on the table were muscular. He was always smartly-dressed and his moustache was always waxed. Percy and his siblings were in awe of their father. Percy said hello and handed the newspaper-wrapped bundle to his mother. She undid the parcel and held up the kippers.

"These are never three ha'penny kippers, they are too small, did you go to Swindlers as I asked?"

"Yes, Mom," replied Percy shaking in his tight boots.

"You go back to the shop and tell them your dad wants a bigger pair or his money back," his father said in his normally forceful way. Now Percy was really shaking.

Percy watched his mother rewrap the kippers and hand them to him; he was now in a panic. He wanted to spill the truth but he dare not, they probably would not have pity on him and the shame would be more than the beating he expected. He fled the house and ran to the end of the street, turning the corner, he felt weak and sat down by a lamppost. His whole body was heavy, his head was bursting and he was scared stiff. He sat on the curb with his feet in the gutter and leaned against the lamppost. He burst into tears and was oblivious to the traffic. After a short while, he felt a tap on his shoulder, and looked up, to see the imposing figure of Mrs Newbury. He had seen her previously; she was a large plump woman wearing a black dress with a clean white pinafore. She was not tall, but from Percy's vantage point, she looked huge. She had a large grin on her face and that with her snow-white hair made her look like an angel.

"What are you crying for, can't you stand the smell of fish?"

Percy stared up at her and decided to confess everything; she was the closest thing he was going to find to an angel today. After he had tearfully recounted the whole story, she looked at him kindly and said,

"Will you ever be selfish and cheat your parents again?"

"No, never, but what should I do now?" He was dreading the obvious reply that he should go home and confess.

Mrs Newbury reached into her pinafore and pulled out three half pennies and gave them to Percy. "Give me the kippers I will have them for my tea, I bet your father eats more than I do. Never be selfish again, now go and get the bigger kippers, and hurry up, or your mom and dad will think you got lost. Don't tell anyone about our transaction."

"What is a transaction?"

"It is what just happened." He was definitely not going to tell anyone.

Percy felt like he was floating. "Thank you, thank you, thank you, I will never be selfish again."

Percy ran all the way to the shop and the same shop assistant served him the second pair of kippers; she gave him a funny look but did not say a word. Percy could see these kippers were larger and feel they were heavier; he realised what a fool he had been to try and deceive his good mother.

Percy entered the house all hot and sweaty, his red face hid his embarrassment when his mother held up the kippers. Percy was feeling very tired but he was so glad he would not be punished.

"That is more like it, you can go out and play now, Percy." When Percy had left, his father turned to his wife and said,

"You know, Dora, we should be more careful when we send the kids on errands, not all shopkeepers are good and honest, I'm sure they take advantage of the kids."

The Runner

Percy was ten-years-old and approaching his eleventh birthday. His father was at war somewhere in France and his mother was really struggling to pay the rent and keep the seven children fed and clothed. She had to take on more cleaning jobs and some washing from the 'big' houses. She had the help of her two eldest daughters but life was a big struggle and she was scared of getting sick. The news from France was not good, the war was not going to end soon and there was no news of her husband. Several of the women in Peel Street were in the same boat and a few were already widows. They occasionally swapped stories but most did not have time for a chin wag; they were trying to earn money to make ends meet. The landlords had to be a bit lenient with the rent as forcing widows and wives of soldiers out on the street could be very unpopular. The government was aware that the war was becoming more unpopular.

The younger children were oblivious to this and they played, as usual, in the street, football, French cricket or running. When one of the fathers got killed or injured, there was a lot of sympathy but the young children did not dwell on the bad news. Percy's elder sisters were very worried for their father but they tried to keep their feelings hidden from Percy and their younger brothers and sister. Most parents in the neighbourhood were trying to keep the grim facts from their children.

Percy was smaller than most of his mates but he was a fast runner and won most of the races in the street. They tried to organise races with other streets but they always seemed to end in a fight. The races in the street were only short and Percy's skill was to be fast off the mark and he could maintain his speed for about one hundred yards. This quickness also helped his football but was not really needed in French cricket. He also practised running when he had to do errands but found that, after about two hundred yards, he tired quickly.

One day, the local bookmaker was passing the end of Peel Street where the boys were having a race. Of course, bookmaking was illegal, but with a few payments here and there, Gilbert was able to make a decent living. Gilbert watched the boys running in the street and an idea came to him. Why not put on races along the canal opposite the soldier's hospital and get the injured soldiers to put bets on the boys? He watched Percy run and picked him out as a favourite who would earn him good money. Gilbert went home and planned this new venture. During most of the weekdays there were horse races and school, Sunday there was church and Sunday school, so the only time was Saturday morning as there were many horse races in the afternoon. He would pay the boys a few pennies and he needed to get to the patients in the hospital to see if there was any interest. The hospital overlooked the cut and the towpath was ideal for running.

The hospital was part of Winson Green Prison and the wing overlooking the canal, commonly called the cut, was for wounded soldiers. Gilbert got one of his contacts to see if there was any interest in a bit of sport with a wager on a Saturday morning. The soldiers were bored and so the response was an overwhelming yes. These soldiers were gambling at cards and this would be another way to win (or lose) money.

Now Gilbert planned how they would race. He would put smaller boys against bigger boys. Percy was much smaller than the other boys, so most of the money would go on the bigger boys. Gilbert was on to a winner but he couldn't let Percy win all the time. Gilbert had to plan so that he always won.

The first Saturday went very well; Gilbert couldn't lose as he took a percentage of the winnings. Gilbert only allowed Percy to race in four of the ten races and Percy won each race. The soldiers were generally going for the bigger boys and Gilbert did not have to encourage them to bet. They would put their bets in a basket which was lowered down from one of the windows. The winnings would be put in the basket and hoisted to the few winners. In the end, Percy got a sixpence and the other boys got a few pennies but they were all pleased and wanted to come back the following week.

Percy ran home and gave his sixpence to his mother, she was very pleased, gave him a big kiss and one penny back. His elder brother, Sam, was impressed and said Percy was the pride of the family. Sam had a club foot and was no good at any sport but he put his energy into learning; he was always reading and going to the library. Their mother had hopes that Sam could get a job in an office as his teachers were always praising him. The problem was that it would be about two years before he left school and they might be destitute before then.

The Saturday races were a great success, especially for Gilbert; the kids had a bit of pocket money and they were also happy. The soldiers were crowded at the windows, and of course, the winners were happy. The bargees were not as happy as they had to wait when races were taking place. Gilbert said those bargees must tell the 'ossies' not to shit when they walk on our runway.

One Saturday, Percy was not feeling well and tried to tell Gilbert but Gilbert was busy taking bets. Percy lost every race that day and Gilbert was so annoyed he pushed Percy into the cut. Percy had not learned to swim and his mates luckily dragged him from the water before he drowned. Some of the soldiers shouted abuse at Gilbert but he took no notice; he was still winning whether Percy raced or not. One of the bargees shouted abuse at Gilbert but Gilbert was happy with the day's takings.

Percy ran home as best he could, his clothes were soaked and seemed to weigh a ton. When he entered the house, his mother was shocked and Percy mumbled that he had fallen in the cut.

"Take off those wet clothes and go straight to bed. I will bring you a warm drink." Percy had a temperature and was sick in bed for a week. There was no money for a doctor but the neighbours helped with potions and lots of advice. Percy's mother was very worried; she had never lost a child during birth but she was fearful that she was going to lose Percy. Word spread about Gilbert pushing Percy into the cut but the races continued. The pocket money for the boys was a bigger attraction than sympathy for Percy.

Several of the boys who raced were Catholics, and at one of the Sunday schools, they talked about Gilbert and Percy. The caretaker overheard and quizzed them about the races and Percy. This man, Liam, was of Irish descent but born in Birmingham and he looked after the church buildings. Liam was a large man but he was deformed, his whole right side was abnormal. His right leg was much shorter than his left leg; his right arm was shorter than his left arm. This was a birth defect that would not allow him to serve in the army. He was a powerful man and had always been much larger than others in his age group. He was disappointed the army would not take him and he had tried to enlist several times. At school, the nuns had allowed him to write with his left hand and that had endeared him to the church. He hated bullies and gambling; the tale of Percy and Gilbert made him angry. He had to see these races for himself and identify Gilbert. Saturday was his free day and the boys had told him the time when the races started.

Liam took a stroll one Saturday morning and observed the races. He identified Gilbert and saw one or two boys he knew from Sunday school. On the way home, he strolled down Peel Street and casually asked one of the boys about Percy.

"Percy's sick, sir, but 'is mom se's 'e's on the mend."

"By the goodness of god, he will be playing football with you soon."

The children looked at Liam and said, thank you, and carried on with their game. Liam then went back to the bridge over the cut and waited to see where Gilbert went after the races. Gilbert went home as there were horse races in the afternoon and he had to collect the bets. Liam started following Gilbert and found that, after a 'day's work', he would have a few drinks in a pub on Winson Green Road. Liam was planning to get even for Percy, who he had never met. Gilbert was a man making money illegally and nearly drowning a boy for losing races, now Liam was really angry. Liam had a plan, and the more he thought about it, the sooner he wanted to carry it out.

Percy was finally getting better but his mother would not let him out to play in the street. He was able to do a few light chores around the house but had to spend many hours in bed; at least he did not have to go to school. Sam would take time to read to Percy while he had to stay in bed but he was itching to get out in the street. The races were going on without Percy and Gilbert was still making money. The meagre pocket money was keeping the boys interested and more boys were coming so there could be more races.

One Saturday night as Gilbert was going home after a few pints in the pub, he was dragged into a dark entry. Two blows to the face and Gilbert was knocked out and sank to the floor. After a while, he came around to find a large woman standing over him. He blinked a couple of times, he was not sure where he was lying on the ground.

"Are you all right, should I call the coppers?"

"No, I will get this settled." Gilbert was still in a daze.

Gilbert found he had been relieved of the day's takings and that upset him most. He had a bleeding nose, possibly broken, and a black eye but the money was gone! He staggered home and vowed he would get the bugger that had stolen his money. This had never happened to him before and he had to think out a plan of action. He would find a 'friend' in the local police and pay him to find the culprit.

Just one policeman, nicknamed the 'bulge' due to his large belly, came around the area asking questions. No children were involved as the assailant was described as a large man. Most of the men not in the army were either at home or one or two were in the pub. It was looking like a disgruntled punter but most of the ones Gilbert knew had alibis. Liam was deformed so he was overlooked, anyway, he did not bet. Gilbert kept asking himself why Saturday night, someone must know that this was the time when Gilbert took the most money The bulge seemed to become Gilbert's shadow and the gossip in the area even got to the police station on Dudley Road. Gilbert gave out a few 'favours' and nothing was said about his protection.

The following Sunday, the collection plate at the Catholic Church was a little larger than normal. Liam passed the plate around but said nothing about the generous donor. After a few days when the bulge had relaxed his enquiries, an envelope was deposited on the doorstep of Percy's house. His mother opened the door and found an envelope addressed to Percy with the words 'get well soon'. She opened the envelope to find five pounds in ten-shilling notes. This would pay off their debts, but should she tell Percy? She decided that she would keep this a secret from everyone, her children, the neighbours, and particularly, Percy. She would pay off the debts very slowly so as not to arouse suspicion, and suddenly, she was happy if only temporarily. The children suddenly noticed their mother was singing again as she used to before their father went to war; they wondered whether he was coming home. Their dad did not arrive, and a few months later, they found out he had been killed in Belgium. None of them really knew where Belgium was but it had entered their vocabulary in a bad way. The two eldest sisters were often seen crying but no one saw their mother cry.

Liam wandered past the cut one Saturday morning to find the races on and the bulge was overseeing the proceedings. Percy never ran along the cut again, and although he missed the sixpences, he decided he must learn to swim before he went down to the cut again. His mother had made it very plain that any more 'swimming' in the cut was either going to result in his death or a long stretch in Dudley Road Hospital.

Jostling 1921

At fourteen years of age, Percy left Dudley Road School in Birmingham. Percy's dad had died in the Great War, and being the middle child of seven, the challenge was to find a job. Johnny, his friend, was smaller and lighter than Percy and he had been offered a job training to be a jockey in France. Johnny's mother had said, no, to that possibility; she believed there could be another war and Johnny would be stranded in France. Percy loved football but there was no future in that so Percy decided to work in a factory. Sport was a good pastime but the family needed money. His eldest sister had just gotten married and started her own life; the loss of her wages was a real blow to the family. Mother and six kids had to pay the rent and eat, the war pension was still not available and the family was constantly in debt. Percy looked at his mother; she was looking old and haggard, and 'we won the war,' thought Percy.

"What are you going to do, Alf?" enquired Percy on meeting his friend in the street.

"Mi uncle has got me a job in a bakery, cleaning out the stables. If I work 'ard I might get out on a delivery round in a year or two. Mi uncle ses the wages are not good to start but there could be some overtime if I work on Sundays. That sounds good to me as I hate Sunday church and Sunday School."

"Does your uncle deliver to the nobs on City Road and in Warley?"

"Yes, he tells me some of them 'ouses 'as two loaves a day, and on Saturdays, they 'as three." The thought of two loaves a day was a dream to Percy and Alf. Percy's mom was always complaining the loaves were getting smaller. Bread was a staple of their diet, and with seven, a loaf did not last long.

Johnny joined them as they strolled aimlessly down the street; they could have been brothers wearing similar rough but not ragged clothes. They all had elder sisters so holes in trousers and shirts were mended but not invisibly. Johnny was the only one wearing socks that day but they all wore the same boots; ill-fitting but durable. These were the 'Daily Mail' boots brought on the 'never-never.' The boys were not old enough to have facial hair but they all had cropped hair, 'short back and sides' was the order of the day generally provided by mom or an elder sister. If you asked them what they wanted besides money, they would probably all have said a moustache waxed at the ends. They all wanted to look like toffs. A neat suit and tie and possibly gaiters would be a suitable dream so they could stroll around getting admiring glances from all and sundry. A motorbike or car would be too much of a dream, even a bicycle would be a real luxury.

'Are you going to France?' Percy asked Johnny. France is where their fathers had died but there was no animosity towards the country.

"I don't think so, mi mom ses there could be another war and she don't want me killed like mi dad. Anyway, she ses them Frenchies can't be trusted and I might get stuck wiv no money so 'ow would I get back?" They all agreed that was a problem, but none of them knew how to get to France, let alone how to get back. They only had a vague idea about France, Belgium and Germany and even knew very little about England.

"Anyway, I 'ave an interview at the Grand 'otel, they's looking for a page boy and mi uncle knows one of the chefs. I will 'ave to live in but I will get four days off a month and they find all mi food and clothes. I 'ope they ave better food than what mi mom cooks."

Percy was in a quandary. "Who do I know who could help me, everyone gets a job through their relatives? I don't know any of mi uncles well enough and mom's family live in Manchester."

"We'll look out for ya when we get our jobs," answered Alf with Johnny nodding in agreement. A week later, Percy's eldest sister, Gwen, visited the house and imparted some important news. Her husband, Bill, was working in a brass factory and he heard through the foreman that there might be a job for a young boy in the near-future. Bill, being a hard worker, was a favourite of Joe, the foreman, and he was told that this news was

29

confidential. When word got out there would be a flood of applicants.

The next day, Percy was outside the factory gates at dawn even though work did not start till much later. The gatekeeper eyed him suspiciously but said nothing. Bill arrived just before seven and greeted Percy; he promised to let the foreman know about his brother-in-law. As Bill clocked in, Percy noticed the time, he knew nothing would happen till after eight o'clock when the manager arrived. Percy was tired but decided not to sit on the curb as the manager might see him and think he was lazy. The gateman was continually watching Percy and might report to the manager.

Just before eight o'clock, a tall man in a grey suit with a stiff white collar and tie turned the corner. This must be the manager, Percy thought, as he stiffened and moved away from the wall. No one in this area wears a bowler hat and carries an umbrella. The man moved purposefully towards the gate and strode past the gatekeeper with a curt nod. Percy relaxed but it was over a half-hour before a thick-set man with a waxed moustache approached Percy.

"Are you Percy?" The man's voice was thick and strong with an Irish accent.

"Yes, sir," Percy responded weakly.

"I am Joe, where does your father work?"

"Mi father is dead, sir, but before he went in the army, he was a foreman tool maker."

"Die in France, did he?"

"Yes, at Wypers, he was a sergeant major."

"Poor bugger," Joe said under his breath.

"Pardon, sir." Percy was on his best behaviour and it was a strain but he had to make a good impression. He was intimidated by this man but did not want to show it.

"Never mind, just go up those stairs and see the manager's secretary and tell him I sent you."

Joe led Percy through the gate, past a scowling gateman and directed Percy to a set of stairs. Percy thanked Joe for his help and then climbed the rickety stairs two at a time. Entering the office, after knocking, he was slightly taken aback.

"Are you the secretary?" he enquired in a halting voice.

"Yes, we don't employ women in this factory," said the man behind the desk.

"The foreman sent me to see the manager."

"Sit down, he will see you in a while," the secretary said curtly.

Percy sat down in a comfortable chair that had a cushion on the seat; he was glad to rest his legs. The while became half-an-hour and Percy was fighting drowsiness, then the office door opened and the manager beckoned Percy, ushering him into a large office. The manager sat in a large leather chair and Percy stood on the other side of the biggest desk Percy had ever seen. Percy had only seen teachers' desks at school and they were tiny compared with this one.

"We are expecting a lot of work in the near future and we need a boy to do a lot of fetching and carrying, do you read and write?"

"Yes, sir, I just left Dudley Road School." Percy thought the manager looked like a headmaster and Percy had just realised that the words fetchin' and carryin' had a 'g' on the end.

"Well, write a letter of application, putting your name and address and the name of your teacher and we will contact you in about one week."

"Yes, sir, thank you, sir," Percy said as the manager waved him out of the office.

Percy did as asked and cheerfully said goodbye to the secretary as he left the office. He felt elated as he descended the metal stairs and he looked longingly into the gloomy factory. He couldn't see Bill or Joe but he felt compelled to wave anyway. The gateman watched him intently and grunted as Percy said good morning. The next morning and for the next three days, Percy was standing outside the factory gate before seven a.m. and left after nine a.m. The manager saw him each day but said nothing until, on the fourth day, when the gateman called Percy.

"The manager wants to see you." Percy bounded up the steps but slowed as he reached the office door; his instincts were telling him to calm down and make a slow entry to give a good impression. As he entered the office, the manager was standing near the secretary and he had a stern look.

"I thought I told you we would contact you in about a week".

"Yes, sir, but I was just practising so that I would not be late when I started work." Percy was not exactly telling the truth but he thought his explanation sounded good.

"Well, I like your perseverance; you can start work on Monday."

"Yes, sir, thank you, sir," said Percy beaming from ear to ear. He wanted to thank Bill and Joe before he left the factory but he could see neither as he descended the stairs. Percy smiled at the gateman as he left the factory but only got a scowl in response. He ran all the way home and told his mother the good news.

'How much will you get each week?"

"I forgot to ask."

His mother smiled, it was a relief to have another breadwinner in the family; they owed money in the local shops and she was still fighting for a widow's pension. The rent was constantly in arrears, and although the landlord understood, the strain was taking a toll on her health. Like many widows, she was angry at the treatment she received from the war office but felt helpless in her bid for a pension. She was not alone in her despair.

Percy found his first week at work tiring although the work was light, mainly sweeping up scraps from around the machines. Constant standing made his legs ache but receiving seven shillings wages on Friday was the best thing that ever happened. He ran all the way home to put six shillings on the table for his mother who kissed him and quietly shed a tear. He gave a penny each to his two younger brothers and a penny to Dot, the youngest. The nine pence remaining he put in a small tin box which he placed under his pillow. He decided he would save all his money although he was tempted to buy some sweets. He told himself that being a working man meant that he had to give up childish things like sweets. Percy daydreamed about what he could buy after a few weeks but he kept changing his mind.

Several weeks went by, and one Sunday morning, he met Alf and Johnny and they decided to walk to the park at Warley. They were all working men, and now they had a few pennies in their pockets, they felt rich. As they started to walk, they chatted about work.

"I'm fed up, each day I shovel 'oss muck and clean the stables of them stinking 'osses and the next morning it is as filthy as the day before. I shall be glad when I get out delivering bread. The stink in them stables makes me feel sick. Oh, I did get a ride on the cart the other day, and as we passed Northbrook Street, there was a long queue. I asked a bloke what they were queuing for and he said, whisky. 'E said he would queue but couldn't afford scotch. Theys were all dressed well and many of them was women," said Alf.

"Mi job is easier except I 'ave to carry 'eavy bags but sometimes the toffs tip me, one gave me a tanner! The food is good and the best is when the pastry chef gives me broken cakes. He makes the most delicious cakes but I 'ave seen 'im put coal on the stove and then carry on making pastry, he tells me it all adds to the flavour. The worst is mi bed, the 'oss air' mattress is so thin I might as well sleep on the board. The only other problem is that if I grow taller, I will lose mi job," said Johnny sadly. "We had a Lord stay the other day, you should 'ave seen 'is shoes. I had to take them to get polished."

"Well, all I do is sweep the floor but I am learning a few things in the factory and mi foreman is a real gentleman. I am going to 'ave 'is job one day," said Percy in a matter-of-fact way.

Suddenly, they were confronted by a tall man in a bowler hat. He towered over them and said in a deep voice, "What do you three think you are doing?"

"We are going to Warley," said Alf.

"You are 'creatin' a disturbance in this residential area and I am charging you with jostling, that is a breach of the peace and I am a police officer."

They were all dumb-struck and each looked at the other.

"You are walking three abreast and causin' a disturbance in this respectable neighbourhood. I want your names and addresses."

They all looked at each other and wanted to run but to where? The policeman, seeing their intention, moved closer and pointed out a man standing across the street.

"You see that man over there, he is also a policeman and if you run away we will catch you and the charge will be resistin' arrest."

35

Meekly, they all gave their names and addresses and were ordered to go home by the policeman. Single file, they ran almost the whole way home and it was not until they reached their street did they stop and consider what happened.

"I don't think 'e was a cop," said Alf and the other two agreed and hoped they were correct

He was a policeman and they found out when, a couple of weeks later, they all received a summons.

Percy was almost hysterical when his mother told him that a man had brought a summons and he had to attend court in two days. Percy explained to his mother and she was sympathetic but what was he to do about work? His mother said the only course was to tell the foreman, Joe, and maybe he would be sympathetic; the police these days were not the poor man's friend. His mother muttered something about class but Percy did not understand. Percy talked to Alf and found he had a similar summons. Alf could lose a day's pay or work on a Sunday for no overtime. As Jonny was always at the hotel, they assumed he also had a summons.

It was about eleven o'clock the next morning when he approached the foreman, his heart in his mouth. Percy had practised what to say but all the niceties were lost as he said,

"Sir, tomorrow, I have a problem; I need a couple of hours off work to go to court."

"Are you in trouble?"

"Yes, I have been summonsed for jostlin' on the City Road."

As Percy explained the problem to Joe, his only thought was that he would get the sack. He heard Joe mutter something under his breath but couldn't make out what he said.

"You go to court and get back here as soon as possible, and if the gateman asks, say I sent you on an errand and I told you last night; it is not worth his job to question my orders," said Joe nodding his head in satisfaction.

Percy was stunned; he could hardly believe his ears and watched open-mouthed as Joe walked away mumbling to himself.

The next day, Percy found himself in court with at least twenty other boys on similar charges. Finally, he was called before the magistrate and stood petrified.

"What are you charged with boy?"

"Jostlin', sir" said Percy almost inaudibly.

"Are you guilty?"

"Yes, sir."

"Fined five shillings, pay the clerk of the court on the way out, next case," the magistrate said in a firm tone.

Percy approached the clerk who was sitting outside the chamber at an old desk.

"What is your name and how much is your fine?" the clerk said in a disinterested way. Percy told him the amount and produced a brown paper bag. Percy tipped up the bag and out flowed almost his whole savings in pennies and half-pennies.

The clerk was dismayed. "You might have left them in the bag, you have made a mess of my desk and now I have to count all these bloody coins."

After counting the money, it was found that there was a penny too much that the clerk gave back to Percy begrudgingly.

Percy ran all the way to work and arrived at ten-thirty. He explained to the gateman that the foreman had sent him on an errand and the gateman looked disapprovingly as he let Percy into the factory. Percy found Joe setting up a lathe and waited till he was finished.

"I am back, sir," said Percy expecting to be in trouble for taking three hours off work.

"How much was the fine and were the plain-clothes dicks in court?"

"Five shillings and I did not see the policemen who arrested us in court."

"No, those slaves of the Warlords don't even have to give evidence; it is all cut and dried, disturbing the peace in a posh area," Joe bitterly spit out the words. Joe was breathing deeply and had a wild look on his face; Percy was a little scared.

"Who was the magistrate?"

"I think his name was Mr Law."

"Fine name for a legal thief; robbing kids and poor widows. We should have killed them off after the war, all the sods called the ruling classes. Never mind, you will get your five shillings back, I will book you plenty of overtime in the next few weeks. They rob us and we rob them."

Alf had a similar experience in court and was fined five shillings. They had all gone to court on consecutive days but Johnny had a slightly different experience.

"The boy in front of me pleaded not guilty and said it was a trumped-up charge with no legal standing. He said, where are the witnesses? The magistrate found him guilty and charged him ten shillings; he said he would not pay so the magistrate said he would go to jail for a week for jostlin' and contempt of court. He screamed and shouted as they took him down to the cells and then I was up next. The magistrate had a grin on his face but he only fined me three shillings and said I should stay out of trouble."

Percy said Joe had called Mr Law a legal thief and they all had a good laugh although they all admitted they never wanted to see his face again.

Teenage Percy

Percy had a job, albeit a dangerous one, catching red hot wire and fixing the wire to a capstan. Percy was agile and very quick to move. One of the workers noticed this ability and asked Percy if he was interested in playing football on the weekend. Percy was very interested; he had previously thought about trying out for West Bromwich Albion or Aston Villa but had been persuaded that he had a steady job and football was not a stable occupation. In the early 20s, footballers were earning more than the average worker but there was no security in their job. His brother-in-law was a very stable influence on Percy; he had helped Percy get his job and was a very good husband to Percy's sister. His advice had kept Percy from an adventure in football. One or two of Percy's close friends had been given trials but none of them had been offered contracts.

Percy's football team was in the Birmingham Works Football Association. Most of the players were ordinary working men but some of the bigger companies hired ex-professional footballers to help their teams. Percy's company did not have such ex-pros but they did well in one of the lower divisions. Once recruited, Percy showed his potential; from a standing start he could beat almost anyone for speed but he was small and light. The coach, Joe, who was the foreman, liked Percy and did not want him to get hurt; his instructions were to pass to one of his teammates as soon as he could. This league was rough but Percy was good; he helped the team win a few games and he was becoming very popular with his teammates. After a few games, they had a cup game and were pitted against a team from division one. This was a team from Dunlop and contained several old pros. Joe warned the team that their opponents may be older (and fatter) but they had the skill and they would not hold back in challenges. Joe was fearful for Percy as he was the smallest and might be singled out for rough treatment. Percy was full of enthusiasm, and the first chance he got, he tried to beat the fullback. Percy found himself flying through the air and landing on his back, well away from the ball. The fullback had hit Percy with his hip and propelled Percy into space. Percy then learned to release the ball very quickly after that episode. After the game which Percy's team lost, several of the opposing players came to Percy and shook his hand. One of the older pros said Percy had what it takes but a couple more stones in weight would help.

Joe was very pleased and so glad Percy had not been injured. Joe said he knew of a team looking for a player to play on Sunday mornings, and as the standard would be lower than the works team, it might be good for Percy.

Joe took Percy to a park on a Sunday morning and introduced him to a new team. Most of the team were Irish from the Irish Free State and most of them lived in the

Hockley area. Percy knew a few Catholics but most of his friends were English and these boys were different. With Joe's encouragement, he mingled with them and found them to be soft-spoken with a kind of sing-song accent. They welcomed him and Joe had told them he would be an asset to the team. Percy enjoyed playing with these boys and learnt a lot about Ireland. Percy had avoided politics with his mother but he listened to his new teammates.

They were plumbers. carpenters, electricians and labourers but they all seemed to treat each other equally. Playing with this team was the first time he saw different parts of Birmingham. The works teams played on their own grounds but this team played in parks. The facilities in the parks were very spartan but the opposing teams got to know each other before the game. A few of the opposing team members asked Percy why he was playing with these Irish lads but Percy's answer that they were a nice bunch seemed to satisfy them. The bigger problem was to answer some of the older men who called them Paddy's and worse names; at these times Joe was his saviour.

Percy was now walking on a Friday evening proudly down Peel Street with his pay packet unopened. He presented it to his mother who gave him his pocket money. Percy was proud that he never gambled or drank lots of beer. He was used to seeing men playing cards on a Friday afternoon and losing half their wages. He was also used to seeing men staggering out of the pubs on Peel Street or on Winson Green Road, probably having spent half the house-keeping money. Most of his friends in the street had jobs but a few were out of work. Percy was always on the lookout for work for some of his unemployed friends. Percy went to the cinema occasionally but he was not yet into dancing. Although he had sisters, he was a bit shy around girls and would rather look than touch or speak.

Percy loved to ride the trams and would spend a lot of his spare time visiting parts of Birmingham he had not seen before. There was a good tram service in Birmingham and he was using it to the full extent. Bill, his brother-in-law, warned him about certain areas of Birmingham that had gangs. Some of these gangs they called razor gangs; race tracks were to be avoided as well as the dogs at Perry Barr. Being small for his age, Percy sort of 'passed under the radar'. The place he liked best was the Lickey Hills, where he could get off the tram and walk straight into the open fields and hills. Percy loved the countryside, and later when he was married, spent many weekends in the country at Arley and Bewdley.

The games with the Irish boys were enjoyable and they won most of the matches they played. One Sunday afternoon, he decided to invite some of his team mates for tea. He forewarned his mother but did not tell her they were Catholic Irish. Percy's mother was a bit taken aback when four Irish boys came through her front door. They were very polite and each one wished her well, one even kissed her hand. She made the tea but would not sit at the table with them. Her attitude changed when one of the lads said,

"Percy's mom, that roll of wallpaper is upside down."

Percy's mother had come into a bit of money; source unknown, and decided to spend a little on a few rolls of wallpaper to go around the fireplace. Each time she looked at the wallpaper she had pleasure in thinking she had spent a bit of money on a 'luxury'. She had looked at that paper a thousand times and not seen what this lad had seen immediately. The lad pointed out the subtle difference in the two adjoining rolls and now she was seeing it anew. She was not upset, in fact, she was laughing louder than Percy had ever heard her laugh. The lad pointed out that he had been a painter and decorator in Ireland but he had to settle for a labourer's job here in England. Dora wished them all well when they left and invited them to come to tea at any time. When Percy came back to the house, his mother was staring at the wall for a long time, she was so happy. Percy couldn't see the difference and couldn't understand his mother's joy but was glad the tea went well.

At home, they did not have a radio but at, work in the manager's office, there was a radio and occasionally they put the radio on the speaker system. The manager was a sports fan and he particularly loved athletics. The 1924 Olympic Games were in France and the BBC was broadcasting the men's races. The factory came to a standstill when Harold Abrahams won the one hundred metres and Eric Liddell won the four hundred metres and then, to top it all, Douglas Lowe won the eight hundred metres. The manager was ecstatic and ordered a barrel of beer for the Friday, after work. Many of the men came to Percy to suggest he try running instead of football but he remembered being pushed into the cut and decided to stay with football. Percy did enjoy a beer on that Friday and was excited about the radio broadcasts. He told his mother they should get a radio but she came out with a list of other more pressing items. Percy decided he would save his money for a radio.

Life around Peel Street was fairly peaceful except when two women took exception to each other. The men were less in number and were generally quieter except when thrown out of the pubs. There was the occasional party or wedding but no one had much money to spend. The friends Percy's age would gather for a chat and a walk to Summerfield Park to have an impromptu kick around but very few liked to ride the trams like Percy. Percy found that his friends were either getting married or moving away from the street. Percy often visited his married sisters who all lived within walking distance but Percy had decided to stay with his mother while she needed him. The landlord of the Sir Robert Peel pub had acquired a radio and Percy would often go to that pub to listen to the radio. He would only drink one or two pints but he would ignore all the conversations and other antics going on and concentrate on the radio. He was saving all his extra cash, which was not much, to buy a radio.

One Sunday after the game with the Irish boys, the captain told Percy not to come to the next game. Percy asked why and was told that they were playing a team of Northern Irish boys and it could get a bit nasty. Percy couldn't understand why there was a problem and asked

45

Joe. Joe smiled as he told Percy a shortened history of Ireland and explained that the Northern Irish boys were Protestants and that religion was serious business in Ireland. Percy was not religious and his mother had not forced him to go to church or Sunday school so did not know the differences in Christianity. He still couldn't really understand why there should be such animosity but Joe was the coach so he had to stay away. As it turned out, the match was abandoned due to an all-in brawl. Joe said he was very glad Percy had not been present as he could have gotten hurt. Joe was very protective of Percy and treated him like a son; a well-loved son.

During one of the works games, Percy was tackled and he heard a crack. He was not the only one who heard the crack. Joe came running over and told Percy not to move. Percy was in a bit of pain but wanted to resume the game. Joe broke the bad news that Percy's leg was broken. An ambulance arrived and Percy was whisked off to Dudley Road Hospital where they set his leg in a huge plaster of Paris cast. Joe had procured a crutch and escorted Percy home. It was not far but it seemed to take forever. Percy's mom was very upset when she saw her poor son (and only breadwinner) come home in such a state. Joe was reassuring and told her the company would find him an easy job while he was in the cast; the only problem was he would not be able to walk to work and so Joe would try to arrange transport.

The first morning, a company lorry came to pick Percy up. It seemed most of the street came out to see the event. There were comments like, 'chauffeured to work; you must be a manager.' Percy was given a job on a pressing machine and he could sit down nearly all day. Actually, he found the job repetitive and boring. After the cast was removed, Percy found that he was not so light on his feet and couldn't go back to catching hot wire so he moved around the factory learning new jobs. He acquainted himself with all the machinery and loved the lathes.

Percy's brother-in-law came to Percy one day and said, "That broken leg may have saved your life, the hot wire was probably going to get you one day. I am sure your sister would have blamed me."

An Older Percy

Percy had joined the workforce at an early age, with little education. His first job was sweeping the floor of a brass factory earning a small wage, most of which, he gave to his mother. She was a war widow with lots of children to feed, house and clothe. She was not alone; there were many of her kind struggling to survive the aftermath of World War One. Percy always thought that his father had been called up, but later in life, he found out that his father had volunteered. At that time, his father was earning good money; three gold sovereigns a week as a fitter in a factory. His wife had pleaded with him to not go into the army but this was the time of the white feather and he was loath to be called a coward. Percy hardly knew his father (although, like all his siblings, Percy was in awe of him) and the only information he received was from his mother and his eldest sister. His eldest sister, Gwen, had only good words to say about their father but his mom never said anything bad but was not full of praise for her husband. Percy's mom was bitter about her husband's 'desertion' and often discussed it with other women. There were many other lonely widows in the area with similar feelings. They were all poor with no husbands and no prospects of getting out of their situation.

Peel Street was a meeting place for the widows, the married women, the children and the teenagers. The men generally met in the pubs; the Sir Robert Peel or the Oak and some went to the Queens Arms in Aberdeen Street. The younger children and the teenagers of Peel Street and Aberdeen Street did not seem to 'get along' but the men mixed well. Of course, there were occasional fights but nothing serious. Percy's job took him away from Peel Street many hours of the day, and when he was home, he spent most time in the house helping his mom do housework. He was growing away from his friends in the street.

Percy interacted well with the factory workers and Joe, the foreman, kept an interested eye on him. Percy moved from sweeping up the factory floor to handling red hot brass wire. This was a job that needed an agile person to grab the wire as it came out of the die and direct it to a capstan. Percy was small but very agile and he had to be as this was a dangerous job. He had long plyers and thick gloves but the only way to control the extruded wire was to catch it with his gloves and quickly transfer it to the plyers. The foreman had noted how quick Percy was on his feet and had promoted him to the job. Percy's brother-in-law had warned Percy that this was a dangerous job but that did not deter Percy. His mother had commented to Gwen that Percy was his father's son; Gwen was of a similar opinion but it was a worry.

Percy's mother was always talking about the war and her hardship because of his father's death. Percy never really understood his mother angst; they had won the war, he had a job and his wages were contributing to his family's well-being. Many women were in his mother's 'shoes', and if they had united, they could have brought down the class system that had led them into a war without winners. The war had been won but at a terrible cost and it seemed the poor were poorer and many widows were forced to live together to afford to live. As it was, the country was short of men and Percy benefitted from that shortage. His job was safe as long as he did not get injured doing it. The demand for brass had not slowed after the war and the company he worked for was doing very well. Industry in the whole of Birmingham picked up and the city was starting to boom again.

Most of his siblings had left home and that left only Dot, Percy and his mom in the house. Life was a little easier and Percy's wages could cover the rent and food but with not much left over for Percy to spend on himself. He loved Peel Street but all his friends were getting married and moving away. His mother was the rock in his life but she could be cantankerous; she always wanted the government to do almost exactly the opposite of what they had done. Percy realised that he was more conservative than his mom, who was almost a Communist. She wanted to get rid of the Monarchy and have the people run the country. One of the workers explained Communism to Percy. He decided that political arguments with his mom were futile and he tried to avoid any topic that would excite her. He was taken aback when a letter came from the War

50

Office stating that his father's grave was in Belgium and would Mrs Moore like to visit the grave and add a memorial. Her reply was no! On the subject of the war and her husband, she was a bitter woman. Percy would have loved to go and he hoped that, one day, he would like to see that grave, and much later in life, he did.

Percy was starting to earn more money and he decided to treat himself to a new suit. He had never had a suit or even a decent pair of shoes so he started saving. He did not tell his mother because she would have found some needier item to buy. After a while, he decided he also needed a shirt and tie so he had to wait a little longer. Finally, he went to a tailor in the city and purchased his whole outfit. Due to Percy's small stature, the suit and shirt were made to measure. Arriving home in his new outfit, he was expecting some kind of praise but his mother was angry.

"Why do you need to dress like a dandy; you've wasted money that could have been better spent. How much did that finery cost? Don't tell me, I will only get angry!"

Luckily, Gwen was visiting and she said he looked handsome and the girls would surely look at him. Gwen was the ideal sister. His mother hardly spoke to him in the next few weeks, and when he wore his suit, she would grunt something Percy couldn't understand.

A hard life finally caught up with Percy's mom and all her children attended the funeral; she had wanted to be cremated but all her children had denied her that last escape. The whole street turned out for the funeral procession; her political and social views were in line with many Peel Street residents and someone was waving a red flag. The family had her buried in Warley Cemetery and they all gathered in the Sir Robert Peel for the wake. Percy felt there was a little tension but he put it down to the funeral.

Dot was now courting and so Percy found Violet. Violet lived near Black Patch Park and was often on Winson Green Road where Percy met her. They had a short courtship and were wed just before Percy's mom died. Percy had planned to find somewhere to rent as his mother could be very abrasive and he was not sure how Violet would take to living with her mother-in-law.

The days after the funeral were a little bit trying for Percy; family harmony was shattered. Sammy, Percy's elder brother, claimed the house in Peel Street and Percy had to quickly find a place to live, quicker than he had expected. He found a two bedroomed house to rent and to welcome his new bride. Percy never lost contact with his siblings but now Percy was involved and surrounded by a new family.

Violet was the eldest sister of a family of seven, and as their mother had died young, she was the 'mother'. Violet's father was alive but she was the driving force in the family and now she had a husband to support her. Percy found that this family welcomed him and took over his life. His own family were fragmented but this family was united and had a cohesion that he had not experienced before. Uncles, aunties, cousins and second cousins were in continual contact. He had married into a large family that was very close and he was married to the local "ruler". He was absorbed and now had to sort out problems that were beyond his expertise. In dealing with his mother's problems, he had sort of withdrawn but now he was drawn into action. At first, it was his in-laws, but later, it was the whole family.

Find my sister a house! Find my brother a job! Is a coalman good enough to be married to my sister? Should my cousin work on the buses as a conductress? There was not only the immediate family but Violet had aunts, uncles and lots of cousins. Percy fitted in very well with all these new relatives who all seemed to live within a two mile radius and were continually visiting one another. Percy found that he was as old, and in some cases, older than Violet's aunts and uncles and their local pub became one of Percy's favourite places where he could meet and socialise with them. The Railway pub and Black Patch Park were the places where many of them met and ironed out many of their problems. This extended family were a friendly bunch and arguments could be solved over a beer or two. Percy enjoyed being a part of the solution to family problems.

Percy often wondered how life could get so complicated; he loved his wife but what had he let himself in for? Work was the easy part; it was within walking distance of his newly rented house, but outside of work, he was 'head' of a new family. He found his newly married sister-in-law a house on the same block as his house; they were renting from the same landlord. He found his brother-in-law a job at his factory and the coalman, who married a younger sister, had a good living and was better off than the rest of the family; he had a car! Two of Violet's uncles had bungalows in the country and the whole family would enjoy holidays in the countryside around Birmingham and Percy was enjoying this country life. Percy had always enjoyed getting out of the city and the air by the River Severn was enjoyable, as it was clean. Rotton Park could be a smoky place with industry cramped in a small area; good for working, but good to get away from.

This was now 1937, work was good and Percy could operate any machinery in the factory. Most problems in the family had been sorted out but there were clouds on the horizon. The talk of war was continuous and the factory manager gathered the workforce together and explained how brass would be of vital importance in a war. The manager stressed the workforce could be reduced if the government brought in conscription. He was hoping that the factory would be seen as supplying important armaments and the workforce would get exemptions.

Percy was now under-foreman in the factory; he had worked on all the machinery and was good at his job. Percy had been fully employed through the depression and had not suffered the hardships of others. Work was increasing due to the importance of brass in the munitions industry. The talk of war involved a push to re-arm the army and to store munitions. Violet was employed in the Jewellery

Quarter, and although they were not rich, they were better off than most. They had no children but did have some nieces and nephews. Percy always had time for children and always had a coin or two for them. Percy loved children and was mystified why he and Violet could have none even though they tried.

War came and many men were being called up into the army but Percy had a job in a vital industry which was needed for the war effort. The foreman, Joe, had decided to enlist, even though he was too old and so now Percy was promoted to foreman. The work in his factory was such that women couldn't replace most of the male workforce and so the men were not called up. His brother-in-law was a bus driver and he was needed to ferry workers to the Spitfire factories and other munitions factories on the outskirts of Birmingham. Percy's sister-in-law was also employed in the Jewellery Quarter making medals and insignia for the armed forces. Although Percy and his brother-in-law were not called up, after work they were both fire wardens. Wardens had to enforce the blackout rule seeing that all windows had black blinds, and if they did not fit properly, the lights in that room couldn't be switched on. They also had to get people to air raid shelters during the frequent night-time bombing raids. Their other duty was to attend bomb sites as quickly as possible to aid the police, ambulances and fire brigade; their local knowledge of inhabitants was valuable after bombs hit houses. There were very few comfortable night times.

The area where Percy lived was full of factories; at the end of the street was a canal and railway lines. The area was a prime target for the German bombers, and although they were aiming at the factories, many houses got hit. Percy never talked much about his duties and the sights he had seen, but there were many civilian casualties in the area. Percy must have seen dreadful sights but the one thing that disgusted him most was looters. He did tell of using his whistle to call the police to arrest two men looting a newly bombed house. The only other reliable story involved his sister-in-law and newly born nephew. When the sirens sounded, Percy would go to each house to urge the occupants to go to the nearest shelter. His sister-in-law had a shelter in her front garden, and as they got to the shelter, Percy took his new nephew while the mother climbed into the shelter. He then handed the baby to his mother, and Percy was standing in the doorway, as a bomb exploded on the opposite side of the street. The blast propelled Percy to the far end of the shelter, luckily missing his relatives.

Percy picked himself up and told his sister-in-law to stay in the shelter until he returned, he then ran to the newly bombed sight. He later came back and hugged his sister-in-law; he had seen the bodies of neighbours he knew well.

Elsie

Elsie was born in 1913 just before World War One. This was a time of turmoil in the world. The suffragettes were pushing their cause for women's rights in Britain. The Irish were starting to look for a break with the United Kingdom. There was trouble in Asia and Mexico was in the midst of a revolution. This was not even a distraction for a newly born. The distraction for her was her family. Later, her mother produced two sons before she died while only in her forties.

Elsie was the third daughter but the fourth child. The firstborn was a boy that had survived but a few months. The next three children were all girls including Elsie, who was the third daughter. The rumour was that the poor produced more girls as they were stronger and the rich produced more boys as they had better care from birth. The poor had less access to doctors as they were expensive; the poor relied on treatment from local women. Modern medicine (as crude as it was) was not available to poor families.

Elsie's family were not 'dirt poor', as their father was working at a local foundry earning enough money to keep them out of debt and out of starvation. It was touch and go, and an extra mouth to feed put a strain on the finances. The eldest daughter, Mary, although only six, did a lot of the housework while her mother was in labour. They lived in Vittoria Street near Black Patch Park, Smethwick. There were plenty of aunts and uncles around but they were all trying to make ends meet and had little time to help other families.

At the back of the house was a small garden, most of which was used for growing vegetables. The soil was poor and the yield was low, and with several children, the vegetable patch could never produce enough to allow the family to live off their produce. The only large garden was at the end house near the railway line. This was occupied by Granny Moss who kept pigs. The girls used to love to play with the piglets but they were only temporary as Granny needed to sell them to make a living. Along the banks of the railway line, the soil seemed richer and horse radish grew very well and the locals would use this to spice up their meagre food supply.

At the end of their street was Black Patch Park. It was not really a park as we know it but an open green area generally occupied by Gypsies. These Gypsies had gathered with their caravans and would go out into the community's selling pegs, potions and herbs. Elsie's dad was a strong socialist and did not believe in superstition, particularly the type used by the Gypsies. He always told Gypsies who came to the door to go away.

Elsie was fifteen when one her friends was dragged into the park and two fellas tried to rape her. Luckily, she got away and raised the alarm. The police were called but a large group gathered and wanted to attack the Gypsies. The police positioned themselves between the two groups. The Gypsies lined up all their young men in front of the older men and asked the girl to identify her attackers. She told the police that none of these men were her attackers. The crowd were dispersed but the anti-Gypsy feeling was still strong.

The local publican at the Railway Inn told the police about two young men, who had a lot to drink in his pub; he gathered they were from Aston. The anti-Gypsy feeling was still in the area and Elsie's dad forbade his children going near to Black Patch Park. For several weeks, the Gypsy ladies did not visit the area.

Elsie, her sister and friends started to 'parade' on Winson Green Road; this was the place to be seen. There was the Winson Green Picture Palace, and if they had money, they could watch a film; if not, they could walk to Summerfield Park. It was a fairly long walk, but in the park, there would be plenty of young men.

Leaving school at fourteen or fifteen, all her friends and sisters (she only had younger brothers) had to find a job. Luckily, her elder sister had a job in the Jewellery Quarter. The company made badges and insignia for the armed forces as well as for other organisations. Elsie was one of the youngest employees but she quickly took to the work. She was on a stamping machine; quite a dangerous job. Her hands were quick and so she was able to avoid getting injured. The foreman admitted to Mary that Elsie was a good worker and could keep the job after a trial period.

Elsie was now contributing to the family income. It was always a struggle but her father always seemed to keep them in the black. Elsie realised that they were in the poverty trap and she wished they could escape. There was plenty of family around but they were all in the same position; they couldn't help. Elsie opened a bank account but she could only save pennies. Elsie used to dream of having money but they were only dreams.

One Sunday when the girls were going on their walk to Summerfield Park, Elsie's left sandal broke. She told the others to carry on, she would catch them up. As she was looking at her sandal, a young man came up and offered help. He took her sandal and said he would fix it. He lived nearby and would be back in a couple of minutes. Elsie was a bit shocked as she watched him disappear. She thought no one would steal a broken sandal. She started to laugh at her next thought; maybe he had a one-legged sister.

Within minutes, he was back with a fixed sandal and a warning that it was only temporary. He said he would like to walk with her but he was late for work. He then ran off and Elsie continued to the park. In the park, all her friends started asking questions; who was this young man, where did he come from and what did he look like? Elsie only had vague answers, and all she could really remember, was that he had his hair parted down the middle and he lived in Aberdeen Street. Other than that she couldn't remember.

The next weekend, they all had enough money to go to the Winson Green Picture Palace on a Sunday afternoon. As they approached the picture house, a man approached Elsie. He said he was the sandal fixer and his name was Tommy.

"I would love to take you to the pictures but I have to go to work."

"What job do you have that keeps you working on a Sunday?"

"I work on the buses and they run seven days a week."

They set up a date later in the week. Elsie's friends were full of questions and Elsie realised he had not asked her name.

"What man does not ask you your name?"

"Maybe he knows it already."

That set off plenty of discussions.

The first date was just a walk but they had to decide where to go. Elsie said most of her relatives lived near Black Patch Park and so she did not want to go there. Summerfield Park was out because her friends might be there. Lodge Road leading to the city centre was acceptable. Tommy pointed out that his elder brother lived in that area but he would probably be at work. After the first date, all her friends wanted to know the news. There was no news and one of her friends said, "He is not romantic, drop him."

Elsie talked to her eldest sister who said, "He has a job, better than a romantic unemployed idiot. If you like him, see him again."

Their father dropped a bombshell. He had found a council house in Warley, a much better location than Vittoria Street. The girls would have a walk but could catch one bus to a bus stop very close to their work. Tommy was not fazed as he worked on the buses and free transport was his right. This house had a larger garden that would allow them to grow more vegetables. Only the boys were disappointed as they would have to go to a new school. Mary was getting married soon and Elsie's second sister, Jean, was also getting married. Elsie would have a whole bedroom to herself. The house was at the top of a hill with a good view. Elsie immediately felt the effect of the cleaner environment. Courting became more pleasant as there were a lot of new places to go. One obligation was a visit to her mother's grave which was in the Warley Cemetery. Tommy helped tidy up the grave surroundings. Tommy also helped them lay out the new garden and that sealed Elsie's future; she would marry Tommy. All they had to do was save enough money and find a place to live; not a short order in 1936.

Tommy was not the most romantic man but he did things without asking. Mary's opinion was that he would make a good husband for Elsie; Mary's opinion mattered. Tommy liked a drink, and so did her father, so they became the best of friends. Elsie's father came with another surprise; he had some money saved and Elsie could have a wedding where all the relatives could be invited. Tommy's family was quite small but Elsie's family was large. The next surprise was that Mary had found them a house to rent just a few doors away from her house.

A church wedding was followed by a reception in the church hall, with a barrel of beer and sandwiches. Someone had a portable gramophone so there could be dancing. Tommy had a good voice and sang a couple of songs. This was the best they could do but everyone enjoyed themselves. The wedding dress was a combined effort from the sisters and aunts, and this marriage brought the family together at the time when everyone was thinking of war. Many of the family admitted that this was the last real celebration before they were being bombed.

Warley was far from the factories being bombed but Elsie was working in a factory in the middle of the bombing. Their new house was very close to factories that were being bombed and Tommy made his new wife move to Warley for a while. Elsie became pregnant and decided she wanted to be in her own home, close to her eldest sister, Mary. Elsie was still working until her eighth month and then, with the help of a midwife and several female neighbours, she had a baby boy. There was a small celebration as this was the first baby born in this set of houses.

Most of the neighbours were retired or nearing retirement age and this boy was a hit with them all. Elsie wanted to go back to work as soon as possible to keep their finances in the black; it was always a struggle. Babysitters were no problem as all the older ladies were happy to look after this boy. One neighbour had a teenage daughter who loved to take him out in a pram, so after a few months breast-feeding Elsie was able to go back to work. As Tommy Junior started to grow, he became a favourite of the whole block. After his first words, mom and dada, he came out with a sentence, 'ain't it cold', that amused everyone. He must have learned it from one of elderly babysitters (who did it for free).

The war was taking its toll. Tommy was not called up as his job (driving buses) was needed for the war effort. When not on duty, he was a fire warden. He generally had the early shift driving workers to factories on the outskirts of Birmingham, to places such as the Spitfire factories. Driving a double-decker bus with no lights down country lanes was no small task. Buses with no power steering and no assisted brakes made his job more difficult. During the nights when most of the bombing occurred, he was on duty. That meant he slept during the day when Elsie was at work.

When the war ended, Tommy and Elsie could resume a normal life, and within a few years, a second son was born. Again, the finances were stretched, especially as they had taken out a mortgage to buy their house. Some free babysitting was available but four mouths to feed and a new-born baby stretched the budget.

Elsie started to take a look at their finances and how they could cut back. Tommy did the Littlewoods football pools at a weekend and Elsie said he should save that money. It was not much money and there was a chance of winning big money. She also wanted him to give up smoking and drinking beer. Tommy was not too happy so he told her to do the pools, and if she won, he would give up Littlewoods and would cut back on smoking and reduce his consumption of beer.

With the pools, football score draws gave three points, and for eight teams, that gave the maximum of twenty-four points. Non-score draws and away wins gave two points and home wins one point. Tommy used to pick ten teams and hope eight teams would give him a good score. Generally, Tommy had problems picking score draws so rarely won anything. He showed Elsie how to pick the teams and he wanted her to try for a month. Her first picks were hopeless, she scored lower than Tommy's average. Tommy was wondering what he would do after the month's trial. The second week, Elsie picked the ten teams; she was not really interested but she was going along to stop this extravagance.

On the second Saturday, Tommy was on an evening shift and did not see the football scores. On Sunday morning, he picked up a newspaper on his way to work. When he had a break, he looked at his coupon and the football scores. Elsie's first pick was a home win but the next seven picks were score draws. His heart was in his mouth as he looked at number nine, it was a home win. Tommy could hardly look at the last score. It was a score draw.

As he sat in a trance, Tommy was called to take a relief duty for a driver who had called in sick. Tommy wondered whether he could transport passengers in his state but he couldn't let people down, so he had to do this duty. He decided that, before telling Elsie, he had to confirm their luck. His duty on Monday morning seemed to drag on forever. When he had a break, he talked to one of his friends who advised he visit Littlewoods office in the centre of Birmingham.

Tommy's copy had to be confirmed with the copy in their possession, but if it was correct, they could have won over twenty thousand pounds. Tommy wanted to tell Elsie but she was at work and he had an afternoon duty. When he arrived home, he was greeted by his two sons and decided not to tell Elsie anything. This was a big problem, so he decided to have a drink with his father-in-law. As they sat drinking their first beer, Tommy spelt out his problem.

"I have had problems all my life and I always wished someone could lift me and my family from poverty. I look at my daughters and they have all escaped. We were never really poor; wait until you know for sure, before you tell Elsie the good news."

Tommy took that advice although he was straining to break the news. Finally, after a few days, a notification came that they were one of several winners. Elsie was about to fill in the third coupon when Tommy showed her the letter. They had to go to the office to collect the cheque. This winning did not seem to faze Elsie; she would pay off the mortgage, look for a new house and throw a party for the neighbours. Tommy met his father-in-law and they decided to sit back and watch Elsie. She was now in control; they had a bank account and surely life was not going to change.

Life did change, but true to his word, Tommy stopped using Littlewoods, he changed to Vernon's Pools.

I Want to Be a Chef

Jimmy was born during the war and was raised by his mother until his father was demobbed. His father came back from the war but he was not the same man; he could get angry and had continual nightmares. Jimmy's mother was not physically abused but was in continual fear of her husband. Finally, she decided to leave and left Jimmy with his father.

An eight-year-old Jimmy was left with his father, Jim. Jim was not able to explain the situation to Jimmy but he told him he would have to do all the shopping and keep the house clean. Jim had a good job in a factory and could get plenty of overtime but he would only sleep in the house and everything was left to Jimmy. Jim spent all his free time at the pub.

Luckily, Jimmy had a girlfriend much older than him who came to his aide with housework. He also had many friends in the street. This was a friendly street and one or two of the older ladies helped him. One did the washing and the other did the ironing. He also had a couple of other friends who seemed to enjoy shopping with him. Jimmy always had enough housekeeping money from his father and he learned to buy a couple of doughnuts from the bakery for himself.

Life was taking a toll, and a couple of times, he fell asleep in class. Jimmy was an intelligent pupil but he was starting to be almost silent in class. The headmaster called him to his study and asked if Jimmy had a problem. Jimmy was smart enough to say that a couple of mornings he did not feel well and had forced himself to go to school.

In time, he worked out an efficient routine and was even able to take on a casual paper rounds when the normal paper boys were sick or away. He relied on a couple of old ladies who lived a few doors down the street. They taught him how to do some basic cooking and he found he liked cooking. His problem was keeping the house clean. He was doing well at school; he was a bright boy when awake. The time was approaching when he would leave his junior school on Dudley Road and go to a senior school, Barford Road. One of the teachers had said he should take the eleven-plus to try to get into a grammar school. He turned that idea down as he realised his dad couldn't afford the school uniform, and anyway, the grammar school was quite far away.

During the summer holidays before going to senior school, his father sat him down, and for once, had a long talk.

"I know I am a terrible father, but you are a very good son. My problem is the effects of the war. I find I am only capable of being in the company of men, but not like that. I am uncomfortable in the presence of women and that is why your mother left. That is why you do the shopping. At work, all my workmates are men, at the pub, they are all men, I will not let a barmaid serve me. I was not like this before the war. I get drunk so I can sleep, as I still have nightmares. Many men came back scared by the war and I am, unfortunately, one of them. This example I am going to tell you may sound funny but it is not; it is a cry for help. A man I know who was in the same regiment came home with a similar problem. Finally, his wife kicked him out and he became homeless and lost his job. One day, he went into Woolworths, picked up an alarm clock and set the alarm. He put the clock in his pocket and it went off as he was leaving the shop. He was arrested and thrown into gaol for a couple of nights; he wanted a warm bed. Luckily, the police doctor saw him and he is now getting some help. That could be me but I have to provide for you so I try to keep my job and pay the rent on time."

Jimmy sat quietly listening to his father; he did not know what to make of the speech but realised his father needed to get it off his chest. He had heard his father say something in the night but couldn't understand what was said and was too frightened to ask. He now realised Jim was having nightmares.

The next day, he visited his aunties. He related his father's chat, and within minutes, they were both in tears.

"In a way, it is a cry for help; war has done this to your father and many others. We are both widows from the First World War; our husbands were killed and the only way we can afford to live is to live together. Many of the men who came back from that war had problems, and now, the Second World War has brought back another crop of mental invalids. These men are not insane but something in their mind has changed and not for the better. Maybe, when you are older, you might be able to help him but now just give him love; it is not his fault he has this problem. Cook him good food and see his clothes are clean and ironed; we will help you with that. We are so glad you told us his story."

After Jimmy had left, the two ladies had a chat about Jimmy and Jim. They were glad they did not inform the authorities of the situation. Jimmy was growing up a sensible boy, and if the authorities had taken Jimmy away, Jim might not have his liberty now. They both had a little cry and made a cup of tea.

Jimmy went back to his father's bedroom and picked out a box of photos. He had seen them before but he wanted to look at his mother. These were pre-war photos and the couple looked happy and his mother beautiful. Jimmy now hated her for not helping his dad; she could have seen the problem, and as an adult, could have helped Jim. He wanted to destroy the photos but he thought that would upset his father.

At Barford Road School in the first class, Jimmy was doing well. As with all senior schools, there was some bullying but he seemed to have acquired two protectors. These were older boys who were leaving school soon as they were fifteen; they had understood Jimmy's situation. Other boys left Jimmy alone and his first year was uneventful. During the second year, his two protectors came back to the school and asked a favour. They wanted him to keep watch while they entered a building, if the police came, he would call out Peel Street. If there was any profit from the venture, Jimmy would get ten percent. Jimmy had to do nothing but keep watch.

It was five p.m. on a cold winter's evening; Jimmy was wishing he was not there. He was standing on a corner when he saw a policeman approaching. He shouted out 'Peel Street' before he was grabbed by the policeman. Then, two more police appeared and he was dragged off to the police station. He said nothing and did not even protest as he was manhandled into the station. He gave his name and address and his father's work address but would say nothing else. In his thoughts were 'name, rank and serial number'. He would answer no questions until his father was present. He realised that might be an admission of guilt but he did not want his words twisted. With his father present, he gave his story.

"I was standing on the corner and a man asked me what was the street next to Aberdeen Street, I couldn't remember at first and then I realised and called out Peel Street, by this time, the man was across the road. Suddenly, this policeman took hold of me (normally he would have called him a cop; American film influence). I did not know what was going on."

"Why were you standing on that corner?"

"We needed carrots for dinner, and as it was late, I was contemplating whether to go to Birmingham Market or Smethwick Market."

"Contemplating?"

"Yes, I had a choice and wanted to make the best choice. When I saw the policeman, I did not run as I had no idea what was happening."

Now Jim piped up and said his son had done nothing wrong, there was no evidence and he was taking him home. The sergeant seemed a little flustered and let Jimmy go. Outside the station, Jim told Jimmy that he was lucky the others were not caught but he had been correct by not trying to escape and saying nothing. Jim said he had no love for the police, having been had up drunk and disorderly and fighting in a pub. Jim had been banned from one of the pubs on Icknield Port Road. and that had calmed him down. The bobbies now knew father and son so Jimmy should be careful.

The next couple of years went smoothly and it was nearing time for Jimmy to leave school. He wanted to buy his aunties a school-leaving present but had no money. His two "old mates' approached him and proposed a similar job to the first. Jimmy was very reluctant but they gave him two pounds in advance. Again, he was standing on a corner when, suddenly, a man in a suit grabbed him.

"Who are you?"

"I am a policeman and you are nicked."

"What for?"

"You are a lookout for a robbery that is now going on."

"Where, I see no robbery?"

His two 'mates' were dragged out of a shop and they were all hauled off to the station. This time, Jimmy spent a night in a cell but not the one occupied by his 'mates'. In the morning, he was taken to court and waited outside while the others were tried. As he entered the court, he saw his father with his head bowed. No court could shake him as much as seeing his father like that. In a way it made him angry. He was now going to be defiant and let them know he was not going to be easy.

"You are charged with being part of a robbery, how do you plead?"

"How can I be part of a robbery when I did nothing?"

"How do you plead, guilty or not guilty?"

"Not guilty."

"Well, we will proceed with the prosecution case."

"Excuse me, sir, why do we not hear the defence case first?"

"That is a very good point, normally out of order. In British law, you are innocent before proven guilty, and so, you need to hear the evidence against you so as to know how best to defend yourself."

"Oh, yes, sir, I will be equipped to refute all the charges."

The magistrate raised his eyebrows and motioned that proceedings should commence. It appeared that his 'mates' had not snitched on him and all the evidence was circumstantial. A couple of times, Jimmy jumped up to speak but the magistrate said he would get his turn. Jim sat very quiet with his eyes glued on the bench and the magistrate; he observed that Jimmy was not intimidated by the proceeding. At last, Jimmy was allowed to speak.

"First of all, I have listened to all the evidence against me, and of course, I am innocent. I was in the wrong place at the wrong time, I was just standing on a street corner. I don't know my co-accused; they had left school before I started, we do not live in the same street and I don't know where they live. I was standing at that corner waiting to see which bus came first. I was contemplating whether to go to Birmingham Market or Smethwick Market."

"Why would you go to the market?"

"Generally, the vegetables are cheaper and fresher in the market and I love roast carrots and parsnips. The best veg are fresh veg, they taste better."

"Well, your culinary delights are not part of this case."

"Sir, I am innocent."

Please stop pleading you innocence."

"But sir, I have no other recourse."

"You, my lad, have given me a dilemma; I think you are guilty but I am going to be swayed by your argument and let you off with a caution. If you come before this court again, you will surely spend an uncomfortable few days in Winson Green Prison, case dismissed.

As Jimmy left the court, he was confronted by two large coppers, they were scowling at him and he was smiling at them. Jim was by his side, proud of his son.

"Sorry, fellas, I am innocent."

Outside the court, his father hugged him and told him he was a marked man. Jim had watched the proceedings and couldn't believe what had happened. The magistrate seemed to be enjoying Jimmy and the police hated every minute. Jim realised he had a very smart son but he was confused about what to do next.

Jimmy also realised he had to stay clean; the aunties advised him that he had to find a job and live quietly. They were proud of Jimmy, and when they learnt of his court case, they celebrated with a Guinness each. Jimmy was their favourite, and for them, he could do no wrong.

Jimmy found a job at Mitchells and Butlers Brewery as a sort of sweeper and handyman. One day, he saw a notice for a young man to be employed in the canteen. Most young men wanted to be draymen or work on the brewing side; Jimmy wanted to be a chef. Mrs Williams was the manager of the canteen, and when she interviewed Jimmy, she found an intelligent young man whose ambition was to be a chef. No other applicant had put his ambition so eloquently. She warned him he would have to be fit; the cooking areas were hot and humid and he would often be on the run for long periods. This is what he needed; a challenge and a way to work out a routine. He was longing to see how food was cooked in bulk.

Now he had the ideal job, surrounded by women and involved in cooking. His salary was not so good but it was all his. His father provided for everything and never asked Jimmy for money. Jimmy opened a bank account, and when Jim found out, he was very pleased. Jimmy was always happy at work and many of the ladies openly expressed their interest in his sexuality (only they expressed it in cruder terms). He had ideas, so whether he was shelling peas or washing plates, Jimmy wanted to make it easier or faster. Mrs Williams was getting lots of suggestions, most of which she rejected but one or two worked. Beer in the batter was a goer, beer in the soup was interesting and beer with the ice cream was not good; some things worked but at least half were non-starters. Mrs Williams loved his enthusiasm and gave him a raise. Canteen food was much the same day by day but she allowed Jimmy to set a menu. There was a menu but Jimmy wanted a printed menu displayed each day.

Jimmy had an ulterior motive; he wanted to visit the typing pool. He had spied a pretty typist and would always take his menus to her. Finally, he asked Audrey out on a date. He took her to an Indian Restaurant for a meal. She was surprised and not keen on Indian food. The decision of where to go was based on extensive research.

During his work in the canteen, he had encountered a dark-skinned lady named Mrs Kaur. She was Indian, a Sikh, and she spoke English with a heavy accent which Jimmy learned to understand. She told him about spices and some of the dishes she would cook at home. She said she would bring him something called a samosa to try. One bite of this samosa and Jimmy was in heaven; it was spicy, tasty and so different from anything he had tasted before. At home, they had pepper, salt, mustard and vinegar to spice up their food but this was different.

"Can you buy these samosas?"

"Not in a shop but there is one Indian restaurant in Birmingham that should have them."

"Thank you, Mrs Kaur, I want to try these again; they have such a different taste to normal food."

The next time Jimmy went to the Bull Ring market, he asked if anyone knew of an Indian restaurant. Someone told him there was one on the Bristol Road. Jimmy realised that he went to Birmingham regularly and never noticed restaurants. He took a Sunday morning to explore the city centre and found there were plenty of restaurants, including two Indian and several Chinese. He looked at the menus and most had dishes that were a mystery to him. Jimmy was not short of cash; Jim paid for everything. He decided he would visit one restaurant a week, starting, of course, with the Indian; he couldn't forget the samosas.

On his first visit, he found that on a Sunday lunch time he was the only patron. He told the waiter this was his first curry and what was the difference. The waiter explained that the Korma was spicy but not hot, the Madras was quite hot and the Vindaloo was very hot. Jimmy asked if he could have a small portion of each and a portion of rice. The waiter explained that they often used chapattis to pick up the food, demonstrating the way. Jimmy ordered a chapatti, and of course, a couple of samosas.

The waiter smiled when Jimmy used the chapatti in his left hand.

"Sir, we use our right hand to eat and our left hand to wipe our bum."

"I am left-handed and I use my left hand to eat and my right hand to clean my bum."

The waiter left, laughing at Jimmy's remark.

Jimmy marvelled at the rice; each piece of rice was separate, none were stuck together.

This was the start of Jimmy's restaurant explorations. He used the same technique of trying several dishes at one sitting and this worked at most restaurants unless they were busy. He also collected menus and acquired a collection. Indian was always his favourite with Chinese a close second.

When he asked Audrey for a date, he wanted to introduce her to something different but that was a disaster. She did not like the food, the background music annoyed her and she felt uncomfortable. Audrey wanted to go to the pictures or a coffee bar. Jimmy hated coffee bars, most of them were 'greasy spoons' and the coffee was lousy. He liked being with Audrey but her likes were not his likes. He took her to an Italian restaurant but the 'spaghetti was too hard to eat' and the coffee was too strong.

Jimmy had met Audrey's parents and her mother was pleased that Jimmy was taking her to restaurants; she was suspicious of coffee bars. Jimmy suggested that he might cook a dinner in their house; he would supply the food and all he needed was a stove and a sink. Mrs Symonds was delighted; this was a different teenager and she was happy Audrey had found an interesting boyfriend. Jimmy cooked a variety of foods, mainly finger foods but with a mild curry. Audrey ate almost nothing, her father couldn't stop eating and her mother was enjoying every mouthful.

The meal was both a success and disaster; Audrey decided that Jimmy's likes were not her likes and they split up. His liaison with Audrey had allayed some of the suspicions of the ladies in the canteen. He now asked Mrs Williams if he could make a few samosas and spring rolls to put at the end of the line. Jimmy stood and explained what they were. They soon ran out and many of the men were asking if there were any more. One drayman came to Jimmy and told him his story of being in India during the war. Jimmy's samosas were the best he had tasted since 1945 but they needed a bit more red pepper. This man also suggested Jimmy try a curry.

The next day, the queue reversed and they were going for the samosas and spring rolls first before the main meal. Jimmy reserved a couple of extra spicy samosas for the Indian veteran. When this drayman tasted them, he was almost in tears, they brought back memories. He told Jimmy he wished he was back in Hyderabad. Jimmy gave him the address of the Indian restaurant on the Bristol Road and they would probably get a new customer.

The night Jimmy broke up with Audrey, he was walking back home from Smethwick. He caught up with a friend who lived in the same street. His friend had just come from night school and was carrying a small case. As it was a pleasant night they had decided to walk home. They strolled along until, near Summerfield Park, a policeman stepped out of the shadows.

"What have you got in that case?"

"Books, sir."

"You can open the case now or we go to the station and we will open it."

"I have no problem, here look, they are chemistry books, would you like me to tell you about organic chemistry?"

"No, bugger off, you cheeky sod."

Jimmy and his friend walked on, and when the policeman was out of sight, they had a good laugh.

"He stopped us because of me; he is now a sergeant but he recognises me from a long time ago. I often get stopped; they are out to get me but tonight was the best.

"We can only walk together only when I have chemistry books," his friend replied.

They both had a good laugh. Jimmy was staying out of trouble, he was more interested in cooking rather than thieving. He had learned that his thieving mates were out of gaol but he was hoping they would not contact him.

Mrs Williams saw the popularity of Jimmy's samosas and spring rolls so she decided to put them on in the manager's dining room. The managers had a separate dining room and menu. The menu changes were an immediate success as she introduced a curry made by Jimmy. The manager of the draymen came to Mrs Williams.

"I have been hearing about this young man. My men are going to the afternoon shift happier than I have ever seen. I've got men talking about taking their wives to Indian restaurants. The draymen all have different ideas but they are all in agreement with this young lad's food."

"Yes, that is all because of one of Jimmy's experiments. He gave some of the ladies his samosas and asked their opinion and most of them thought they were too spicy. He cooked up a special batch and asked if the men would assess a free samosa and the ladies would assess the same samosas. He sat them down and gave them each a Samosa from the same batch. They all filled in a questionnaire and he found that the ladies liked the samosas less spicy and the men liked them spicier. When he announced the results the next day, the men stood up and cheered. I have never had a cheer in my canteen."

Jimmy now viewed his experiment and realised Audrey may have found the food too spicy, but then she did not like Italian food. Her father, her mother and his father had no complaints about his cooking.

The manager's dining room was lapping up Jimmy's dishes but Mrs Williams had a problem. Each month, the board would meet and they had dinner in a separate dining room. They normally had smoked salmon or roast beef and Yorkshire pudding but could she put on one of Jimmy's curries and could she add samosas and spring rolls to the entree menu? She did and it was an immediate success. One of the board members came to her and was effusive in his compliments. Jimmy was introduced to this man, and after a short discussion, the man said he had a brother who owned a hotel in London and Jimmy might find a job there. Jimmy approached Mrs Williams and her advice was to take any offer.

The manager of the draymen came to Mrs Williams and asked what was happening. He had men spending more time in the canteen and willing to work later. Mrs Williams said that her canteen had been a place where men came in, ate their lunch and left. Jimmy had transformed that into a meeting place where men would ask about the menu, swap recipes and laugh a lot. She related one instance where one man had told Jimmy his wife would not cook a samosa recipe. Jimmy had told him if he cooked the samosas himself, he did not need a wife. There was a roar of laughter and the man said, if I tell that to my wife, she will kill you. Now the whole canteen was laughing.

Within two weeks, Jimmy had an offer of a job. He gave his notice and told the canteen of his good fortune and thanked them for all their support. When he said that he had left the recipe of his samosas, there was a cheer.

Mrs Williams was sorry to let him go but thought he had a great opportunity.

"I have never seen such a happy canteen. The serving staff are enjoying serving and a bunch of rough draymen loving having lunch here."

With that, there was loud applause.

The hotel was a large one and Jimmy had to learn their routine. He was hired as an under chef but had to start at the bottom. Jimmy did not mind peeling spuds and was always thinking of making tasks faster and easier. This was a different place to the M&B canteen; there was a hierarchy. He had a small room in the hotel, and of course, meals were no problem. He did not have much spare time but the area around the hotel was interesting. He was missing his dad and his two aunties. His dad was happy to let him go and Jimmy had arranged with the aunties to carry on the washing and ironing and he had persuaded Jim to pay them. He had also got them talking, and when Jim found out about their husband's deaths, he was at ease.

Jimmy was talking regularly to the chef, a French chef from Lancashire. He persuaded the chef to put on a few Indian dishes. At first, there was some resistance but a group of Germans loved the dishes. This group were staying for a week, and when Jimmy put on his samosas, the restaurant filled with Germans who were not residents. Samosas and beer became the evening menu. The hotel was becoming popular and was attracting other nationalities than German. There were even a few Indian customers who wanted their curries a little hotter. One customer introduced him to cumin.

One night, a visiting rock band came to the restaurant, and after their meal, wanted to see the chef. The Lancastrian chef admitted that the dishes were Jimmy's creations and when this Brummie introduced himself there was lots of laughter; most of the band was from the Midlands. There was a long conversation and they were all telling Jimmy he was a star. Suddenly, the hotel became a hot spot and the restaurant could hardly cope with the new custom.

Word had spread, and soon, Jimmy was poached by a bigger upmarket hotel. His new job was basically director of food preparation and delivery. Now, he was not very involved in the food preparation, but more, in the presentation.

He suddenly felt the need to go back to Birmingham. He did not let anyone know he was coming and went straight to the aunties. They greeted this well-dressed handsome young man. Jimmy had picked up twelve Babychams at the outdoor at the end of the street. The aunties promised not to drink them all in one go. Jim was in the Belle View pub so Jimmy wished the aunties goodnight. The bar of the pub was crowded, but when Jimmy walked in, it went very quiet. Jim was so happy to see his son, he split his beer. Jimmy hugged his father and ordered two beers.

There was the usual ritual of, how are you and vice-versa, when Jim said come around the other side of me. Jimmy was a bit confused but he did what was told.

"The bloke the other side of me is one of them. He might get a bit too close for comfort."

Jimmy looked and saw a well-built man with a good beard. He looked like the sailor on the Players cigarette packet.

"Oh, yes, we have a few of them in London, but not too many in working class pubs."

Jimmy did not say that his boss and at least three waiters were 'one of them' and many of the regular customers were of the same persuasion.

"You look very smart in that suit; by the way, what brings you to Brum?"

"This is my working suit, I often wear an apron and a hat. I am here because our kitchen is being refurbished and I thought I might spend time with my favourite dad."

After another couple of pints, Jim was dragged home sober. The next morning, Jimmy cooked the best breakfast with what he could find and vowed to do some shopping while his dad was at work. He decided to go to Smethwick Market, and when he got off the bus on Cape Hill, he saw an Indian shop selling spices. When he entered the shop, he recognised the lady behind the counter but she did not immediately recognise him.

"Hello, Mrs Kaur."

"Ah, Jimmy, I not recognise you in suit, where you now?"

"I am the deputy chef in a large hotel in London and I am visiting while they are fixing up the place."

"You make me very happy, this shop is success because of you. Men from Mitchells and Butlers come here to buy spices; they bring wives who want to know how to cook. They ask first about samosas, now curries and biriyani and how to make chapattis and parathas. I even give demonstration at Warley College."

"Yes, but it was your samosa that started me; I am indebted to you. They have been a success wherever I go."

"You such a good boy, my two sons hopeless, and my husband, lazy and hopeless. They no help in the shop and I am glad to be alone here. Take anything you want free-of-charge."

"No, Mrs Kaur, I cannot be seen to get anything free, it is seen as a bribe."

Mrs Kaur laughed, she knew all about bribes.

After purchasing some spices, he went to the market where one of the lady stall holders commented on how smart he looked. Then, a lady behind in the queue asked if she knew him.

"Yes, I am Jimmy, Mrs Symonds, how is Audrey?"

"Audrey is OK but some of the dead beats she goes out with are not so good. You know my husband says the best meal he has ever had in our house is the one you cooked. Of course, I disagree with him but he is correct. I will tell Audrey I met you, but if I tell my husband, he will ask why I did not ask you to cook dinner."

Back home, Jimmy cooked dinner and took two plates and a couple of Guinness to the aunties. He bought a bottle of wine for himself and a few beers for his dad.

"Can I try your wine, in France we used to drink wine? We drank anything we could get? Some of it I liked but some were like vinegar."

"Yes, Dad, France has plonk and good stuff, I suspect you drank a lot of plonk. Would you like to go to France?"

"Now, you have put me on the spot. France has good and bad memories. I have lots of mates under the soil and visiting their graves could be a bad experience for me. Many of my nightmares have gone but a visit might bring them back. Maybe in the future we could go."

Jimmy understood, but on reflection, he had never taken his father anywhere.

In the morning, the aunties brought the plates back and thanked Jimmy for the food which they found delicious. They also told him that the way the food was presented, they were almost afraid to touch it and wished they had a camera. Jimmy explained that he cooked tasty food but presentation was important. He had been studying the Japanese way but he thought they might not like their food. He promised to send them a photo of a feast he would prepare when he returned to the hotel. Jimmy's five days were a success and he was able to find lots of places he remembered, but most of his school pals had moved away to places like Tamworth and Hereford.

The months went by and the chef resigned and Jimmy was made chef. The chef was going to Spain to open a restaurant. Lots of people seemed to be retiring to Spain or Portugal. Now, he was more-or-less his own boss although the chef had given him plenty of liberty.

One morning, Jimmy received a call from the aunties; Jim had a massive heart attack and was dead. They would lay him out and they had contacted a funeral home. Jimmy was in tears and said he would catch the first train. On the train, he was regretting not visiting his father more often. They had never gone to France, in fact, they never went anywhere together. Now, he suddenly felt alone.

Reaching his home, he found the aunties had done a wonderful job and the funeral director was very professional. Jim would be buried in Warley Cemetery next to his parents. Jimmy had never known his grandparents, and although not religious, he liked the idea of a family area. The aunties and a few of his pub mates attended the funeral and Jimmy treated them all to a 'slap-up do' at a local club, 'no drink restrictions'. The aunties informed him his mother had been there at the back during the burial but he was glad he had not seen her as he might have become abusive. Now, he had to clear the house of personal belongings. The only thing he wanted was the photos, Jim's army uniform and a set of cufflinks that brought back memories of his dad getting dressed for the pub. He asked if the aunties would get rid of the rest however they pleased, and of course, they agreed.

Back in London, he tried not to dwell on his father's demise and concentrated on work. He organised everything so he could take a week off and go to Spain. In Spain, he relaxed at his friend's place, but on a couple of occasions, he had to cook and serve in the restaurant. Holidays were not for him so, back in London, he was happy. He decided he should make others happy. One day, he arranged with the hotel manager to book a room for two nights and have a chauffeur booked for two days. The manager asked if this was for a girlfriend and Jimmy told him two.

On a Sunday he went to Birmingham and stayed in a hotel. He visited the aunties and told them they were going to London for two days and he would pick them up in the morning. They should pack a few of their best clothes and they would need no money. The next day, he picked them up in a taxi; a first for them. They had never been on a train and had never been to London. A taxi took them to the hotel and the manager was surprised to see two old ladies, but of course, he was very polite. They had lunch with Jimmy and then they were to be taken around London.

"Tell the driver if you want to see anything special, he will show you all the sights and he will bring you back to get ready for dinner. At the dinner, Jimmy came and sat at their table for a while. The other guests were wondering if these ladies were related to royalty. Jimmy explained they would get Babycham which would be poured out and brought in a glass, and if they wanted more, they should tell the waiter. If one of the other guests would want a glass, it would be explained, that was the last of the bottle. The waiters were all on it and loving the subterfuge.

The next day, they would have the driver; they had seen Buckingham Palace, the Houses of Parliament, Tower Bridge and the Tower of London. When asked what else they would like to see, they surprisingly said the dock area where their husbands had been sent to France and Woolwich Arsenal. Jimmy decided to join them. They stopped at a café in Woolwich and Jimmy was taken by the fact that the docks were the highlight of their tour. At the evening meal, the same procedure was followed and other patrons were coming up to the aunties to say hello and some of them were bowing. The next morning, Jimmy put them on the train with taxi fare in Birmingham.

Arriving back at the hotel, the manager asked were they relatives.

"No, these two ladies set me off on my career; they helped me in so many ways, they started to tell me how to cook. They helped me to manage a house; I owe them so much it is a debt I can never repay. My father taught me how to manage money and never objected to my way of doing things even when I was in trouble. I am sure I have done better than all of my school mates except maybe the fellow who studied chemistry."

Kidney Stones One

Ken lived in Ladywood with his mother and elder brother; his father had been a gunner on a Lancaster bomber that had been shot down in World War Two. His mother and brother, Brian, were very proud of the father although Ken hardly knew him. Brian was ten years older than Ken but Brian was like a father. Brian always played with Ken and taught him new tricks and games. Ken worshipped Brian. They lived in a 'two-up-two-down' house and so Brian and Ken shared a bedroom. Living so close, they had a strong bond that the age difference did not reduce.

Brian worked in a factory very close to home; he had left school at fifteen and was an apprentice fitter. He went to college one day a week and went to night school two nights a week. He was studying for his Ordinary National Certificate, and if he received it, he could get a better job. Brian often talked to Ken about his job but always stressed that Ken should stay at school as long as possible.

"School is short term but work is long term. Get a job you enjoy because that is going to be for most of your life. I see many older men in repetitive jobs who hate life; you must not be one of them."

Ken was in junior school and was second in his class. The first in the class was a girl whose mother was a teacher. He liked the girl but hated that she was better than him. At his age, there was really no homework but Brian used to ask if there were problems Ken couldn't solve. The major problem was that Ken was left-handed and the old pen nibs were sticking in the paper so he couldn't write fast. Brian solved that problem by buying him a Biro. Now his problem was spelling. The local accent often meant that some English words spelt as they were spoken were wrong. Brian used to sit down with Ken and say a word and ask Ken to spell the word. Brian would then correct the spelling. Their mother was so proud of them, particularly Brian, who should have had further education and become a teacher. His mother thought he had a natural gift for explaining things. Finances had dictated Brian leave school and find a job to support the family income.

Ken was coming to the end of his junior school at Dudley Road and was preparing for the eleven-plus to go to grammar school. He tried the exam while he was only ten but failed. Brian took him through some of the questions he found difficult and told Ken he would surely pass next time. Brian was so patient and Ken started to get close to being first in the class. When he took the eleven-plus a second time, he passed.

Although his mother and Brian were working, it was a struggle to buy a school uniform. They were so proud of Ken. Brian got his Ordinary National Certificate and a better-paying job. In the first year at grammar school, there were three classes and the pupils were selected alphabetically by surname. At the end of this first year, they were selected by position in the classes. Ken went into the top stream and, throughout his school life he was always near the top of the class.

When Ken was in his third year, Brian started to get back pains. Sometimes they were quite mild, but at other times, he was in real pain. Ken used to rub Brian's back with a pain-killing cream which occasionally worked. These pains were spasmodic and there were long periods when they did not occur. During one period of pains, a doctor gave Brian a cortisone injection and that did not work. Summer was approaching and Brian was going camping with his mates. Ken had a part-time job delivering groceries to earn a little pocket money.

Ken was at home when Brian and one of his mates appeared. Brian was in agony and passing blood in his urine, he was also occasionally vomiting. Ken was in a panic, his mother was at work and Brian's mate wanted to go back to Cornwall. Ken convinced the driver to take them to Dudley Road Hospital and then go back to the camp. Ken was in tears although he tried to hide his emotions, and in the emergency room they said they would do tests and Ken should get his mother. Ken was loath to leave Brian but he had to get his mother. Before he caught the bus to his mother's work, he had a good cry; his fantastic brother was in agony. He had watched his brother bent over in pain that made him shake uncontrollably and that scared Ken.

When Ken and his mother returned to hospital, they were informed that Brian had a kidney stone stuck in the ureter. They had carried out an IVP (Intravenous pyelogram) and the nurse showed them the X-ray. Ken was mesmerised; he could see the stone, the ureter, the kidney and the bladder. He decided, at that point, he would try to be a doctor. The doctor had given Brian morphine but could only give him pethidine to take home. The hospital had booked an appointment at the Queen Elizabeth Hospital where there was a Renal Unit; the only problem was that it was in two weeks.

At home, Brian admitted that the morphine worked but the pethidine was not too good. Ken was worried so his mother sat him down and had a chat. This was not life-threatening and it might be best if he treated Brian normally. After one week, Ken decided to take Brian to the Emergency at the Queen Elizabeth Hospital as he couldn't stand to see Brian in pain. Although Brian did not have an appointment for a week, they did another IVP. This showed the stone to be moving back towards the kidney so they admitted Brian immediately. They would operate the next day and Ken learnt a lesson; be pushy.

Ken couldn't visit Brian on the day of the operation, but the next day, he was there bright and early. He had to wait in the waiting room as he was too early for visiting hours. He was fascinated by the comings and goings and decided this was a good place to work. Brian's words, 'work is for a long time so pick a job you enjoy', were remembered. Brian was in a big ward and seemed to be half asleep although he said hello to Ken. His bedside neighbour said Brian was still under the influence of the drugs given him during the operation and he should be better tomorrow.

Ken started to talk to this man called Roy.

"I am a stone maker, this is my third operation. I asked them to put a zip in my belly so they can get easier next time. I'll show you one of my stones."

The stone in a small vial seemed so small and Ken said so to Roy.

"Yes, it is small, but look closely, and you will see it is jagged and that it is why it does not have a smooth ride down the ureter. Even the smooth ones have to pass through the penis."

Roy probably thought that Ken would feel squeamish, but the opposite, Ken was more interested. The next day, Brian was more alert but still in pain.

"They gave me a new drug beginning with Z but I can't remember the full name. Anyway, it worked but then I had some funny visions; there was a little bird sitting on the end of my bed and there was something growing out of the wooden floor. When I told the nurse, she said, "You're having no more of those pills!""

Brian couldn't show Ken his scar but said it must be a foot long, maybe the surgeon had big hands. Brian laughed with some pain but Ken thought there must be an easier way to get to a stone. Brian thought he would be out in a few days but there was a complication. Brian developed a blood clot in his leg, and first, they gave him Heparin (snake venom), and then, he was on Warfarin (rat poison).

Ken asked lots of questions of the nurses about the drugs and how they treated Brian.

Visits to the hospital heightened Ken's interest in kidney stones. He visited the local library and the central library in Birmingham, missing two days of school. His form master asked him about the problem.

"I woke up OK and Mom left for work and then I went to the toilet and then I couldn't leave. My brother is in hospital so there was no way to tell the school. In the afternoon I was better. The next day was a repeat but I will catch up."

The master was satisfied that Ken had some kind of food poisoning. He caught up easily but decided his obsession with kidney stones had to be a weekend study. Brian came home, and when Ken saw the scar, he was astonished. Ken did go back to the hospital to visit Roy; he was still there, they had him in some sort of study.

Ken was even more convinced that he should become a doctor. A careers advisor came to the school and Ken asked about medicine. The advisor was not very enthusiastic and suggested that maybe Ken should consider another option. He would need three A levels and then many years at university. His friend had asked about the diplomatic service and been told NO CHANCE. Later in life, this friend had visited many countries and found some embassy staff were often not very intelligent.

O-level exams were no problem. Ken had eight passes but asked his mother whether he could stay on at school. She was so happy and said, whatever it cost, they would be able to pay. Brian was so proud of his brother and he put money aside although he was preparing to get married.

The A-level class was divided in two groups: Arts and Science. Ken obviously chose Science. The career adviser told Ken that three subjects with labs would be difficult. Ken was not daunted, he wanted to get into medical school. Brian found the mathematics beyond him, and of the other subjects, chemistry started to make sense but all he could do was encourage Ken. The A-level exams were a good test and Ken's mother wondered whether Ken could handle the pressure.

The exams were all over and Ken could relax but all he wanted to do was visit the renal unit in the Queen Elizabeth Hospital. He had a whole ward of friends and had seen more kidney stones than the average surgeon. Several nurses asked him why he came to this ward and his reply was that he wanted to be a renal surgeon.

His A-level results were three As and one B in mathematics. His mother read the results and was in tears; he was one of the first (in his family and the street) to go to a grammar school, and now, he was the first to go to university. Brian was so proud he told all his mates and organised a party in the local pub.

Ken had to put his renal studies on the back-burner and concentrate on general medical studies. One of his tutors was very impressed when Ken was asked to write an essay on a medical problem. Of course, he wrote on kidney disease. Ken sailed through his medical studies, and when it came to further studies to be a specialist, it was, of course, renal studies. The Queen Elizabeth Hospital had a large renal unit and Ken fit in as the youngest member of the team; renal studies were not very popular. He watched the large cut and extract and wanted something less invasive.

Key-hole surgery and laser treatment were now coming into vogue. Ken studied the literature and decided to concentrate on these. He went to France and Germany to study their approaches. After returning, he applied for university and hospital money to get some of the necessary equipment and was quickly able to show that recovery times were greatly reduced. The hospital management were very happy; less time in hospital was a great cost saver.

An army surgeon was visiting a patient in the hospital when he learned of Ken's work. He approached Ken and asked if he would talk to an army medical unit as some soldiers had kidney problems and it was often a problem in the field. Ken took up the offer and gave an informal lecture and talked to many of the medical officers.

After spending a couple of days talking medicine with army doctors, he went back to the hospital. A week passed and a general came to talk to him. In the field in some countries, he would not name them, they had a few soldiers either pass kidney stones or be sent home for treatment; would Ken be able to fly into a combat zone to assess the situation? Yes, Ken could take some time off but he asked,

"How big is the problem?"

"We do not know, our record of casualties is good but health casualties are not so well-documented, because no one has assessed them."

"Is there an X-ray facility where I am going?"

"The Americans have such a facility and they will let us use it."

"Give me a couple of days and I will square it with the hospital authorities."

"It has already been squared with the hospital authorities, as you put it."

"Then I am ready to go at a moment's notice."

Ken told his mom and Brian and impressed on them this was a secret. His mom was a bit apprehensive but Brian was excited. "You are taking my kidney stone to a combat zone. I hope it comes back intact. More importantly, I hope you come back intact."

"Don't worry, I will be in a bulletproof tent." They both laughed and hugged, his mother was not so happy.

Ken was provided with body armour and he realised a problem, weight. The plane landed in a very dusty airfield surrounded by army vehicles. They asked Ken what he would like to do.

"Collect as many men as you can, both British and American, I would like to give them a lecture."

Ken showed them Brian's stone and told them how much pain they could be in for days if the stone started to pass. Several soldiers were cringing, even some of them shutting their eyes. Ken explained this study would be voluntary as he wanted to see how many soldiers had stones. He showed them the positions of stones that could cause problems and the ones that might cause problems later.

The next day, the major running the X-ray unit said he had never seen so many soldiers wanting an X-ray, he even had soldiers coming in from the field who had heard about Ken's lecture. The X-ray unit worked overtime that day and the next and the general in charge jokingly said to Ken,

"You are costing us a lot of money."

Ken's reply was, "How much would it cost if a soldier in pain was killed because he couldn't concentrate on the job at hand?"

"That is a very sobering point I will relay up my chain of command."

Ken was shocked by the results, as about five percent of the Brits had stones and about eight percent of the Americans. He could identify that at least eight soldiers should be immediately shipped home for treatment. There were two soldiers who he would treat on base. The commandants, both British and American, were impressed and now started to have their team thinking about diet and fluid intake.

Back in the UK, Ken's mother was relieved and Brian welcomed home his stone, and of course, his famous brother. A few weeks later, Ken was invited to Washington, to the Pentagon. There, he showed the kidney stone and talked about the pain but emphasised the psychological effects. A man on combat duty who was having pains couldn't function one hundred percent, in fact, with renal pain he might not be able to function at all. Identifying potential soldiers was important, not only to him, but his whole platoon. Initial screening was very important but it was also important for any health problem. His lecture went down very well and officers were coming to shake his hand. One officer relayed that a friend had witnessed his talk at the base and had seen veteran field soldiers wince, and close their eyes. The important message was that they all enjoyed his information.

Arriving back in the UK, he was in the local newspaper. His mother was so proud and Brian said his little stone did it all.

Ken's reply was that Brian's agony did it all. "Your pain gave me all that I have accomplished."

Kidney Stones Two

Brian was born in 1929 in Birmingham. His father had been killed in World War Two not long after his brother, Ken, had been born. Life was a struggle for his mother until Brian left school at fifteen His small wage as an apprenticed fitter helped keep them solvent. Ken was looked after by neighbours while Brian's mother was at work. These elderly neighbours did their job for free; just part of the community spirit. During his apprenticeship, Brian was able to have one day at a technical college, and when he finished his apprenticeship and received his Ordinary National Certificate, he had an increase in pay so that Ken could go to grammar school.

Brian had a thirst for knowledge and took extra courses at night school. He loved helping his brother with homework and other problems. He was like a father to Ken and he wanted children of his own later in life. His mother was very pleased with her boys but she regretted her husband couldn't see them grow.

Late in his teens, Brian started to get backache, he thought it was muscular although he did no heavy lifting. One doctor gave him a cortisone injection but that did nothing. This ache would come and go, and occasionally, it was very strong. He learned to live with the pain. He had friends who decided to go to Cornwall for a camping holiday at Newquay. Four of them went in a friend's station wagon; it was about a seven-hour drive, and when they reached the camp site, Brian had severe back pain. He excused himself for not helping with the tent pitching. In the morning after a sleepless night, he started to pass blood in his urine. He persuaded his friend to take him back to Birmingham and the blood in the urine did the trick.

Somehow, the trip back was shorter, but all Brian could do, was lie across the back seat. When they arrived home, Brian stumbled out of the car and promptly vomited, the pain was worse than before. He looked up to see Ken's face, he looked in more pain. Ken insisted they go to Dudley Road Hospital and Brian's friend left for the long journey back to Cornwall.

In the hospital, they stuck a needle in the back of his hand and whisked him off to do X-rays. Brian did not care what they did, he was only semi-conscious. They gave him morphine and the pain eased and he was able to sleep. The next day, he felt much better and was going home with Ken and his mother. A stone was lodged in the ureter. The X-ray revealed the stone and where it had lodged. They gave him an appointment at the Queen Elizabeth Hospital (QE) Renal Unit in two weeks.

He was given pethidine as a replacement for morphine, and in two days, he realised it was not doing the trick. No matter whether he was lying down, sitting or walking, the pain was getting worse. Ken persuaded him to go to QE and they did another IVP (Intravenous pyelogram), which showed the stone moving upwards to the kidney. This was dangerous as it would make surgery more difficult. They kept him in hospital, gave him an enema and said he would have an operation the next day. He was given morphine that allowed him a good night's sleep.

After the operation, he had new pains, and although morphine had an effect, every time he moved, he winced. Ken came to visit but all he could say was hello. He put on the headphones and listened to music which had a slight soothing effect but all he wanted to do was sleep. Suddenly, he felt cold and the nurses put another blanket on his bed but now the weight seemed to be pressing on him. The following day, the nurse explained that they would give him a new drug to kill the pain as morphine was addictive. The nurses tried to move him but he was in too much pain.

On the third day, they were able to lift him and he could dangle his legs over the bed but the pain was incredible. More of the new drug did kill most of the pain but had an interesting effect. As the nurse left the ward, he had strange visions that seemed to lessen the pain.

When he asked the nurse about the little bird, she said, "You are having no more of those pills, I will talk to the doctor."

The next day, the surgeon visited and the nurses rolled Brian over so the scar could be examined and he winced and cried out. The surgeon told him not to be a wimp and

Brian's reply was that he wished the surgeon some of his agony but not in those terms.

Ken visited every day and saw the scar; it was more than a foot long. Brian was enjoying Ken's visits as he was introduced to most of the other patients through Ken. One day before he was supposed to go home, Brian sat on the edge of his bed and dangled his legs. He noticed that his right leg was giving him pain and looked swollen. He told the nurse and there seemed to be a panic. The nurse explained that he had a blood clot and he would need a fast-acting blood thinner made from snake venom.

"You are joking."

"No, I am not, and after your blood thins, you will have to keep it thin for a while, which will mean taking rat poison."

"Now, you are really joking."

"No, I am not, do not tell the doctors what I have said. I saw you were an intelligent person and should know the truth."

"I am in love with you."

"Sorry, I am married."

Brian regretted his remark but put it down to the drugs. He now had to spend another ten days in hospital with numerous tests. Ken was disappointed but said he would go look up thrombosis and the drug treatment. On leaving hospital, Ken presented him with lots of information. His mates visited and said they had a good time although it rained for one week, but as they were going to leave, the weather got better and the next week was sunny. Brian showed them his stone and they couldn't believe anything that small could cause so much pain.

Brian was back at work within two weeks; he noticed Ken had an obsession with kidney stones. Brian felt a little embarrassed at what he had said to the nurse but he started to think the straightforward approach with women was the best. He soon found out that the nurse might have been a bit of an exception and he should be a little more subtle.

Brian was watching Ken enjoying school and doing well. In a way, he envied Ken but he decided to take all sorts of night school classes, including one on the history of Birmingham and the Black Country. He really enjoyed this course more than the engineering courses he normally took. He met Barbara at one of the dances at the Ladywood Reservoir dance hall. She was a good dancer and a good listener. They started courting and Brian met her parents and liked them both. He went to the pub with her father, Ted, they had a good conversation. Ted was also a fitter. During their conversation, Ted did warn Brian that Barbara had been a difficult child occasionally having periods when she was almost uncontrollable. If Ted was warning Brian, he did not take heed. Brian had a party when Ken was accepted at the University of Birmingham but Barbara declined the invitation.

Three years passed by and Brian became engaged to Barbara. Several of his friends declined the invitation to his engagement party; they had been alienated by Barbara. Brian realised she could be strong in her opinions but she was right to have her own views. Ken also came in for criticism but he could hold his own and loved to argue with Barbara. The engagement lasted over two years due to one or two problems. One problem was another kidney stone. Luckily, this operation required key-hole surgery conducted by his brother. This was one of the first operations that Ken tried this kind of surgery and even Ken was nervous.

This was a large stone that was blocking the ureter and produced several pieces presented to Brian as a present. Another problem arose when Brian and Barbara were visiting her parents. There was a rather loud argument and Brian sided with her parents as he thought Barbara was wrong. Brian was in the dog house for quite a while. Finally, they were married and found a flat. Brian started to enjoy married life for a couple of months. Another visit to her parents changed his peaceful marriage.

Barbara picked on some trivial thing that her father had said. Brian tried to intervene as he thought Barbara was being too critical. That set Barbara into a rage that lasted until they got home. In the morning, Brian had forgotten the previous night, but apparently, Barbara had not. She now started to tell Brian he was never on her side. Brian was glad to leave for work. In the next week, there was constant tension, culminating in a scene in the kitchen. Barbara was washing the crockery when Brian mentioned she had missed a bit of food on one of the plates. The next thing he knew, he had a plate flying towards his head. He ducked and it crashed into the wall. He caught the next plate and decided to leave. He spent the night at his mother's house.

Brian had to confront Barbara, but when he did, he saw such hatred in her face he backed away. The next day, he left work early and went to the flat to pack some of his clothes. That evening, he went near the flat to see the rest of his clothes on the grass outside the apartment. Brian couldn't think what had caused his wife to turn into a manic.

Brian went to talk to Barbara's parents and Ted told him that his mother could fly off into uncontrolled rages. Ted said that Brian should move out for a while and see if Barbara's mood would change. That confirmed Brian's opinion and he started living with his mother. Barbara made several almost obscene phone calls; her language was such that, when his mother picked up the phone, she couldn't believe what she was hearing. Brian asked Ken to take their mother to his flat then he changed the phone number. A couple of times, his friends had seen Barbara waiting outside the factory and Brian exited through a back door.

He wondered if he should approach the police but she was still his wife. Shortly afterwards, the police contacted him. Barbara had been to a pub and picked a fight with another woman. The police were called and they had taken her into custody. At the station, she had attacked the policemen and then the police doctor. He had suggested she needed to see a psychiatrist. Brian visited the police station and confronted Barbara, he asked her for a divorce and she became apoplectic. The police sergeant said she would have to go to a mental hospital; she couldn't stay in the cells as she was a danger to herself and everyone else.

Brian kept asking himself what he had done. Ted and Barbara's mother were on his side, telling him it was not his fault. Brian decided he must get away; he wanted a new life. The company he worked for had been taken over by an American company and he saw an advert for a job in Canada with an associate company. The job was initially for one year but he could apply for immigration status at the end of the year. The job was in London, Ontario, on the River Thames. Brian thought that was ideal as he had one year to assess his situation. His mother and Ken agreed he needed a break and they were happy for him to go to Canada.

London was a small but growing city. Brian found an apartment, bought a car and settled into his new job. The job was easy but the whole factory needed rearranging; machines were placed wrongly and often breakdowns were lengthy due to difficult accessibility to fix broken parts. The manager was very flexible and allowed Brian to change the positions of some of the machines. Outside work, Brian was enjoying Southern Ontario. His first trip was to Niagara Falls. The falls were impressive but a little disappointing; a visit in winter was much more impressive. Lake Huron to the north and Lake Erie to the south were both easily accessible. The area he liked best was near Kitchener where the Amish lived. Their lifestyle impressed him and brought back his history courses.

One day, Brian was introduced to an American visitor named Troy. Troy had heard of the changes that Brian had made that had improved the smooth running and profitability of the company. Brian was unaware that this was the big boss who owned the company and no one informed him. Troy told Brian that he loved the way he talked and the way he had rearranged this factory. Would Brian come to Atlanta Georgia where there was a similar factory? A green card could be arranged, and if Brian did not like the position, he could come back to London or could return to Birmingham. Brian looked at his manager and he was nodding that he should accept. Brian said, yes, but had a lease on his apartment. Troy indicated that was not a problem and an apartment was awaiting him in Atlanta.

Brian had to plan his journey and his manager advised that, first, he should go to Windsor, cross to Detroit and then head south on Highway 75, that would take him to Atlanta. It was over seven hundred miles from Detroit to Atlanta so Brian would have to sleep overnight somewhere; Cincinnati was suggested or somewhere close.

Brian enjoyed his journey but did not like the big cities and stayed overnight in a small town near Cincinnati. Detroit was a big disappointment; he crossed from Windsor on the bridge to Detroit. He found himself in a poor area and was glad to get out onto Highway 75.

Atlanta was a large city, and luckily, the factory was on the edge of the city. Brian had noticed that Atlanta was much warmer than London and he would not need his woollen sweaters. At the factory, he was met by Troy but he was still unaware that this was the big boss. The apartment selected for Brian was very upmarket and spacious. Brian was worried about the rent but Troy said he owned the apartment and the first few months would be free. Brian had landed on his feet.

The workforce was very friendly and Brian was often asked to repeat what he had said; they understood but just liked to listen to him speak. Brian was starting to get the impression that Troy was important. One day, Troy invited Brian to dinner and said he should take a taxi as they might have a few drinks. As the taxi pulled up to the house, Brian couldn't believe what he was seeing. The driveway had been long but this was a mansion. Troy met him and introduced his wife, Rose.

"May I call you Rose?"

"Certainly, young man, I would be disappointed if you called me anything else. I just love your accent."

"My accent is from Birmingham, England, and in fact, we have a dialect where some words date back to Shakespeare's time."

"Please come in and I would love to hear more at the dinner table."

The meal went very well and Troy hardly said a word. Brian was enjoying this dinner; the food was good and he said it was, 'bostin grub', and he was stuffed. He then said his last comment was from Birmingham, but if he used a Black Country term, he would say, 'bostin fittle'. Rose enjoyed the translation and admitted she had learned new words and new phrases; she would try them out on her friends. Brian talked about his life and both Troy and Rose were enjoying his company. Dinner was followed by drinks and Troy had the best whisky and brandy. They talked very little about work, and when Troy brought up the subject, Rose objected. As Brian left, Rose said he should come again and meet their daughter.

Rose contacted her daughter, Chantelle, and said she should come to dinner to meet Brian. Rose was very impressed with this young man and his accent was bewitching. Chantelle was studying to get a master's in history, her major was in American history but she had an interest in English history. Rose couldn't believe Brian had left school at fifteen; Troy pointed out that he left school at sixteen but that fell on deaf ears.

The factory was starting to improve with some of the suggestions and rearrangements Brian had made. He explained to the workforce what he was trying to do; half of them were listening but all of them were enjoying the way he spoke. At this dinner, Troy picked him up and delivered him to Rose. She was in a very good mood and was asking Brian to teach her new phrases.

"When we are leaving, we say, 'tarra a bit', which means, 'good bye for a while'. In the Black Country, sometimes we use words dating back to Elizabethan times such as 'bay' or 'baint' which means 'not', such as in, 'yo bay, om ya'. That means, 'you are not, are you?'"

"I have to get a pen and write these down, I am learning a new language."

As Rose went for a pen and paper, a very attractive young lady entered the room. Troy introduced his daughter, Chantelle, called Charley in the family. Brian was on the front foot straight away and said Charley looked like Rose. He also told her he wanted to wait for Rose so he could do a comparison.

"My mother had told me about your accent but had not warned me about you."

"I am sorry, I was just trying to make an impression and you have seen through me, let us start again."

At this point, Rose entered the room and welcomed Chantelle but was more interested in getting Brian's phrases. Troy was almost silent watching the interactions. The dinner was just as good as the first and the after-dinner drinks were just as good but Chantelle did not drink. She offered Brian a lift home and asked whether they could meet for lunch; of course, Brian agreed. Chantelle picked up Brian at the factory the next day and took him to a very upmarket restaurant. Brian admitted he had little money on him and he was still waiting for his credit card. Chantelle said it was her treat and she just wanted him to talk. Brian was a bit confused but started to tell her about Birmingham. Chantelle paid the bill and said that was the most entertaining lunch she had ever experienced.

During the next weeks, they had many meals together and Brian paid for at least half of them. Chantelle confronted her father.

"Daddy, Brian is the man for me; I love the way he talks, I am interested in what he has to say and I must see the places he describes."

"Charley, slow down, he is at least ten years older than you and he is still married. You have only known him a short time."

"Yes, he has described his marriage and the age difference is not important to me. He is the only man who just talks to me; he does not try to impress me, he does not talk down to me, he is so natural. All the other guys I have dated had some agenda, he has none."

"Well, this man has captured the two ladies in my life. Your mother wants to go to England but not London. She wants to go to Birmingham and get a chauffeured car and see all of England. I made the mistake of telling her it was a small country. She has a list of places as long as your arm."

"We will also go to England for a couple of weeks. Brian is looking into getting a divorce with the help of his brother and, surprisingly his in-laws. I can't wait but he says he has a lot of work to do before a holiday. By the way, I hope you are paying him well."

"I am assessing his worth."

Chantelle let Brian read her master's thesis which she was to submit in a few weeks. Brian found a couple of mistakes but said it was a good read and he learnt a lot, but then he was not a professor of history, he just loved History. Chantelle was very pleased he understood some differences between American and English spelling.

At weekends, unless Brian was busy, they would go out to the countryside in Chantelle's new Mustang. Georgia was very suited to convertibles except when it rained. Chantelle was a good driver but a little lead-footed and picked up a speeding ticket on their second drive. The policeman took her particulars and asked Brian if this was his car. Brian told the officer the car belonged to Chantelle and the officer asked Chantelle what Brian had said. After the policeman had left, Chantelle said she had never laughed at a speeding ticket before.

A few months passed and Troy and Rose went to England. The plan was to stay two weeks but they stayed three. Troy said they had visited several castles, three cathedrals, a few factories (one of which he owned) and lots of pubs. One taste of English beer was enough but he had found several malt whiskies he had not tried before. His comment was that, if that was a holiday, give him work any day. Rose had filled several diaries and now she was busy writing about their trip and a 'new' language.

Brian approached Troy and asked if he could take a couple of weeks off work to go to England.

"If I say, 'no', I will lose a daughter so, of course, you can, with my blessing."

Ken had done most of the work and a divorce was awaiting Brian's approval. Their mother would stay with Ken so Brian and Chantelle could stay in a two-up-two-down house built in Victoria's time. Chantelle was excited but Brian warned it was a bit small. He also said his mother's bed was pre-war.

"If you are trying to turn me off, you are doing the opposite."

They had slept together in Chantelle's apartment but her bed was huge. The apartment was also huge, with a floor space as big as his mother's whole house. Brian was a bit apprehensive about the next few weeks but he need not have worried.

They landed at Birmingham Airport to be welcomed by Ken and his mom. The mother was a bit shy but Chantelle gave her a hug and that squashed the nerves. Ken was very polite and handsome with not much of an accent. He explained he would drop them at their mother's house and come back later to pick them up for dinner. Brian realised he had not told Chantelle about the house, except it was two-up-two-down.

"The house is one of seven all joined together perpendicular to the street. We have to walk up an entry and enter the back yard through a gate. There is another entry on the other side of the houses to enter the front but we don't use that way."

"Are you trying to confuse me?"

"No you will see soon."

Brian let Chantelle walk up the entry and go to number six. As she was walking, the lady from number four poked her head over the fence.

"Allo, luv, oh, it's Brian, ow yow bin doin?"

"Very well, Mrs Rogers I have just come from America."

"Did yow see Niagara Falls, I saw it at the pictures last wick."

Chantelle was watching this encounter and Ken was smiling. They entered the backyard and the door that led to the kitchen. Chantelle was taken aback by how small the kitchen was. The bathroom and the toilet were adjacent to the kitchen and the other direction led to the living room. Ken excused himself and said he would be back later.

"Well, this is cosy, you will not be able to escape me. Who was that woman and what exactly did she say?"

"Mrs Rogers is from Dudley which is in the Black Country not far from Birmingham and I will take you there. Their accent is different from mine and she has been our neighbour for many years. She is lovely and harmless but a bit nosey. She was asking me how I was and the pictures are the cinema. Now, I suppose you need a shower so I will check it out. You have to stand in the bath and hold the shower head; be careful you don't slip in the bath. I will put on the heating. You might think this is Victorian, but when I was young, the toilet was outside and the bath was a large tin bath. This house has been 'modernised' only in the last few years."

"Well, this is an experience that I need, to get into English history."

After a difficult shower that needed Brian's help, they were picked up by Ken who said the next shower should be at his place. Brian was starting to think that they should have stayed at a hotel. The restaurant was in an upmarket hotel on the Hagley Road. The menu was extensive but

Brian wanted roast beef and Yorkshire pudding; he had missed that in Canada and America. Ken told them about his trip to the Pentagon with Brian's stone.

"You mean part of your body has been in the Pentagon?"

"Yes, but it was part I lost a long time ago."

They all laughed and Ken told them about his work. Chantelle was very impressed and wanted to see the hospital. Brian said they would visit the hospital and the university, but first, he had to see his wife. Ken nodded his head as though that was not a good idea. Chantelle said she understood and the subject was changed. Now, Brian's mother joined in asking Brian about Canada and America, it lightened the mood.

Arriving back at the house, Chantelle was surprised at the size of the bed.

"That looks cosy, you will not be able to escape me."

"I never want to escape you."

The next day, they went to Birmingham on a double-decker bus, which Chantelle thoroughly enjoyed. Brian took Chantelle to the museum and said he would leave her and be back in about one hour. Brian took a bus to the asylum. As he entered and signed into the visitor's book, he was greeted by a nurse.

"I will take you to Barbara's room, but if she gets excited, you should leave. She is on tranquillizers but she can still get aggressive."

The nurse unlocked the door, and as they entered, Barbara was sitting on the bed. She looked very thin and

119

was just staring at Brian. He stared back and then he noticed her blank stare was changing. The nurse told Brian he should leave as Barbara was getting excited. As he was leaving, he heard a scream and his name repeated several times. He was glad to get outside the building, and once in the grounds, he had a couple of deep breaths. His walk to the bus stop and his journey into the city was filled with visions of Barbara's face.

He arrived at the museum, found Chantelle and said, "I need a drink."

They went to a pub close to the museum. It was not the best pub in Birmingham but Chantelle liked the atmosphere. After a whisky, followed by a beer, Brian told Chantelle his experience that morning.

"Well, I think you have satisfied yourself she is beyond hope, now, let's go back to the museum. I am as interested in the building as in the exhibits."

Brian hired a car and they went to a market in Dudley. Brian informed Chantelle this was real Black Country and she should listen to the sounds.

"I hardly understand a word they say, what are spuds?"

"They are potatoes. I will take you to a real local pub where the landlady brews beer in the back of the pub. I will try to tell you about this dialect."

"I am getting used to going to a pub for a lecture."

"I will ignore that remark."

The pub was called Ma Pardoes and this was not a posh pub. They were greeted by the landlady and Brian explained that his American guest did not drink beer but she wanted to know about the Black Country dialect.

"Welcome, ma wench, yove cum to the right place."

"Wench is a girl or young woman, now, let's get down to some of the finer points. Letters at the beginning of words are often dropped. The letter 'h' is almost never pronounced and the letter 'g' at the end of the word is lost. How becomes "ow' and house becomes "ouse'. Living become 'livin' and working becomes 'workin'. Words with an 'a' are changed to an 'o'; I think it might come from old German, so man becomes 'mon', am becomes 'om' in 'yowm', you am or you are. There are also some old words, 'such a yon wench is bostin', the girl over there is a good looker."

"I think I might need a strong drink to understand all this. Can we go back to the market so I can have another try at listening to what they were saying?"

The next few days they spent time in the car going to Warwick Castle, Coventry Cathedral and Stratford upon Avon. They were able to see a play at the Stratford Theatre and Chantelle was entranced by the performance. Brian asked if Chantelle wanted to see anything more as time was approaching when they would leave for America. The only place she wanted to take a more in-depth look at was Birmingham University. She wanted to contact the history department. She was adamant she would be back.

Talking to Ken and his mother on the last day, Chantelle said she was awed by the history all around Birmingham. The language and attitudes were so different that she had to come back, as she wanted to know more. Ken confided in Brian that he had met a 'good one'. Ken and his mother were unhappy that Brian and Chantelle were leaving but they would meet again soon.

Arriving back in Atlanta, Troy explained that Rose was giving a lecture at some women's gathering and apologised for her absence. Brian thought nothing of it but Chantelle said her next lectures would have a lot more information. Arriving at the house, Rose was home. Chantelle immediately went straight to her; she had so much to tell. Brian was left with Troy who pulled out his new malt whisky. Troy explained this whisky was worth the trip to England. He had difficulty finding it in the US but had found a supplier. Brian's message was that he had visited the factory in Birmingham and they needed some new machinery.

"You want to spend my money."

"Yes, but this is an investment."

"I have a lot of factories in our country and I think we should look at them with your expert eye."

Meanwhile, Chantelle was telling her mother that she had missed Dudley Market. Chantelle was going to do a master's in history on Black Country History. She was going to talk her dad into letting Brian change the factory in Birmingham while she studied. Rose was very happy, she was now a celebrity talking about a 'new' English.

Brian received his divorce and the wedding was planned. Everything was going well, when disaster struck. Chantelle and Brian were going on their visit to the country when the Mustang was clipped by a truck as they entered the freeway. The Mustang mounted the guard rail and hit a brick wall.

Troy had to go to the crash scene to identify the bodies. He noticed there was hardly a scratch on the rear of the Mustang. He would not let Rose see the bodies until the undertaker had 'fixed' them up. He contacted Ken and invited him and his mother to the funeral, which would be delayed until they arrived. Rose shut herself off for two days, she was so upset. Troy spent most of his day in his office in a sort of trance. He couldn't think what to do next and this was a new thing to him.

Ken and his mother arrived in Atlanta and were taken to Troy's house. The mothers had a long sobbing hug and they all retreated to the lounge. Ken felt the need to take charge and said he would like to see the bodies the next day. If he thought it suitable, he would allow his mother to see the bodies.

The funeral director showed Ken the open coffins and Ken took his mother to see them. She kissed them both and quickly left. Ken spoke to the director and said he would put something in Brian's coffin, something that belonged to him. Ken produced two small vials of kidney stones and placed them near Brian's kidneys.

"I am returning these, they have made my career but belong to you, farewell, brother."

Renal Surgeon

Ken became a renal surgeon after he saw the agony his brother, Brian, suffered passing a kidney stone.

His elder brother, Brian, had been killed in a car crash with his fiancé, Chantelle. This happened in Atlanta, Georgia, and Brian was buried there. Brian's first marriage was a disaster and his wife was in an asylum. Brian and Chantelle were to be married when the accident happened. Ken and his mother had gone to Atlanta for the funeral and met Chantelle's parents. Ken had kept in touch with Troy and Rose. Troy would often call at all hours of the day and night. Ken did not mind as he liked Troy and Rose.

Ken had become a senior surgeon at a hospital in Birmingham. He had developed key-hole surgery and laser surgery, more or less, getting rid of large-scale 'open 'em up' surgery to get the kidney stone out. Ken had also shown how kidney stones could affect soldiers in the field, both the British and American armies. His expertise in the field had him giving lectures on kidney disease in the UK and abroad. Ken's mother pointed out that, although he was successful, he was still a bachelor.

Ken liked his lifestyle; he could go anywhere he wanted, eat in the best restaurants and pick and choose his friends. The only problem was that he did not have many friends. At work, he was respected and treated courteously, but at home, he was isolated in his flat with little interaction with his neighbours. His mother suggested he should take a break and go somewhere and relax. Two days by the sea were about as much as he could take; he was not a beach person. He had visited many cities in Europe and was not a great holiday maker. It occurred to him he should see a bit of America.

One phone call from Troy had him thinking he should visit Atlanta and also Canada. His brother loved his stay in North America and Ken thought he should take a look. Ken arranged with Troy to stay for a week in Atlanta. Troy and Rose were very happy to have him visit, in fact, they were excited about accommodating him.

Rose had isolated herself when Chantelle was killed. Chantelle was her only daughter. Troy had told Ken he had several factories in America and one in Canada, and if he wished to travel, he would be accommodated anywhere he went. Troy's request was to find him a new malt whisky. Rose's request was for him to talk at one her ladies' meetings, of course, using a bit of dialect. Two problems; Ken knew nothing about malt whisky and he had lost much of his dialect.

He consulted a colleague who was a whisky drinker and decided to go to a market in Smethwick to listen to the people. His colleague found a special malt whisky from a small distillery. He described the taste as having a slight taste of peat but not as strong as Laphroaig. The twelve-year-old was the one he liked. Ken ordered two bottles; he had never tasted Laphroaig.

Walking in the Smethwick Market, he was asked if he was lost, he had forgotten to wear old clothes.

"Are you lost, luv?"

"No, I have come to the market to refresh my memory of how people speak."

"Well, yow've cum to the right place, tek care there could be pickpockets about, bastards."

"Thank you for that advice."

Ken had forgotten how friendly the local people were. He checked his wallet. The only time he spoke to people was at work. Most of his patients were silent unless they said, 'Ouch', in which case, they needed more anesthetic. He had forgotten potatoes were called 'spuds' and cauliflowers were 'collies'. Practising the local word sounds made him laugh. It then occurred to him that he spoke to his mother regularly and she had a local Birmingham accent slightly different from the Smethwick accent. Many of the nurses were from Birmingham and he listened to what they said but not how they said it. He suddenly became interested in sounds and words.

If he was going to talk to Americans there would be some ordinary words they may not use. Phrases such as 'a two-up-two-down house' with a coal house in the back yard, which you had to reach by walking up an entry, would be foreign to Rose's friends. Some houses had coal cellars with a grating in the street. Birmingham had lots of cuts (canals) with barges carrying goods and people. He started to amuse himself by finding words he may have used as a child. Suddenly, he realised he had become isolated, he even had his groceries delivered.

Now, he started to do his own shopping, and on one of his trips, he went into an Indian shop in Smethwick and was served by a young girl. She had the most distinct accent that made him listen very carefully. It occurred to him she had probably been born in Smethwick and had picked up the strongest accent he had heard.

Work had taken a back seat as he prepared to go to America. The first week would be easy with Troy and Rose. The second week he would go to London, Ontario, and hire a car. Troy had accommodation lined up for him in that city. He would be able to see Southern Ontario. The third week, he would be based in Toronto and maybe drive as far as Montreal. This was new to Ken and he felt excited; there was some structure but a lot of freedom. He was so used to structure in his life and this was like going back to his childhood. Money was no problem as he spent little of his salary.

The last time he went to Atlanta with his mother for Brian's funeral, he had flown economy class. This time, he flew business class to New York and then to Atlanta. It was all so easy and somehow less tiring. He was met in Atlanta by an excited Troy and Rose. Rose was hugging him and saying he was not like Brian but there were similarities. Troy was still apologising for Brian's death. Ken was in a good mood; he was learning to relax. Troy had to sample his malt whisky when they reached the house and agreed it was different.

"You might find it hard to get."

"I will put my agent on to it and I will send a message to the manager of my factory in Birmingham; this is going to go down well in my whisky club."

At dinner, Ken was introduced to Taylah, Troy's niece. She was staying with them while studying history at the university. Her parents lived in Birmingham, Alabama. She was following in Chantelle's footsteps and had met Brian a few years ago. Taylah was a good-looking girl and Ken was very happy to talk to her about English history and life in Britain. Rose was listening and commented that Ken's accent was different from Brian's.

"When we were young, we both had a Birmingham accent, but as we grew up, mine changed. University and then the medical profession softened my accent and made it more like what we call BBC or Oxford English. I suppose I did not notice the change and fit in with the mode of speech of my colleagues. Since your invitation to talk to your ladies, I have been back to my birth area and listened to how people speak. In a way, it has opened my eyes and now I am listening more, thank you."

Troy was listening and had to butt in.

"You have probably just made my wife a friend for life; she has this obsession with language, thanks to your brother."

"I thank my brother for many things, including making me the man I am."

The dinner went very well and Ken preferred brandy to whisky; that was no problem for Troy, he had an extensive cellar. Troy was amused when Ken told him many English people kept coal in their cellar before the clean air act in 1956. One of Ken's uncles was a coal man and saw his business collapse when they stopped coal being burnt in fire places in most of Birmingham. That gave Ken an idea to talk about (fog) smog in his lecture. Taylah was asking lots of questions, particularly about the Black Country. Chantelle had told her about this area of England. Ken was tired, and finally, had to excuse himself and go to bed.

After Ken left the table, Rose was saying this young man was going to slay her ladies. Taylah was telling her uncle she had to go to England after she graduated from university. Troy was still sampling his whisky.

Ken's lecture was a great success and he had to cut it short as he had too much to say. He was used to giving lectures to students and thought fifty minutes was suitable for young students and was surprised these older ladies were listening intently after one hour. Taylah was in the audience with a friend and both were clapping vigorously at the end of his lecture. There were many questions; one lady said her mother was from England and talked about dripping.

"I have forgotten what it is, can you enlighten us?"

Ken smiled and said, "When you roast meat, the fat lands in the pan. If you take this liquid and let it cool, the top becomes solid, that is the fat. Underneath, will be a jelly, we normally spread that on bread with maybe a pinch of salt."

"Ooh, I will go home and try that."

"I don't think you should eat much animal fat."

Another lady asked, "What is a whistle and flute?"

"That is cockney rhyming slang from London and it means a man's suit."

Rose butted in and told the audience that Ken was tired and she had to cut the event short.

Ken told Taylah he needed a drink so Taylah and her friend took him to a bar. Ken could not believe his eyes; they had Bass on draught. They were serving it in pints so he ordered one, then he apologised and asked what the ladies needed. He could not believe he had ordered his drink first; he must be in holiday mode. Both girls did not drink beer or spirits so they wanted Coke. He apologised for his behaviour but explained when he saw English beer he forgot himself. The girls giggled but said nothing. Ken watched as the barmaid took a glass from the fridge and poured an ice-cold beer. He then asked the barmaid for a bottle of beer to be put in the fridge.

"But it is warm."

"No problem I will drink and pay for both beers."

Taylah and her friend watched as he drank the warm beer, to them, it was very unusual. When the bottle of beer was finished, he touched the pint glass and it was still too cold so he cupped it in his hands. All the time, the bar maid had been watching this beer on the counter getting warm. Ken explained that at ice temperature the beer was tasteless and to get the full flavour it had to be just below room temperature. These girls were sitting at the bar loving everything he said. Later, Taylah told Troy the story and he said he could not stand English beer.

Rose was getting lots of complements from her ladies and several said they had to visit England, others were amazed he was still a bachelor. Troy wanted him to stay longer. He had taken Ken into the countryside to get a 'feel' for Georgia. He insisted that he would drive and would not let either Rose or Taylah drive. Ken was enjoying this holiday. After Ken left Atlanta, Taylah told Rose that she was in love with Ken.

Ken flew from Atlanta to Toronto and hired a car and decided to drive straight to London. In London, he was met by the manager of the factory owned by Troy and taken to a flat. It turned out that Troy paid the rent on the flat occupied originally by Brian. He used it for visitors and did not seem to care when it was empty. Ken realised that Troy was very sentimental. Ken's first venture was to the Amish country. He had bought several books but he had to see for himself. Seeing these people had Ken enthralled, they were so different. He went to a restaurant with Amish cooking and it reminded him of Germany; plenty of potatoes. There was a lot to see in Southern Ontario but he had to come back to Amish country again.

Ken went to Windsor and looked across the river to Detroit but took Brian's advice not to take a closer look. Ken loved the cleanliness of Ontario; even the cities were clean. He started to notice he was looking at things differently. In Birmingham, he would not notice litter, but here, he was surprised when he saw it. Roadside signs became important; some were hilarious but others had a good message. Ken was feeling he was changing. Even the beach at Grand Bend had him watching and enjoying the antics of the beach goers.

After a week in London, he moved to a good hotel in Toronto; at least they had parking for his hired car. This was a big city with good restaurants and lots of entertainment. After a couple of days, he wanted to get out. He wanted to drive to Ottawa and then Montreal. These were long drives but he was enjoying the scenery. Ottawa was the cleanest city he had ever seen. Montreal was so different, he decided his next trip would be to that city.

Flying back to England, he was asking himself why he had not taken a longer holiday. He decided his next holiday would be in Canada, possibly Quebec.

In Atlanta, Rose was thinking of visiting England again. Troy had procured more malt whisky and was introducing it to his club with much appreciation. Troy was not interested in golf, unusual in Georgia, but he was invited to talk about whisky and England at a good golf club. He was now thinking of a trip involving a tour of whisky distilleries. Taylah was sure she was going to England to study Black Country history and she was also now studying English Language but not finding much about dialects.

Back in Birmingham, Ken settled into his routine and was finding it dull. He told his mother about his trip and was now starting to listen to how she spoke. Being away for three weeks had allowed a back-up of operations, and so, he set his mind to clearing the backlog. His colleague asked him about the malt whisky. Ken advised him he should try and contact the distillery and get a commission from orders coming from Atlanta. Later, his friend came back and said he had a free bottle from the distillery.

A few months passed and Troy said he was planning a visit and Taylah wanted to visit for a month to see Birmingham. In a phone call, Troy asked if it was possible for Taylah to stay with Ken's mother, Troy would pay. Ken answered that staying with his mother was OK but payment was not necessary. Troy's answer was that it was important to him. It was settled that Taylah would come with Troy and Rose and then they would go to Scotland, leaving Taylah with Ken's mother. Ken booked them into the Grand Hotel for the first night.

The greetings at Birmingham Airport were very warm; Rose and Ken's mother were kissing and hugging as the others watched on. Rose was saying that Doris had raised two special sons and she wished she could have had a son. Troy was thinking the same. Ken introduced Taylah to his mother. There was then another bout of kissing and hugging. A taxi to the Grand Hotel had Troy in raptures. This was a black cab that accommodated them all and luggage which was not insubstantial. Troy insisted they should all have dinner together. Ken pointed out that he should take Taylah to his mother's house; it may not be suitable.

Taylah was looking at the streets and houses in the drive from the hotel with great interest. She had never been outside Georgia and Alabama and never in a poor city area. Now, she was seeing new sights. One sight that had to be explained was a bombed area; there was one at the end of the street where Ken's mother lived.

As Taylah walked up the entry, none of Doris's neighbours were there to greet her. Entering the house, was to her like going into the previous century. Ken's mother showed her around the house and the bedroom where she would sleep. This room was tiny compared with her bedroom at Troy's house or home in Alabama. The room had wallpaper, which was new to her. The stove in the kitchen was, to her, something out of a museum and the water heater above the sink was something she had never seen.

Ken had brought the luggage from the street and Taylah told him she would love living in the past. Ken warned her that having a shower was going to be an experience, and if she needed a good shower, she should come to his place. Taylah was thinking that might not be a bad idea. Ken said to settle in and he would pick them up to go to the Grand Hotel in the evening. Taylah sat in the small bedroom and was writing notes about everything. These notes were going to fill several letters to her friends in Atlanta.

The meal was good and Troy found another whisky he had not tried. He chatted with the barman who showed him the range of whiskies they had. Troy had little interest in the meal. He told the barman he would be back in a week. Rose was listening to Taylah tell her about the house and wanted to see it the next day, but Troy reminded her they were off to Scotland the next day. Ken's mother, Doris, was telling them about the house and how they rented it before the war. When Brian was earning money, they bought it with the help of Ken. She knew it was tiny compared with Troy's mansion but she lived alone surrounded by helpful neighbours and was contented.

The next day, Doris asked Taylah what she wanted to do.

"I would like to see the hospital where Ken works and the university."

"Well, we will walk to Dudley Road and catch a number eleven bus. From the bus, we will walk near the hospital where Ken started his career and on to the university and then catch a bus to the city."

"I am in your hands, let's go."

On their walk, Taylah asked about one of the buildings.

"That is a bakery and now we are passing a pub."

"I love that smell of the bakery and I would love to visit a pub."

"Yes, we can always get freshly baked bread but you will have to let Ken take you to a pub as I don't drink. Pubs have bars that are only meant for men and a smoke room where men and women sit together."

"I forgot to bring my dairy; I can't wait to write this down. Will we see many more sights that should go in my dairy?"

"You will see many new sights and will do this plenty of times so just enjoy for the first time."

Doris loved having a very polite young lady with her. They entered the bus at the back and Doris said they should climb the stairs to the upper deck. She explained this was normally for smokers but they would get a good view if they could sit in the front seat. They did get the front seat and Taylah was excited. The conductor came to give them tickets and Doris paid.

"What did he say? I only caught a couple of words."

"He asked me where we were going and told me the price for two tickets, which I paid."

"What is 'luv'?"

"It is just a greeting; I find hard to explain but there are others like 'ducks' and 'darling'; you will hear them often."

Taylah loved this ride and she saw so many pubs she lost count. Doris pointed out they would leave the bus before the Cadbury's Chocolate Factory. Taylah had only tasted Hershey's chocolate and had never tried Cadbury's chocolate. They reached their destination and they descended the stairs.

The conductor said, "'Bye, love, don't get lost, I hope youm not ailing."

Taylah asked what the conductor had said to her. Doris explained that he saw she was going to the hospital and hoped she was not sick.

"I am so glad you are with me. I am lost and feel like I am in a totally foreign country with a different language."

"You will find your way but please ask me if you don't understand."

Doris was remembering when Ken was asking questions and Brian did most of the answering; now she was the teacher. Doris had forgotten to tell Taylah to put on good walking shoes but then she was young. Taylah was impressed with the hospital and the bell tower of the university. All the buildings looked so old she would have to investigate them at a later date. She was regretting she had not brought her note pad.

They caught the bus to the city centre and Doris took her to the Bull Ring market.

"I don't understand much of what they say but I am starting to get the rhythm of their speech. I need to buy something and see how it goes."

Doris stood back and watched Taylah buy a scarf. She wanted to intervene but she kept quiet. She was amused by the palaver and how two people were trying to understand each other. When the deal was done, Doris thought that Taylah had been cheated but she kept silent. Taylah was happy with the deal and so Doris did not give her opinion.

Taylah was happy to get back to Doris's house; she had so much to write in her diary. Double-decker buses were her favourite and she described them in great detail in letters to her friends. Arriving back at the house, there was no dinner prepared so Doris asked whether Taylah could eat fish and chips. Taylah loved these fish and chips wrapped in newspaper. Now, she had to fill in her notes.

Ken had decided to give his mother and Taylah a day or two on their own; he was busy anyway. Actually, he was dying to see Taylah. He called his mother but they were out. Doris was taking Taylah on the full circle of the number eleven bus. She pointed out the Cadbury factory and now Taylah had to try the chocolate. Taylah had taken her notebook and it was filling up fast. The conductor seemed to talk the whole journey and Taylah understood about fifty percent. Arriving back at the house, Ken was waiting; he had his own key.

Doris said she was tired after that trip. She realised that leaving the young ones was a good idea.

Taylah said she had to change but she was ready to go anywhere Ken would take her. She said she would like to go to a pub. Ken said that the pubs in this area could be a bit rough so they would go to the edge of Birmingham. Taylah did not care; Ken was giving her shivers. Ken's choice of the Hen and Chickens on the Wolverhampton Road was a good one as they could sit in comfort and silence to discuss Taylah's impressions. Suddenly, Ken was interested in Taylah and he could not put his feelings into any order.

This was different; he was being told about Taylah's experiences and her problems with living in Birmingham. She loved to live in history but it was difficult. Ken was not to know that Doris thought Taylah would find it difficult at first but would adapt. Doris was thinking of a daughter-in-law.

"Pounds, shillings and pence, it is so complicated. Your mother tells me it will help my mental arithmetic. I am hopeless at maths. What I do love are the buses and conductors; those guys talk incessantly and now I'm beginning to understand what they say.

"Funnily, I haven't been on a city bus for years but mom is a regular user. Did she take you to the market?"

"Yes, she took me to the Bull Ring, that was an experience, she has promised to take me to another market but I have forgotten the name."

"She will probably take you to Smethwick Market. You should hear slightly different accents from Birmingham."

"Yes, one of your mom's neighbours was talking to her and I could hardly understand a word she said."

"Yes, she is from Dudley in the real Black Country, and if you are going to study Black Country history, you should get mother to take you to their market."

"I think I have led a very sheltered life; I have never been to a market in Atlanta or Birmingham Alabama. My mother rarely shops, she orders things to be delivered. The only things I have shopped for are clothes. Your mother showed me the bakery and their bread was so tasty. What I really loved was a jam doughnut; we have doughnuts but not like that. The butcher's shop was interesting and she

139

showed me a shop where they used to sell whale meat and horse meat. Have you ever eaten whale meat?"

"I suppose I have but I have certainly eaten horse meat which is a delicacy in some parts of France."

"Your mother said she would not take me to a pub, but here we are, and it is so nice and quiet."

"Yes, this is mid-week, but at weekends, this place will be swinging with a live band. I will take you to a real country pub soon and you will see a different style. The pubs in my mother's area are more working-class places; they can be friendly but are much rougher."

Taylah was not sure what Ken meant with that last phrase but she thought she would have a look for herself when she found her way around. The first week passed very quickly and Troy and Rose were back in the Grand Hotel. Troy could talk about nothing but whisky and the distilleries. Rose loved the countryside and the quaint houses and one old hotel where they had stayed. She was adamant she wanted to see Doris's house. Ken was taking a few days off and would pick them up, take Troy to his factory and take Rose to his mother's house. Then they would go for lunch in the Gypsy's Tent near Hagley. He described it as a large country pub. Ken would phone them and book a table for four as his mother would not come.

Early in the morning, Ken picked up Troy and Rose. Troy said he would chat with the manager. Chat was a word he never used but had picked it up on his trip to Scotland. There were many words he did not understand and the accents were very difficult. He had only been to this factory once before. He explained he had bought out a company and this was part of the group and he had intended to visit with Brian before his death. Ken said he would take a look when he picked Troy up later. Rose was excited to see Doris's house. She was shocked when Ken told her about the bombed area at the end of the street. Her eyes were everywhere as they walked up the entry.

"Allow, lov, ow bin ya Ken, your mom 'as a smasher with her as a lodger."

Rose said she caught some of that but what was a 'smasher'? Ken explained she meant Taylah was a good looker. Rose smiled and said that was a new phrase for her diary. Entering the house, Rose thought of the past. She explained that, when she was young, her parents had a small house and then her dad got rich. Taylah took her on a tour and the first place was the shower and the second place was her bedroom. Rose sat in a chair and started to tell about her childhood. Ken saw a glint in her eyes that turned to tears. Rose stiffened up and told Doris it was a pleasure to come to her house. Leaving the house, Rose and Doris hugged and kissed; Rose was quite emotional.

Ken, Rose and Taylah had a good look around the factory. Troy said he had to have more discussions with the manager and he would come by taxi the next day. Troy liked the taxis. He also loved the Gypsy's Tent which did not have a malt he had not tried but the view of the countryside impressed him.

The next day, the ladies decided to pick Rose up from the hotel and take the bus to Dudley. Doris thought that there may not be a full market but there should be a small market during weekdays. Rose loved the bus (a Midland Red) as they had a front seat on the upper deck. There was a small market and Rose bought a tee shirt that had Black Country on the chest. She did not care who it fit, she would frame it. Walking around, there were plenty of shops and Rose bought a few things that would remind her of Dudley. Then she spied a pub and said she wanted to visit, even if it was not the one Chantelle talked about. Doris said she was not familiar with pubs but she would ask where the ladies could sit. They found a quiet room and Rose insisted she would buy the drinks. Doris and Taylah did not drink alcohol so Doris suggested a pop or fruit juice.

"What is pop?"

"Something like fizzy lemonade."

"I will have a pop."

Rose went to the counter and ordered two pops and a sherry. Then there was the problem of payment. Rose was bemused by the money and Doris told her to give the barman a pound note and wait for the change. This was the first time she had to count money. The other things she had bought had a price which she was told. This barman did not tell her how much to pay. Rose was so happy as they caught the bus back to Birmingham; she had understood some of the locals and did a bit of shopping. Listening to the conductor had her enjoying the ride. Troy was waiting anxiously, of course, he was in the bar. They parted with the knowledge Ken would take them out the next day.

Ken took them to Clent Hills and the Fountain Inn where they had lunch. Troy, again, could not find a malt whisky he had not sampled so he tried an aged Johnny Walker. They were all impressed with the oak beams and the décor of the pub. Rose asked if Chantelle had visited this pub. Ken said he was not sure but he would have expected Brian to bring her here. Rose said she felt her presence. Troy did not look happy.

Troy and Rose were leaving and Taylah had another two weeks. She decided, after her uncle and aunt left, she would try to get around on her own. Rose was almost reluctant to go home; she said something had clicked in Birmingham and she was going home to an empty house. Troy could not wait to get back and give a slide show of distilleries; he also had some ideas to improve his factories. Ken and Doris were invited to come and stay at any time; they would be most welcome. There were lots of hugging and kissing at the airport and also lots of tears.

Taylah had two weeks to find her feet; she had decided she had to come back after the first day. She decided to go to the university, have a look around and then find Ken in the city. She caught the Outer Circle number eleven bus. Doris had told her she could come home on the same bus. Taylah knew that as she had done the full circle. The university buildings were not very old but they looked it to Taylah. She found the history department and was able to talk to one of the professors. After graduation, she would have no problem doing a master's degree in Black Country history. He warned her, that as a foreign student, she would have to pay tuition fees. She had no problem and he confided they loved foreign students who paid fees.

Next, she took the bus to the hospital and found out how to get to the renal unit. The receptionist asked if she was a patient.

"Not yet, I hope never but I am here to see the senior renal surgeon."

She was directed to his office and had to wait in the outer office until he finished an operation. Ken was very happy to see her and invited her into his office while he wrote his notes.

"Did you come on your own?"

"Yes, I decided I had to try to get around on my own. I visited the university and found the history department."

"Good, we will go to my flat, and after I have changed, we can go for a meal. By the way, you have not been to my place."

"No, I had an invite for a shower but I have mastered your mother's shower."

They both laughed at that comment.

Ken took her to his flat and offered her tea, which she drank with only sugar. Taylah looked around the flat and realised it needed a woman's touch. The flat was on the second floor with a view of the university. She realised from her observation of housing in Birmingham this was an upmarket area. Ken's furniture was minimal and Doris's furniture was more comfortable. Ken had changed and he looked so smart. He asked if Taylah had tried Indian food and she answered in the negative. He warned her it could be spicy and hot. She said she had eaten Gumbo and liked spicy food. Ken said they would take a taxi as he did not drive when he had a drink.

The taxi driver was a chatty fellow and Taylah enjoyed his West Indian accent. The ride was quite a short one but the sights were different in the early evening with the street lights starting to come on. Everything seemed to have a softer look. Ken told her this was his favourite restaurant as it was the first Indian restaurant he had visited with his brother. Taylah understood Ken was not afraid of talking about his dead brother.

The restaurant was half empty being a week day. The staff knew Ken well but this was the first time they had seen him with female company. Ken asked what she would like and Taylah told him to order what he thought she would like. He had no idea what she would like but he decided not to order any hot curries but several samosas, which were his favourite. As they chatted, Taylah was enjoying the food. For a drink she wanted only water. Ken had two Kingfisher beers during the meal and a brandy at the end of the meal.

"Your uncle likes whisky but I prefer brandy."

"Yes, my daddy likes whisky and my aunt likes sherry. My mother does not drink and she is always telling me about the dangers of alcohol. To be frank, I tried wine and disliked it. Daddy's whisky was too strong and I was not keen on beer. Coming here, I realise I have led a sheltered life but I am glad here we speak a similar language. I am not sure how I would fare if it was Russian or Arabic. What surprises me is that, here, I feel freer, maybe because no one knows me and I am a bit different."

"You will soon go back home, will you come back?"

"Most certainly, I have already been to the university history department, and once I have my degree, they will welcome me. If your mother will have me for a short time, I will find my own place."

"Why not stay with me; I have two bedrooms and my place needs a woman's touch."

Taylah had a shiver go down her spine; she was so excited by that comment it was so unexpected.

"I have to get my degree first but I only have two courses left and I will be here as fast as a bullet."

Ken was enjoying this meal and he was surprised by his invitation. The taxi ride to Doris's house was quite short but it ended with a kiss from Taylah.

"I will have to pay for the next meal, may it be soon."

"We will see about that but it will have to be soon as you will be going home. On Saturday, I will pick you up and we will get out of the city and go into the country, so now, good night."

Taylah walked up the entry and felt she was flying. Doris greeted a grinning Taylah and realised she'd had a good evening. Doris was worried Ken was a bit of a loner and she was looking forward to grandchildren; all her relatives had grandchildren.

On Saturday, Ken picked up Taylah and took her to Worcester. They went to the cathedral to see where King

John was buried. They walked along the River Severn hand in hand, and as it was approaching lunch, they went to a pub called the Cardinal's Hat reputed to be the oldest pub in Worcester. Ken said he would have shandy as he was driving.

"What is a shandy?"

"Basically, half and half, lemonade and beer, try one, and if you don't like it, I will buy you a fruit juice."

Taylah liked it as it took away some of the sweetness of the lemonade. Ken told her it may not go well with lager but she should try it in America and set a trend. He was laughing inside at how unserious he had become. They followed the River Severn to Bewdley where they had lunch and another shandy overlooking the river. Taylah was in heaven but she had to pay for the lunch, protesting it was a chance for her to use pounds, shillings and pence. On Sunday, Ken took his mother and Taylah to a pub at Upton-on-Severn and told them to drink in the peace and quiet. Doris said that peace and quiet could be had many places but they should smell the countryside. Ken had been outdone by his mother. Taylah said she had never smelled the surroundings and Doris had put another good thought in her head.

Doris said she loved the countryside, as she thought her ancestors came from Evesham.

"Evesham is on the River Avon and I am not sure whether they were farmers or boat people."

Ken said, "You never told me that."

"Well, you never asked and I don't think you know much about our ancestors."

Ken had again been outdone by his mother.

"Wow, I have to talk to my parents when I get back home; I know nothing about my ancestors."

Ken took Taylah to the airport and she was crying while hugging him. He was also unhappy to see her leave. She said she would complete her courses and be back as soon as possible. She also had to find some personal history; who were her ancestors? Ken was also now interested in his ancestors. Doris was at the airport and told Taylah she was welcome to come back and stay as long as she wanted. Taylah was having second thoughts about leaving but she had to come back with a degree to get into graduate school.

Arriving at Atlanta Airport, she was met by her parents and Rose. Troy had some problem in the factory which kept him away. Her mother, Elvira, thought Taylah had changed and Rose thought it must be Ken's influence. Her father, Josh, said he now had a grown-up daughter and what did she want to do now?

"I want to marry the man I love and I will live wherever he wants to live. Firstly, I have two things I must do: I want to get my degree and I want to know about my ancestors."

Josh was not so happy about that last statement.

"Troy and I came from a dirt poor family and we have left that behind."

"But Daddy, you both have made it out of poverty so you must have something from your parents."

This put a bit of a dampener on the arrival so Rose changed the subject.

"What did you learn in England?"

"I have several diaries full of my observations. I felt I was living in history and I was living in a country where we spoke the same language but differently. In some ways it made me realise we do not appreciate our history and now I want to know both histories."

Elvira said she wanted to know more about this man. Taylah said she would like to sleep before she told of her feelings; the flight had been tiring. They all retired to Troy's house. Troy was there to meet them in a happy mood, his problem at the factory had been solved.

Josh involved Troy in a very deep conversation and was worried about their past. Troy's response was, did they have anything to be ashamed of? Josh made Troy promise to tell Taylah only the barest details and leave her to talk to her mother and aunt.

The next day, Taylah was up bright and early and was having breakfast with her mother well before the others woke up. She was asking her mother why her father was unhappy about looking into the past.

"I think he was not happy with the past and does not want to relive it. When I met him, he was working in our cotton warehouse. My father promoted him to manager and I met him and we married, not to the liking of my mother. Your father's mother had died in child birth when he was young. His father was a blacksmith and struggled to bring up two boys and your Aunty Jessica. I think your great-grandfather was a miner but I am not sure. I have no idea about your grandmother."

"Thank you, Mother, I think I will leave my father's side as a mystery. How about your family; where do they come from?"

"My father and his father before were cotton merchants. My grandfather married a Spanish lady and that is why I am called Elvira. I think my grandmother was rich and that is how we did well in cotton. I met her once and she was beautiful but very prim and proper. I think you should put this ancestor tracing in the background and resume your studies."

"Yes, Mother, I can try later but I need to get my degree. I want you to meet Ken. I am sure you will like him but I love him."

The others all appeared for breakfast, and so, their discussion terminated. Troy was full of beans, telling them all Ken's brother had made him a lot of money. His factories were turning out more produce faster and orders were being fulfilled without any delay. Rose was having fun with her ladies group and they all wanted Ken to come back. Josh was saying he had to get back to Birmingham, Alabama, as some new state regulation might affect his business. Elvira said she would stay a few more days as she had to have a serious discussion with her daughter.

After Josh had left, Elvira wanted to know more about Ken. Troy and Rose knew him well so they had a discussion with the four at the table.

"I know Ken more than anyone else so I am going to have my say. I first met Ken at the funeral of his brother and my cousin. I was very close to my cousin and had met Brian several times, and when I met Ken, I knew they were very different persons. When he came to visit my aunt and uncle, I saw a very intelligent and educated man. My friend and I went to his lecture and I fell in love with him then. It was not love at first sight, as I had seen him before, but it was the way he dealt with people and situations, he was so at ease. My trip to England opened my eyes to another world and he was there to explain it to me. He is very understanding and gentle. I am going to get my degree and go to live with him."

"What are you saying? That is not what should happen; you are throwing yourself at a man who may not marry you."

"Mother, you do not know this man, you have to meet him. If I throw myself, I am certain he will catch me."

Now, Troy and Rose thought they should lighten the mood. Rose was offering to take Elvira to England but Troy said that Elvira and Josh should go to England and see for themselves. Troy was betting they would enjoy themselves. Elvira was not convinced; she thought Troy and Rose were too liberal.

Elvira left for Birmingham and Taylah sat down with her aunt.

"I know my mother is a bit straight-laced but my father surprised me when I mentioned ancestry."

"It is complex; in this society many look only towards the future and forget the past. My husband and your father were never really poor. Their father was a blacksmith and Troy learned to make things and that started him on his career. Your father worked in a warehouse and used his skills to get to manager. Your great-grandparents came from the north and I think your great-grandfather was a miner. My parents were not rich. I remember when I was little sitting on my father's horse-drawn wagon. Then my father had several wagons followed by horseless trucks. That brought us out of poverty. When I went to Doris's house, it brought back memories of our first house and I could see my mother and father. I know nothing about my grandparents."

"Thanks, Aunty, but what is your opinion of Ken?"

"I am married but I would marry him in a minute if he asked me. I am joking, but I can't find fault with him, but then I do not know him very well. At the funeral, I saw a man with a strong character, and when he visited, I saw a very educated man. My question to you is, where would you find better?"

"Yes, Aunty, I have not looked but I am certain there is no one out there better than Ken. I love Doris and know she wants grandchildren and I am very willing to give them to her. The important thing to do now is getting my degree."

The next two months were filled with her courses. She used a bit of her knowledge of Birmingham city life to fill in one of her essays about urban living. That essay got her an A and the tutor wanted to know more. Aunty Rose was always involving her in discussions with her older lady's group.

Elvira was the problem, and so, Taylah had to encourage her parents to visit Birmingham, England. She wanted to be there when they visited. Her father was dragging his feet and that gave Taylah time to finish her degree.

One lunchtime, Taylah was doing her usual walk, when a man on a bicycle pulled up next to her, it was Ken. She nearly jumped out of her skin.

"What are you doing here?"

"Well, I thought I should meet my future in-laws, and as they haven't come to see me, I thought I should come to see them."

Now, tears were streaming down Taylah's face. "Is that a proposal?"

"Well, it is only temporary if your parents approve. Anyway, I need a pillow for my knee."

"My parents have no say in this. I love you and want to marry you; they can disinherit me if they want. By the way, where did you get the bicycle?"

"Rose's neighbour lent it to me. I would have liked to have ridden a horse but there was not one available. Can you not go to class this afternoon, I would like to talk to you?"

"I can cut class as I was only going to the library."

They hugged and kissed while Ken was trying to balance on the bike. Passers-by were smiling and giving encouragement. Taylah had her car and the bike would not fit in the car so Ken had to cycle back to Troy's mansion. Taylah arrived first to be greeted by Rose who told her she had the ideal man. Ken arrived a bit out of breath and returned the bike. The neighbour told Rose that was the most romantic story she had ever heard.

"The reason I am here is because I cannot stop thinking about you and you are disturbing my thoughts and sleep. I have just been promoted to the head of the renal unit and I told them I needed two weeks' holiday to prepare me for my new job. They agreed and Rose only knew when I was on the way. I arrived just after you had left for university. Rose is getting tickets to go to Birmingham, Alabama, tomorrow. She insists she is coming. This is going to be a big surprise to Troy when he comes home."

"I am shell-shocked and I have invited my friend to dinner tonight. I hope you do not mind, I could cancel."

"Do not do that. I am sure Rose can cope."

Troy arrived home to find a surprise visitor and a single malt whisky he had not seen before. Ken told him he was getting to know about whisky but he did have help at the duty-free. Taylah's friend was surprised to see Ken, and when Taylah told her the story, she was in tears. She told Taylah to find her a husband like Ken.

The next day, they caught the flight to Birmingham to be met by Elvira and Josh. Ken was straight on the front foot, he gave Josh a firm handshake and kissed Elvira's hand. He said he would answer any questions they had, but he wanted to marry their daughter. Rose and Taylah were quiet and were smiling at each other. Over lunch, Ken did most of the talking, telling them about kidney stones and his brother. Josh was on-side, Ken had come from the working class to be at the top of his profession. Elvira said she would like to get Ken alone and ask some questions.

"It is my pleasure and would not expect anything less from a mother who is looking after her daughter's future."

Rose was restraining Taylah from saying anything. Ken could look after himself. Then Ken produced another malt whisky for Josh and the luncheon broke up; Elvira and Ken adjourned to another room.

"Where did you find this man, you have my blessing."

"Thanks, Daddy, I hope Mummy does not give him a rough time."

Rose now said, "Don't worry about Ken, he can hold his own; Oh, how I wish I had a son like him."

Elvira questioned Ken for a couple of hours and they both emerged smiling. Taylah rushed up to Ken and gave him a hug and a kiss. Elvira said she could not find fault with Ken but he had a different way of speaking.

"He has his way of speaking English that is different to the way we speak, but that is one of his charms. You have to go to England, and if I can talk Troy into it, we four could go together.

"I have persuaded him to get married here as I want a big wedding; Josh is going to find this wedding expensive."

Ken was sitting with Taylah on a large swing on the balcony; Taylah was almost sitting on his lap.

"Did my mother bully you?"

"No, she asked very good questions. She was worried about how you could adapt to living in a foreign country and whether I could give you the standard of living you would need. I was tempted to say you would have to go to work but I restrained myself. I told her, although I had a two-bedroom flat, sorry apartment, I was planning to buy a house. She asked me about children, she was keen on having grandchildren. I told her I thought two would be sufficient but we would have to consult you. She thought that was funny. I agreed to have a wedding here and I would only bring my mother. Then she started to ask about my mother. There was nothing I could not handle."

The evening meal was full of laughter and Josh was enjoying his whisky and Ken could enjoy Josh's brandy.

The next day, Taylah took Ken on a tour of the city. They ended up at the botanical garden. Being a week day, it was quiet and they could sit and discuss in peace.

"I have now fulfilled my mission of coming to America. You could call it mission accomplished. One of my friends told me that it was generally the mother-in-law who could be difficult, and especially, as you are an only child. I had to meet your mother and get her to like me. I knew Rose was on my side so I needed her help. Once you have graduated, I would like them to come to England to see where we will live. Your mother asked a lot of questions about where we would live. I am planning to buy a house, and now I am in charge of the renal unit, I am sure I could get a good mortgage. I would like to keep the flat but that would depend on finances. The flat would be more convenient for you to go to university."

"I have money, I have an inheritance from my maternal grandmother."

"I want you to keep that separate and only use it in an emergency. You will be going to university and there may be some incidental expenses. Now, you just get your degree and come to me as quickly as possible."

"I will be there with my skates on and my boots blacked."

"Looks like you picked that up from my mother."

"Yes, I can't wait to talk to her again; she can introduce me to so many sayings and customs."

"Now, we must leave as I have to look at some baby photos. I told your mother I was not sure what our babies would look like and she was preparing photos to show me."

"You scoundrel, you have charmed my mother better than anyone could."

"Well, let's go."

"Yes, sir, anything you say, sarge."

The next couple of hours were spent viewing photos and eight millimeter films. Rose whispered to Taylah that she knew Ken would charm her mother but she was surprised he had done such a complete job. She also said she had never seen Elvira so relaxed. The next day, they caught a plane back to Atlanta, and within three days, Ken left to go back home. Taylah was upset but now she had to complete the courses to get her degree.

Later, Ken said he had found a house but he would not make any decision before Taylah had seen the property. Taylah was thinking, what a man! Her graduation was in one week and she had her flight booked for two days later. Her parents and Rose and Troy came to the graduation and there was a party at Troy's house in the evening. Taylah invited a couple of friends and one of her mother's distant relatives who lived in Atlanta. Rose told Taylah how she overheard Elvira talking about Ken to her relative. She was full of praise for this Englishman and she could not wait for grandchildren.

Taylah left for England and her father was promising to come after he made some contacts in London. Ken was at Birmingham Airport to greet her, he did not bring his mother as he wanted to take Taylah straight home. He gave his mother the excuse that he would have to go straight from work. He felt guilty as he rarely told his mother falsehoods.

After minor hugging and kissing at the airport, the serious stuff started as they entered Ken's flat. They were both aroused but Ken slowed it down by showing Taylah her room with a new double bed.

"I thought if you did not like this bed you could sleep with me in mine."

"Thanks for the bed but I had planned on only sleeping with you. Now, let's try your bed."

"I think we should have protected intercourse before we are married."

"Good idea, I am already on the pill but a second barrier could be a good idea."

Taylah was laughing at this temporary pause in the inevitable.

"I must have a shower as I have been on a plane for several hours but I will be quick."

Ken was amazed at how everything was going smoothly. He could not believe how he was acting. Taylah had changed him from being careful to being free. Taylah emerged from the shower in the nude and motioned that they should go to the bedroom. Suddenly, Ken was self-conscious; he was still fully dressed but the object of his desire was standing naked before him. He followed her, trying to get rid of his clothes as fast as he could. There was no time to put on his condom as she was on top of him holding his penis. Taylah took charge, and after a little resistance, he was inside her. It was all very quick as they were both excited and there was no holding back.

Lying on the bed, Ken let Taylah do all the talking; he needed a breather.

"I had a few boyfriends; they were useless and never got past first base. I was in a sorority house and all the girls were talking about losing their virginity but I was not interested. It was one of the reasons I went to live with Uncle Troy. The first time I saw you at the funeral, I did not get to know you. The next time at the dinner table, something clicked, I even told my friend. That time in the bar with the cold beer showed me you had a strong character and then you were all I could think about. So, here we are and you have fulfilled my expectations."

"Well, thank you, I suppose you can thank my mother for letting me know I should think about you. She told me I was too alone, and here, was a beautiful polite girl who was not afraid to learn new things. I should get to know her and take her out. As soon as I got to know you, I felt myself loosen up, and suddenly, I was saying things that I would be too shy to say before. When you went back to America, you were all I could think of. I wanted to propose but I had to get to know your family. Rose was my ally, she gave me lots of information. She told me my brother had changed her life and she wanted to help me change mine. Also, I like your mother; she asks straight forward questions and does not get emotional. I think she will make a good mother-in-law. So, here we are."

They both lay on the bed smiling until Ken said they should take his mother to dinner. Doris was very happy to see Taylah and they kissed and hugged. They went to the Indian restaurant but all Doris would eat was egg and chips. Taylah was eating more spicy dishes and loved them. The next day while Ken went to work, Taylah was planning what to do with the flat. She found a laundry and clothes lines but no pegs. She thought Ken might not know there was a laundry; he had all his clothes dry-cleaned.

Ken told Taylah that, when he had a suitable ring, he would propose. One of his cousins was in the jewellery trade and he would get some diamonds to show Taylah and then they would work on a design for the ring. Taylah was excited she was going to help design her own ring. One lunchtime, Ken took Taylah to the Jewellery Quarter and introduced her to Jack, a cousin. He had a selection of diamonds on loan and Taylah could pick what she wanted. There was one square stone that took her fancy.

"Where do these diamonds come from and how do you have them?"

"South Africa; sent to Amsterdam for cutting and brought to the UK by a Jewish friend of mine. These stones are on loan. I meet him in a local pub, and on a hand shake, he loans me the stones. We will negotiate the price when you choose a stone. Now, we have to design a setting for the stone and pick the gold we will use. Nine carat is harder and so wears well, many people prefer that property, especially if you are a working mother. Fourteen carat is softer but still wears well. Any gold of a higher carat is softer, and in my opinion, not suitable for a ring as it deforms easily."

"Wow, that is a lot of information, what do I have to do?"

"You have picked the diamond now I want some basic information such as the width of the ring and how you might want it set. First of all, let me go to my friend and negotiate a price. This is a good quality stone and I know my friend would not offer me any rubbish."

"Where is this pub? I want to see it."

"It is just down the road but it is a very working-class pub and particularly raucous in the evening but lunchtime should be OK."

Ken took Taylah to the pub, and while they were there, the Salvation Army ladies came collecting for the poor. Taylah was delighted to see with what respect they were treated and they collected plenty of money. Ken told her the Salvos were well-treated even in rough areas. She could use them in her studies of the Black Country.

With the designed ring in his hand, Ken proposed to Taylah. She thought it was so romantic and wrote several letters to her friends and family about the whole episode. They now had to plan for the arrival of Troy, Rose and Taylah's parents. Ken had them booked into the Grand Hotel and had tickets for a variety show at the Hippodrome Theatre. He also had tickets for the Shakespeare Theatre in Stratford. He had hired a minivan to take them all to Stratford and the country pubs. Taylah was excited to show her parents this different Birmingham.

The four were arriving at Birmingham Airport and Ken said they should take two taxis to the Grand Hotel. Taylah would sit with her parents and he would sit with Rose and Troy. Everyone was hugging and kissing but Elvira held Taylah at arms-length, looked intently at her and then gave Ken a big kiss. Taylah was shocked and looked at her father who was laughing. Troy was happy they were taking black cabs; he was telling Josh to enjoy the ride.

Ken and Taylah left them at the reception and said they would be back with Doris for dinner. After checking in at the reception, Troy went straight to the bar and found his favourite barman. He introduced Josh and they had a couple of whiskies. Rose was a little put-out but Elvira was admiring the architecture.

Doris met Elvira and Josh; she was getting used to the Grand Hotel, a place she never thought she would visit. At dinner, Doris sat between Rose and Elvira with Ken next to Elvira. Taylah sat opposite, between her uncle and father. As soon as they were seated, Elvira took Taylah's hand to look at the ring.

Ken said to Elvira, "Don't blame me for that ring, it's your daughter's fault."

"I was just admiring a simple but attractive ring. I think I like it better than mine."

Ken looked at Josh and he was smiling. Now everyone was talking. Doris was telling Elvira about Ken's early life and both Elvira and Ken were listening intently. Elvira told Doris she had a fabulous son and she was so glad her daughter had met him. Elvira said she was glad to be in Birmingham but it was a little cooler than she expected. Doris told her to come to her place tomorrow and she would lend her a cardigan.

Taylah had planned to take a city tour but that was in the afternoon so she took her parents to Doris's house in the morning. This was their first treat on a double-decker bus. From the bus, they walked near the canal with a railway line behind the canal. Taylah explained the bomb site at the end of Doris's street. As they walked up the entry, they were greeted by the lady from number four.

"Tay, youm lookin' good, ow ya bin?"

"I cor complain. I've got a bostin' ring."

"Wow, that's a smasher, tell Ken es a lucky bugger."

"Firstly, I did not understand what she said and I could hardly understand what you said."

"Yes, Mother, I am practising my Black Country speak and that lady has promised to show me some old photos. Mrs Rogers comes from Dudley and I will take you there to hear how people speak."

Doris greeted them at the gate and showed them her house. Josh was silent but nodding his head at the things he was being shown. Later, he told Taylah he had been taken back to his childhood and it was a funny feeling he would have to digest. Elvira was interested in the kitchen and the bathroom. Taylah told her to have a shower was quite a performance but she had learned to enjoy it. Now at Ken's place, it was not so much fun. A suitable cardigan was found and Elvira was very happy to get warm. Elvira said she had never worn a cardigan.

The bus tour of Birmingham was in a coach not a double-decker bus but the tour guide had an authentic Brummie accent. Rose was enjoying herself and Elvira had to ask Taylah some questions. Troy was pointing out the pubs to Josh; there were one or two old ones that interested Josh. After the bus tour, they went back to the hotel to await Ken.

When Ken arrived, he suggested either a pub dinner or going to his favourite Indian restaurant which was licensed. Taylah suggested the Indian food might be too hot but her mother intervened and said she liked spicy food. Troy said he had not eaten Indian food so, "let's go." Ken was hoping the restaurant would not be full.

Ken ordered plenty of dishes and some were very mild dishes. The samosas were to everyone's liking and he had to order more. There was plenty of food left over and Ken asked for a doggy bag. Elvira could not believe what she was seeing; she had assumed that the left overs would go to the garbage. Taylah explained that this food would not be wasted and would probably provide tomorrow's lunch. Now Josh took up this approach; he was happy that no food should be wasted. Taylah was seeing a new father.

The next day, Troy and his brother were off to Troy's factory and then to see other factories. The ladies were off to Dudley Market. Luckily, the ladies got both front seats on the upper deck of the bus. Taylah sat with her mother and Rose had the seat to herself. Taylah answered a lot of questions. She pointed out the boundary between Birmingham and Smethwick and this was supposedly the start of the Black Country. The conductor was very talkative and Taylah did a belated translation. Elvira was enchanted by the whole atmosphere and the journey, it was all so new to her. In the market, Taylah was in her element, trying to copy the Dudley dialect. Rose and Elvira bought some small things with Rose doing the paying. Rose loved getting used to the money. Finally, Rose spied the pub and said, "Let's get a drink," she was beaming from ear to ear.

Entering the pub, the barman recognized Rose and greeted her.

"Look I have come thousands of miles to be greeted by a barman; I almost want to be a regular. I love that phrase. What are you two drinking?

"I am having a shandy, and Mom, I think you should try one."

"What is a shandy?"

"It is half lemonade and half beer. Don't worry, the beer is quite weak but it takes away the sweetness of the lemonade."

"OK, this is all new to me so I will give it a try."

Elvira said she enjoyed the shandy and it was refreshing. Rose had her sherry and a chat with the barman. Then she noticed pickled eggs and Scotch eggs; she asked for one of each and a knife. They all sampled the eggs; they had never eaten these before and they all enjoyed them (there are pickled eggs in America but not in areas frequented by Elvira).

Back at the hotel, Josh was in a happy mood; he had seen some investment opportunities. Of course, he and Troy were at the bar so Josh asked the ladies what they would like to drink. Rose said a sherry and both Taylah and her mother said a shandy.

"What is a shandy?"

When it was explained to Josh, he was surprised.

"We have been here about forty-eight hours and you have accomplished more than I could do in thirty years; getting my wife to try an alcoholic drink."

Everyone was laughing, even the barman.

The next day, Josh was going to London; he had made some contacts in the City of London. Troy was going to his factory to take the workers to a pub at lunchtime and treat them to a drink. The ladies were going shopping without Taylah.

Troy said he had eaten a ploughman's lunch and he had a great time at the pub and was going to do that again. The ladies had found the Birmingham Market near the Bull Ring and planned to go again.

After two days, Josh came back from London. He was in a very happy mood. He had met some interesting bankers and could not wait to go there again. He told Elvira that they had to spend time in London. She said it might be possible after the wedding. Now she wanted to get home to plan the wedding.

The trip to Stratford was a great success and trips to country pubs had Elvira trying different beers in her shandy. At the airport, Elvira was telling Taylah how she had enjoyed herself, and in some ways, been liberated.

A few months passed and Ken, Doris and Taylah were off to Birmingham, Alabama. Elvira had everything planned. Troy was to be the best man and Taylah would have her best friend as bridesmaid. The church prepared and the reception would be in a large hotel. In the church, Rose sat with Doris on the groom's side. Taylah's

Aunt Jessica came from New York with a friend and they would sit with Doris. The bride's side of the church soon filled up and many were taking advantage of the pews on the groom's side.

The wedding went without a hitch and the reception was a great success. Jessica took one look at the engagement ring and told her friend she wanted one like that. Taylah told her aunt she might have to go to Birmingham to get something similar. Jessica said they were going as soon as their film was finished.

After a few months in Birmingham, Ken and Taylah welcomed Aunty Jessica and her friend, Ivan. Ken was bemused by this couple but they loved his Indian restaurant. They bought several pieces of jewellery from Ken's cousin; he was doing good business. Jessica asked many questions about their life and asked if she could write an article for a New York publication. Ken said yes but he should get a copy before publication. Taylah was getting to know her aunt as they had only crossed paths when she was young.

After Jessica left, Taylah told Ken she might be pregnant. Ken said they should wait a couple of weeks and do the test in the hospital. The test was positive and Ken suggested they try ultrasound. It was relatively new but he was using it to look at kidney stones. Taylah had not really had morning sickness but the ultrasound showed a very small fetus.

Taylah phoned her parents and told her mother she was pregnant. There was a scream at the end of the line and then lots of questions. Taylah told her mother that, if it was a boy, they would call it Brian, and if it was a girl, they would name it Chantelle. Elvira might want to consider second names but that was in the future.

After a couple of months, Ken encouraged Taylah to have a second ultrasound scan. He was interested in how the baby was progressing. This scan showed there were twins and one might be a boy. On being informed, Elvira said there were twins in her family. Doris could not remember twins in her extended family. Elvira wanted to get on the next plane but Josh wanted to wait a while as his contacts in London were looking at new business. Taylah said there were months to go so her mother should relax. Elvira could not relax and all the family and her friends knew the news.

Josh and Elvira went to London but Elvira only stayed one night and was soon sleeping in Ken's second bedroom. Taylah was still studying, writing her thesis and was felling little discomfort. Ken promised when Taylah was in her last days of labour Elvira should come, and if Josh could not come, to bring Rose. Ken had a very soft spot for Rose. Elvira gave him a kiss and said she would not miss the birth of her grandchildren.

Finally, the time arrived. Elvira and Rose did not have to share a bed as Ken's new place was a three-bedroomed house. Rose was reading Taylah's thesis and loving every word. Taylah was going to submit it after the birth.

Four anxious individuals were in the waiting room as Ken decided he would not go into the delivery room, even though he could. Sometime after the birth, they were called into the delivery room.

Taylah said, "Meet Brian and Chantelle; they will not be able to marry each other but this is the best I could do."

Teddy Boy

It was approaching Christmas 1955 and I was just fifteen. My parents, my uncle and aunt were invited to one of their friends who was having a party. The living room was full so Doris (their daughter) and I escaped to the kitchen. She was my age and I was infatuated with her. As we were chatting, a fellow entered; he was a friend of Doris and he was a Teddy Boy. He had drain pipe trousers, thick sole shoes, we called them big 'boppers', bright yellow socks and a pale blue coat that came to his knees. The coat had a leather collar. A string tie and a black shirt made up his attire. He was in the Ladywood gang and told us stories of his exploits. Doris had heard it all before and pulled him up on some points. She emphasised she was not his girlfriend and that put my mind at ease. He said that on Saturday the gang were going to Nottingham Ice Rink to have a fight with the local gang. He invited me and I declined as I had a job on Saturday (a lie).

Terry worked on a stall in the Bull Ring but he would give up work for a good fight. He bought his clothes in the centre of Birmingham; there was a tailor who specialised in Teddy gear. Terry had left school at fifteen and would soon own his own barrow. I did not tell him I went to school in Smethwick, as I knew the Smerrick mob had a few fights with the Ladywood mob. A flash point was Summerfield Park especially when there was a fair. Victoria Park in Smethwick was also a meeting ground for gangs.

Terry was smaller than me and I asked about the others in the gang.

"They are all taller than me but they think I am their mascot. If there is a good fight they protect me, but I can fight. Some of the gang carry razors and knives but they only use them when necessary."

I thought he was boasting, but Doris saw my frown, she confirmed that she had seen a few knives and razors. She said the gang was stupid and ignorant; Terry was quick to defend them. While we were talking, Terry said he would get some drinks. He came back with two beers, one of which I shared with Doris; she did not really like beer. She had also left school at fifteen and was working in a shop. The shop was a clothing store and she thought the dresses and ladies' suits were so old fashioned. She wanted to design a new type of clothing. Terry said he was wearing a new style clothing. Doris told him in no uncertain terms that this was Edwardian dress except for the colours. She then told him about the Edwardian period and said he should read some history. His reply was that he had stopped learning when he left school. She looked at me and shook her head. My feeling was that his clothes must have cost a fortune and I really liked his coat, although I thought I couldn't wear a pale blue coat.

It was time to leave and I did not fix up a date. Doris's father said they would get together at Christmas time, so I would see her again. The next week, there was a fair at Victoria Park and I went as one of my friends was working on a stall. I was enjoying the fair when I saw Terry and decided to go home. I warned my friend at the stall that there could be a problem. The owner of the stall had told my friend that they were prepared for trouble, and if a fight broke out, he should hide with the cash. I later found out that two gangs had gathered to clash but the fair men had stepped in and then the police arrived and the gangs dispersed.

Christmas came and Doris and her parents arrived. Unfortunately, I was with my two cousins when Doris arrived. They were teasing me and I was reluctant when she said she was going dancing and would I come. I missed a chance, and later, I cursed myself. Her going and my staying did not stop my cousins from teasing me.

Later, I heard she had gone to London to be a fashion designer. A few years later, I was studying in London, and one day, I went to Carnaby Street. The clothes were way out, and as I was looking in a shop window, I spied Doris. I went into the shop and said, "Hello Doris".

She turned to her fiend and said, "This is the bloke who would not go dancing with me on Boxing Day."

"You missed your chance, mate."

I was obviously now blushing and Doris said, "Let's go for coffee; my colleague will look after the shop."

Our coffee break was a long one. Doris did most of the talking, she was married to a man she called a 'show off'. She had become pregnant and married a most unsuitable man. Into her fourth month she had a miscarriage and was glad not to have a child like her husband. She had come to London to be a clothes designer and was creating women's clothing which was becoming popular when she met this man. There were plenty of men but this one took her fancy.

"It was my fault I fell for his spiel, and of course, I became pregnant. I forced him to marry me but he just did what he wanted, and when I had a miscarriage, he couldn't care less. He struts around this area in outlandish clothing and thinks he is the bee's knees. I see him occasionally when he wants money. By the way, I am Shanelle now not Doris; I always hated that name. I now have a good clientele who know me a Shanelle and Doris is in my past. How come you are in London?"

"I am studying but I live in Ilford. I come to London often but this is the first time I have been in Carnaby Street. I am blown away by the clothing and was thinking about Teddy Boy gear; by the way what happened to Terry?"

"Terry was in a pub near the Black Patch Park when he got into an argument. He was glassed and the cut was across his cheek and down to his throat. Luckily, they kept him alive till the ambulance arrived. He was in hospital for weeks; one of my friends visited him and was surprised he was alive. I think he gave up being a Ted. The last I heard, he was in Portugal. I think the place is called Faro."

The next time I visited Carnaby Street, there was a man in outlandish clothing in the shop. Shanelle introduced me to him; he was her husband. He talked to me in a very strange way and I wondered if he was batting for the other side. He had caused Doris to be pregnant so he was a real man; maybe he batted for both sides.

Doris winked at me and said, "We missed each other and now we are going in different directions." Her husband looked confused but I left with Shanelle for a coffee with a smile on my face.

I saw Shanelle a few more times and we mainly talked about her husband. She had kicked him out of the flat and had no idea where he was living. He might be squatting in the area. She wanted a divorce but that would probably have to wait a while. Shanelle missed Birmingham but she was now part owner of the shop and wanted a shop of her own.

While in London, I met another Brummie. One day, I went to an Indian restaurant in the East End. I was ordering my meal when the waiter asked if I was from Birmingham. I told him I was and spent a lot of time in Smethwick. I had obviously said the correct word as he started to laugh. I was a bit bemused but he explained.

"I am from Smethwick; I was born there. I am a Sikh but I was born in Smethwick. My dad and mom came to England and my dad found work at the Birmid. I don't miss the Birmid but I do miss Smethwick. I have a lot of school friends in that town and most of them have not left."

"I know that factory; not a pleasant place. I remember passing the factory and smelling horrible fumes. I understand there are many Sikhs in the area and there is a Sikh temple on the High Street in Smethwick. Do you get back often?"

"I have not been back for a while but you have put a thought in my brain. When you ordered your meal, I listened. I suppose Smethwick is not Birmingham but I can identify the accent and we don't get many customers with your accent. After leaving school in Smethwick, my dad arranged for me to work in the factory. It was so dirty and the fumes were intolerable. I left and went to live with relatives in London near Heathrow. My family are always trying to marry me off to some Sikh girl. I am resisting although there are some good-looking Sikh girls so I am regarded as a rebel."

I finally finished ordering my meal and we promised to meet the next day at a pub close to the restaurant. It was his day off and he felt comfortable in that pub. The East End had a mix of nationalities and I had heard a few racial slurs in that area. One of my Indian friends was often harangued from passing cars.

The next day, our talk ranged over so many subjects but it always came back to Smethwick and Birmingham. Jagtar went to school in Smethwick till he was fifteen. His job at the Birmid lasted two years but he talked his parents into letting him go to a less polluted environment, to his relatives in London. Once there, he could breathe more easily and found a job in a restaurant. At first, his uncle and aunty were easy but then they started to try to find him a wife. There were some lovely girls but he wanted to find his own wife. His aunt told him that was not the way it was done. He moved out and came to the East End. He had found an English girl and was considering marrying her. I counselled him on mixed marriages but I asked if I could meet her. I felt guilty when I thought he might have an easier life if he married a Sikh girl.

The next week we met in the pub and she was a beautiful young girl. She was Irish and she was in England on her own. I was worried she was lonely and had found Jagtar to take her out of her loneliness. My misgivings were communicated to Jagtar but I was so wrong. They were soon married, and as far as I know, still together with two children. I should have realised Jagtar was more than half English. I now try not to make snap judgments where mixed marriages are concerned.

I had lived in many countries and one of my honeymoons was spent in Portugal. We were staying in Lagos on the southern tip of Portugal, and as part of our holiday deal, we had a Morris Mini to drive about the country. The Mini was a good car to travel around on country roads. There was plenty to see, and once I had learned to drive in Southern Portugal, we could go anywhere. We had flown into Faro Airport and were taken by bus to Lagos so I knew Faro was not far.

I went to Faro with my wife with the purpose of finding Terry. We first went to the fish market which was very interesting. We were both used to strong smells, having lived in Africa. The fish smell was overwhelming as it was a hot day but we were not too uncomfortable. The variety of fish on offer was interesting. After leaving the fish market, we walked to the centre of the city and looked into a few cafés with no luck. I saw a restaurant that looked a bit 'upmarket' and decided to have lunch. As we entered, I saw Terry behind the counter, he was talking to some waiters, he looked very smart in a black suit.

"Hello, Terry, what is a Brummie doing here?"

He looked at me with a frown.

"Doris and Nottingham Ice Rink, do you remember? That was a few years ago at Christmas time."

"Oh, yes, please have a seat I will be with you in a couple of minutes."

We sat down at an empty table, there were other customers in the restaurant. Terry came to join us after a few minutes.

"One of the waiters called in sick and I was instructing the others what to do this evening, I am the manager and part owner here. You have picked a good place for lunch if I say so myself."

"You have done very well I remember you had a barrow in the Bull Ring."

"It is a long story, and if you come tonight, I will treat you to a meal and tell you the story. I will bring my Portuguese girlfriend, we don't get many Brummies here and you have made my day. I now have to get back to the staff. I will send a waiter with good English to take your order."

We had a drive back to Lagos and my wife asked me about Terry. I said he was a Teddy Boy I once knew. My wife not being English, I had to explain Teddy Boys. Most of my explanation was about dress and nothing about gangs.

That evening we met and the four of us enjoyed a great meal. It tasted better when Terry told me it was on the house. My wife talked mainly to Terry's girlfriend while he told me his story; she was listening.

He was doing very well in the Bull Ring and soon owned his own stall. He was still involved with the mob and enjoying the camaraderie. One night in a pub, he had an argument with a stranger, and before a punch was thrown, Terry had a broken glass in his face.

"They saved me but my pale blue coat was a ruin. I spent about three weeks in hospital, and when I came out, I gave up being a Ted. I did a course in bookkeeping and that helped me on the stalls. I was keeping the books for several of the stall holders. We noticed an increase in pilfering and a group of us decided to keep an eye out on our stalls. We caught a couple of young 'toe rags' and a little hint that a knuckle duster might rearrange their faces scared them off. We never saw them again."

My wife interrupted and asked, "What are 'toe rags' and what is a 'knuckle duster'?"

After a brief description, he continued his story. I was not sure how much his girlfriend understood but her English was quite good. Now, I realised the ladies were both listening to the story; maybe his girlfriend had not heard the whole story before or maybe a second dose would let her into things she had missed.

"We caught an old lady, I think she was a "klepto", we couldn't hurt an old lady so we warned that her son or daughter might get punished, that was the last we saw of her."

"What is a 'klepto'?"

After another explanation, then Terry carried on with his story.

"The stalls were doing well and I had a couple of cousins helping me although it was hard graft. I did not drive at that time and they did most of the carrying. Running a stall is OK in the summer and at Christmas but in October, November, January and February it is cold, windy and generally raining; a miserable time for me. I had made some money so, one October, I decided to go to a warmer place. I ended up on the Spanish South Coast. It was so cheap and I travelled by bus along the coast until I crossed the border and reached Faro. I really enjoyed travelling on the buses and I was about to move on when I met one of the Ladywood mob called Gerry. I came for a meal at this restaurant and he was the owner. He had a local partner who signed the place over to Gerry then disappeared. At the time I thought nothing of it. Gerry offered me a job, in fact, he offered me a partnership, I was expecting he would want some money but he said he had other business and the restaurant was tying him down. I told him I would run the place and keep the books. He had a gaff upstairs and he would move out and I could live there; he would live on his boat."

"What is a 'gaff' and what is 'graft'?"

Another explanation and he was off again.

"I couldn't believe my luck, the only problem was that I couldn't speak Portuguese. I soon learned some basics and the place was making a good profit. One day, I hung a photo of me in my Teddy suit and put on a rock 'n' roll record. There were not many people in that day but no one complained. Two men came to pay and said they enjoyed the music. Then one noticed my photo and asked who it was. I told him it was me and tried to explain Teddy Boys. Their English was quite good but it was hard work. They loved my pale blue jacket and asked where they could buy one. I told them of my tailor in Birmingham and these clothes were made-to-measure. The following week, I had a booking for a large party, and when they came, they wanted me to play rock 'n' roll. Two of the men said they were going to England soon and asked me the address of my tailor. I thought nothing of it, and about a month later, two men walked into the restaurant fully dressed as Teddy Boys; it sent a shiver down my spine. One had my pale blue jacket and the other had a green jacket. I have never liked green but he looked fantastic.

At the next block booking, there were several men dressed as Teds and their wives were dressed in short skirts. They wanted me to play rock 'n' roll all night; their favourite was 'Rock Around the Clock'. Suddenly, I had people coming from as far as Lisbon asking for the address of my tailor. I thought I should write to him to ask for a commission. Now, at least twice a month I have a full house. The waiters love it as the tips are about five times normal.

Gerry would come by occasionally; he told me I was doing a great job, he had heard there was a rock 'n' roll club in Lisbon where they dressed as Teds. I would show him the books but he was not too interested; a couple of times he said he was short and asked me for a few thousand. He offered to take me fishing on his boat, but as I can't swim, I declined. I never asked him about his business and he never told me anything.

A few times he brought a couple of men to dinner, of course, he never paid. One man was old and ugly and the other was young and not good-looking. I realised by the talk they seemed to be Spanish. My waiters confirmed they were Spanish and one waiter told me they were probably thieves."

"How can you tell Spanish from Portuguese?" My wife was asking the questions.

"There are a lot of 'sh' sounds in Portuguese, and anyway, I would ask the waiters. Like a good bookkeeper, I would keep an entry when Gerry had his freebies. Normally, Gerry would show up about once a month, and on the last occasion, he said he would soon make good money and we could fix up the restaurant. I had been slowly changing this place with some of the profits. About three months passed and no Gerry. One day, the police came a visiting; they took me to the station and asked me questions, in fact, it was more like an interrogation. I was there six hours and they wanted to find Gerry. I told them I had not seen him for about three months, maybe they should look at his boat. One of them laughed at that comment but I was none the wiser. They asked me about his business but I could tell them nothing except he rarely wanted any money from the restaurant. We went around in circles several times and they asked me whether I had been on his boat. I had not been on the boat and I told them I couldn't swim. That obviously was amusing to them. They let me go, but the next day, they were back again but at least we stayed in the restaurant. I showed them the books and the last time Gerry came in with two men. They had a book of mug shots and I went through all of them."

"What are 'mug shots'?"

"I immediately identified the ugly old man and then the younger one and I said I thought they were Spanish, They were Spanish and they were father and son. They had also gone missing. The police then told me some divers had found Gerry's boat about five kilometres out on the bottom of the sea. There was a big hole in the hull. No bodies had been washed up on the coast. Did I know anything about drugs? I denied knowing anything, actually I knew nothing. They said they had a warrant to search the restaurant and my flat. I told them to go ahead and they found nothing but left my place in a mess. They had opened every drawer and wardrobe, they had tipped up my bed and even looked under the carpets. I had a job to put everything straight. The waiters all laughed when I cursed the police."

We relaxed for the coffee and port and then Terry resumed his story.

"Gerry's bank account has never been touched. I have never had any correspondence from him. The police come around occasionally, and when I go to England, the customs go through my luggage with gusto. I am sure they are tipped off by the Faro police. Whenever I am in Birmingham, I ask about Gerry but none of my old mates has heard from Gerry and I think he is mutton jed."

"What is 'mutton jed'?"

"It means dead in Cockney rhyming slang, I will explain later."

I thanked him for an interesting story and would recommend any of my friends who were visiting to pay him a visit. I also admired his restaurant, he was obviously doing a good job and this restaurant was one of the best in Faro. As Southern Portugal was becoming popular, he would be getting more English visiting and probably more Brummies.

"I am sure lots of Portuguese are visiting Birmingham, by the way, I have lost touch with Doris, do you know where she can be found?"

"When you go to London try Carnaby Street and ask for Shanelle."

Carnaby Street

Doris was born at home in Ladywood early in 1941 during a bombing raid. The area where her father and mother lived was close to factories, and sometimes, the German bombers would miss the factories and hit houses. Luckily, her house was never hit. Both her mother and father worked in factories, and as soon as Doris was old enough to be looked after by a neighbour, her mother was back at work. The neighbour had retired and was glad of a little extra money. Her husband was a train driver; he was driving after retirement age but was now relegated to shunting goods wagons around the area.

Doris's dad, Tom, worked in a factory making parts for Spitfires and so was exempt from call-up. Her mother, Ivy, worked on a press making parts for cars and lorries. This was a dangerous job but she was good at it and could get plenty of overtime. With both parents working, they were not well off but better off than some of the people in their street. Doris was being looked after by Mrs Beasley and had not a care in the world. Her only problem was cod liver oil. She would get orange juice which she loved but she would often spit back the cod liver oil at Mrs Beasley.

She would laugh and admit she would probably do the same.

After 1943, the bombing of Birmingham decreased and the air raid shelter had less use. The fire wardens would still come around to check that no lights were showing from the houses. Many of the blinds were not efficient so many houses could have few lights on at night. This was not such a problem in summer as it was light till ten o'clock at night. The problem was in the winter when it was almost dark at four o'clock in the afternoon.

One of their more affluent neighbours had a pram. They had a son and a daughter. Olive, the daughter, used to take Doris out in the pram. Doris was growing fast and always jabbering away but no one could understand her. Mrs Beasley said that she talked to her all day and Doris would answer back but she had no idea what she was saying. Olive, who was thirteen, said the same; she could not understand Doris except when she said moma or dada. Ivy was getting a little worried that Doris was not talking.

One Saturday morning when Ivy was off work, Olive came around with the pram.

"Look, moma, pwam."

"You little bugger, you can talk."

After that, words came thick and fast and Doris was talking to anyone who would listen. Olive would take her shopping and she knew all the ladies. There was still rationing but Doris would always get a sweet. As soon as Doris started to walk, Mrs Beasley had a job to catch Doris and often had to enlist the help of Olive to catch her. Olive would take her to the park to play with a ball. Doris did not want to kick the ball, she wanted to pick it up and run with it. Olive showed her boys playing football but she still insisted on picking the ball up and running with it. Olive and Mrs Beasley were of the opinion that this girl was an independent strong-willed girl.

The war ended and there was a street party and Doris was entertaining everyone. Mrs Beasley had taught her some rhymes and she was telling them to all the adults. After that, Doris was four-and-a-half and was starting infants school. Mrs Beasley was picking her up from school and giving her tea. She made the most delicious cakes and the best were the fruit cakes. Dried fruit was hard to get just after the war but Mr Beasley had contacts. He had just retired but he had lots of friends on the railways.

One afternoon when it was raining, Doris saw him cleaning his dominoes and she asked him whether he could teach her to play. He was delighted and many afternoons they would play dominoes. Mrs Beasley told her husband to let Doris win occasionally, but he said she was so good he did not have to let her win. At school, she was good at arithmetic but poor at writing. She was left-handed and the pen nibs would stick in the paper. Mr Beasley talked her teacher into letting her write with a pencil and he bought Doris several pencils.

One day after dominoes, Doris said that she wanted to draw. Mr Beasley gave her a piece of paper and suggested she draw the fireplace with the clock on the mantle shelf.

He was astounded at the finished drawing and called his wife to look at it. He asked Doris whether he could keep it, and of course, she said yes. Then he asked her to write her name on the bottom; he was going to show it to his sons. After a couple of days, Doris had a pad with plain paper from one of Mr Beasley's sons. Dominoes and drawing took up a lot of time while it was raining and it rained quite often.

On the sunny days, she would play with the other children in the street; there were so few cars they were rarely disturbed. The girls played hopscotch, skipping and French cricket. When the boys were playing football, Doris had a tendency to pick up the ball and run with it so the boys decided she could not play with them. Doris was growing fast and she was taller than most of the boys her age. Her mother told her that some of her ancestors came from Scandinavia where girls could be taller than boys. That sparked an interest in maps. She dragged Mr Beasley to the library so they could borrow some maps; she was too young to borrow books. He admitted to his wife that he was learning about Europe.

Doris was ten-years-old and everyone was talking about the eleven-plus. This was an exam allowing children to go to grammar school. The teachers were telling Doris's parents she should take the exam but they were resisting as they could not afford the uniform and the other clothing required. Very few children in their area went to grammar school for that reason. Mr and Mrs Beasley could understand but they were unhappy for Doris.

Doris could more or less look after herself, but if there was bad weather after school, she would go visit the Beasleys. She went for the dominoes and the cake and to also learn new card games. Mr Beasley was finding her a fierce competitor.

On one of her visits, Doris saw a woman's magazine that had been given to Mrs Beasley. She was fascinated by the woman's clothing and she sketched some of the dresses. Mr Beasley asked if he could keep a couple of the sketches. He joked that when she was famous he would sell them for a lot of money.

"If I become famous, you are welcome but you might have to wait a long time."

Now, Doris was visiting the library often to look at the women's magazines. She determined that when she left school she had to work in a clothes shop.

This was a time of the Teddy Boys and many of the older boys were dressing in these outlandish clothes. Their suits were of bright colours, not the normal black or brown. Their trousers were tight around the legs and they were wearing large thick-soled shoes. Their jackets often had leather collars. She knew a couple of these boys and Mr Beasley told her that they were wearing a copy of Edwardian dress. That sent Doris off to the library and she was now consumed with the history of dress. All the time, she was making sketches and Mr Beasley was keeping a scrapbook.

Doris was going to leave school at fifteen and Mr Beasley, through contacts, got her a job in a clothing store.

Doris's parents were grateful to Mr Beasley, he was telling them they had a very intelligent daughter and she was going places. It was also about this time that Doris's father started to use his authority. Doris was now being told to be home by ten-thirty and her parents wanted the names and addresses of her friends. Her father had suddenly become very protective. Doris was earning money and could go to the ice rink or dancing and was not worried about the curfew.

Many places, including some pubs, closed at ten p.m. and being home at ten-thirty was no problem. Doris only had an occasional drink of Babycham but she disliked beer and whisky was too strong. She actually spent many hours in the library. Doris was now interested in the newspapers and they had a lot of information about fashion in London. She talked to her mother about clothes but it was not one of her mother's interests, her mother was interested in a new house; not in Ladywood. Doris's friends were all working but their major interest was boys. She found most of the boys she met to be uninteresting. The Teddy Boys were just showing off the way they looked but had no real interest in their clothes.

Doris decided to take a night class at a local college. This class was teaching girls how to use a sewing machine and how to sew. Doris's boss was very enthusiastic and allowed her to leave early on her night school day. Doris soon mastered the machine and started to try some of her new ideas. The older lady teacher was not too impressed but agreed that Doris could sew and cut cloth. Doris was still sketching and Mr Beasley was the recipient of lots of sketches.

About this time, her mother received a letter from one of her friends who had moved to London. She had a daughter slightly older than Doris. This daughter was looking for someone to share a flat in London. Doris's dad was not informed of this news but Doris was keen to try something new. She gave in her notice and received a good reference from her boss. Her father was not told till after she had left for London; he was not well pleased. Doris's mother had recognised they were holding Doris back; they should have let her go to grammar school.

Doris met Hazel and they were immediate friends. Hazel worked in a department store and told Doris to go around the fashion shops; she would surely find a vacancy. Doris did just that and quickly found employment. She was interviewed by the shop owner and his wife. She showed them some sketches and straight away had the job. They said their shop was in a transitional area. Their shop in Carnaby Street was selling ready-made ladies' and gents' clothing but they were noticing a younger set of people were coming to the shop. They wanted to brighten the place up.

Doris had found the ideal job. The back room had a sewing machine and she was encouraged to make some ladies' clothes in bright colours. By this time, hemlines were rising above the knee so she made a couple of simple dresses in red and pink. As soon as they were displayed in the window, they were sold. The owner suggested she look around the local shops to get an idea of prices. He also suggested, although he liked the name Doris, maybe she should find a flashier name to put on a label in the dresses.

Doris did go around some of the local shops and got an idea of prices. She had been selling her dresses too cheap. All the time she was thinking of a new name. While looking in the shops, she saw some perfume and there was her mother's favourite, Chanel. She then decided to spell it differently and came up with the name Shanelle. Her boss liked the name and also liked the idea of putting up their prices.

Even with higher prices, her dresses were selling like hotcakes. The boss suggested she try men's clothing. He gave her a bright print and asked whether she could make a man's shirt.

"I don't think I would wear a shirt that outlandish; it has fishes and flowers in the same print. Where did you get it from?"

"This is a sample from a new supplier; when I looked at it I just shook my head and he gave me a free sample."

Shanelle made the shirt and was afraid to put her label on it. When displayed in the window, it was sold within minutes, even Shanelle was shocked.

The boss asked, "Can you make a pair of shorts in the same material?"

"Surely, you are joking."

"No, the man who bought the shirt said he wanted a pair of shorts in the same material and then maybe long trousers. In all my time in this business, I have never experienced anything like this."

Anything Shanelle made sold almost immediately and she was spending most of her time cutting cloth or sewing; she had little chance to see the customers. For a laugh, she made a tie, a bow tie and a cravat in some outlandish material. They hardly made the front window before they were sold.

Shanelle had been in the shop for a couple of years doing a roaring trade, when the owner asked her to stay after the shop closed. They had a proposition; they wanted to retire and would Shanelle take over. Their house was in Surrey and they were tired of the drive to London every day; the traffic was getting unbearable. Shanelle would take over the business, and if she liked, could slowly buy them out. Shanelle would need an assistant and their accountant would instruct her on how to keep the books. The upstairs apartment that they used sometimes would be part of the rent, which was reasonable, and Shanelle could move in and live there.

Shanelle's head was spinning and the rent was not much more than Hazel paid for their flat. She could hire Hazel and they could live above the shop.

"Since you came, our turnover has boomed. Whereas we had a slow steady business, we are flat out every day and we want a rest. There is no hurry, think it over and we will come up with a more detailed plan."

Shanelle hurried home to talk to Hazel; everything was happening so fast. While telling Hazel she remembered she had never been in the upstairs flat. Hazel was also excited she would be working with Shanelle who she was still calling Doris. She had watched Shanelle operate and she knew they would succeed. Shanelle was still going to the library to learn more about fashion and was always coming up with ideas.

Now Shanelle was in a planning mode. There was a lot of old stock that she would have to offload and she wanted to see the customers while she was sewing. The old stock was good stuff and might sell better in a place like Birmingham. Before she signed the contract, she told the owners she wanted to visit her parents and take some stock with her. She also wanted to visit a tailor in the centre of Birmingham who was making Teddy Boys' clothes.

Back in Birmingham, her father was unhappy she had not told him she was going to London but happy she was doing well. She was telling her friends her good luck and was wondering if they believed her. She was also thinking the story was too good to be true. A few of the men's clothing shops were interested in her old stock and the Teddy Boy tailor surprised her by saying some of the Teddy Boys wanted normal suits as they grew older and more prosperous. She could easily offload the old stock, Birmingham was a different market. She told her old friends to organise a trip to London and come visit Carnaby Street.

Hazel had resigned from her position and was now working for Shanelle. The upstairs flat was well decorated and much better than the flat in which they lived. Shanelle had moved the sewing machine into the shop so she could see Hazel serve the customers. Hazel had worked for a large store and could not get over these outlandish customers. She was really amazed at what the men were buying for themselves.

Shanelle was learning a lot from the accountant and with her half share of the profits she was buying into the business. The accountant was shocked by the profit being made and advised she could take out a mortgage to buy the whole business. Shanelle was cautious as the interest rates were high and she had plenty of time to get into debt. It was a wise decision as the interest rates started to increase.

Shanelle and Hazel were being invited to all sorts of parties, and at one, Shanelle had a bit too much to drink and was cajoled into bed. This man could talk the talk and Shanelle let herself go. Intercourse was nothing to write home about. He ejaculated but Shanelle felt nothing much. She was to regret that night.

One of the customers came into the shop in a really short skirt and announced this was the time of the 'mini'. Shanelle realised that none of her dresses were that short. She walked around and saw skirts so short you could see the knickers. Now this was a challenge; how to design very short skirts that did not show everything. She designed knickers attached to a very short skirt. She took some of the dresses she had made and shortened the hem line. Sales took off but there was a problem, Shanelle was pregnant. It had only been once and the bloke had never contacted her again. Hazel was disappointed; she had thought that party was crap and had gone home alone.

Hazel was a calming influence. She told Shanelle to contact this bloke who was called Archibald and tell him of the problem. Archie was a strange character who seemed to float around the area. He did not live in any particular place and was a confirmed squatter. Finally, when Shanelle contacted him, he was talked into marrying her but he would live his own way and would not be financially responsible for the child. They were married in a registry office with Hazel as witness and Ivy present. There were no representatives of his family. Shanelle's father had refused to attend the wedding; he had learnt she was pregnant. This was a strange wedding.

After a couple of months, Shanelle woke up with strong pains and she aborted the foetus. Hazel shut the shop and called an ambulance. They kept Shanelle in hospital overnight, and when she was released, there was more bad news. Mr Beasley had died and was buried while she was in hospital. In some way, his death was more important than the miscarriage.

Shanelle was quiet for a few days and made no new clothing. Hazel was selling a few items but some dresses were not selling. Shanelle shortened the hems and decided to put that cloth with the fishes and flowers around the waistband. Hazel told her she hated them but they were quickly sold out. Hazel now admitted anything Shanelle made would sell.

Hazel and Shanelle were sitting together one morning planning what they could put in the window, when a very handsome man walked into the shop; by his accent he was obviously French. Hazel took a deep breath and asked him what he wanted. She was regretting she had not been too polite.

"You English come straight to the pointy, I love it. I am here to see some of your new creations."

"Do you have a shop in London or somewhere else?"

"My somewhere else is Paris and I have a few shops."

"I am sorry, I just took you as a normal customer."

"If you keep talking I will cry but I am here to do business and my love for you will have to take second place."

Shanelle was watching and loving Hazel getting compliments. Hazel was blushing so much Shanelle was deciding that would be the colour of her next line.

The man introduced himself as Clément and was in London to look at new fashion. He heard Carnaby Street was the place to come and Shanelle's shop was worth a visit. He looked at the clothing and asked Shanelle what would sell and the slow movers. Shanelle was quickly on the front foot and asked what was selling in Paris and Hazel was her partner, not just some sales assistant. Shanelle had sensed that Clément was interested in Hazel. Shanelle showed him some of her drawings and her little workshop. Clément said he had a workshop with ten seamstresses and they could produce anything he ordered but he needed inspiration. Now he was looking in London, he was seeing something new but he could not understand this new movement.

Shanelle was telling him about the evolution of fashion, much of it she had learned in the library. Hazel told him about this new breed of customers. He sat down and took it all in; he was learning. After that lecture, he invited them to dinner but it had to be at a French restaurant. The girls did not care as a free meal could not be ignored.

They went to Soho to a French family restaurant. Clément was in his element asking lots of questions about the menu. Shanelle was watching Hazel who could not take her eyes off Clément. Shanelle realised Hazel needed a talk about the birds and the bees. After a very good dinner with many dishes Shanelle and Hazel had never eaten, Clément invited them to Paris. He gave them his business card which was in French, but on the back, it was in English. Shanelle had to have her own card, she had not thought of it before. The girls admitted they did not have passports, and as soon as they had them, they would come to Paris. Clément asked if he could take a couple of dresses to Paris. He would put them in the window of one of his shops in central Paris. When he sold them, they would get the full selling price.

On the way home on the Tube, they were both excited. Clément had kissed both their hands but seemed to take longer over Hazel's hand. Shanelle was up very early in the morning, sewing a special dress she had designed. The hemline was lower than the mini; the colours were of pastel shades less bright than her normal dresses. She picked out a simple dress and packed the two together and awaited Clément's arrival. Hazel was in the post office getting passport forms. Luckily, she returned before Clément arrived.

"I will display these two dresses for about two weeks and I will have a notice saying Shanelle of Carnaby Street London. After two weeks I will sell them and you will get a cheque in Francs. I am sure there will be interest and look out for French ladies coming to your shop."

Shanelle was on the front foot, "I can't wait, I have always wanted to visit Paris, the centre of fashion."

Hazel wanted to speak but all she could say was thank you as he kissed her hand.

Before Clément had come to the shop, they had discussed about taking on a young girl to help with the sewing. Shanelle was farming out some of the simpler dresses to a 'sweat' shop in the East End but she hated to use them. The shop was now opening on Sundays and closing on Wednesdays and they had a second machine in the back room. Now the possibilities of selling in Paris meant they could be 'snowed' with work.

Shanelle went to a local college and asked about sewing classes in the evening. She introduced herself to one of the teachers, presenting her with one of her new business cards. Shanelle was looking for a bright girl who could sew and cut cloth. She understood these girls were already working, but if she found a suitable girl, she could give her a good wage and conditions. The teacher picked out a girl and quietly asked her to stay back after class.

The girl was called Lucy and she only had a part-time job in a fruit shop. She was excited when Shanelle gave her a card and asked her to come by the shop one evening after six p.m. Shanelle would give her a trial and pay her for her time.

"Thank you, miss, can I come tomorrow?"

"Yes, by the way, I am Shanelle and you are Lucy, actually I am a Mrs but first names only, see you tomorrow."

Shanelle thanked the teacher and said she hoped Lucy was suitable. The teacher replied that Shanelle should open a factory, as all these girls would like a decent wage. That gave Shanelle all sorts of thoughts.

Lucy arrived a nine a.m.; she was obviously nervous and could not wait till the afternoon. Shanelle gave her a cup of tea, introduced Hazel and told Lucy to relax. Then Lucy was given a pattern of a simple dress and asked if she could cut and sew the dress and not to worry if she made mistakes. Lucy asked if she could have a pencil and paper so she could sketch how the dress might look. Now Shanelle was beaming, and when she and Hazel left the room, Shanelle said she was hired, no matter how the dress looked. She had started sketching long before she could cut and sew.

After a couple of hours, Lucy came into the shop and presented a dress, she hoped it was good enough. Shanelle and Hazel looked it over and there were a couple of mistakes, easily rectified.

"You have the job if you want it. It is a five-day week, nine to six and you start at twelve pounds a week, and after three months, you will get a raise. There will be plenty of overtime if you want. Now you can pick the days you want to work except we would like you here on Saturdays. We close on Wednesdays and open on Sundays so you can think about the days you want to work. By the way, I forgot you have an hour for lunch, do you agree?"

Lucy was bouncing up and down shouting, "Yes, yes, yes!"

Then she asked whether she could have a drink of water. Shanelle reprimanded herself for not thinking about a drink for Lucy. When Lucy left, Shanelle turned to Hazel and said she thought they had hired a gem. Hazel's reply was that they should talk to the accountant. He thought the pay was generous and the conditions unbelievable; he had never heard of any young employee given the option of when to work.

The news from Paris was very good; the two dresses had elicited many enquiries from old and new customers. Clément could have sold them both on the first day of their exhibit. He was surprised that the simple dress was getting as much attention as the better dress. They could come to Paris anytime and bring some dresses with them. Shanelle decided to splash out and phone Clément. She asked him about the ferries and he laughed, replying that he always flew to London. There was more laughter when she told him they had never flown and neither of them had been out of England. He advised them to take the train and ferry as they would see more.

They now had their passports and were planning to spend two nights in Paris. They would shut the shop on Monday, Tuesday and Wednesday; Lucy could have Monday off.

"On your day off I want you to walk around the shops looking at prices and styles. Take your pad with you and do some sketches. You look like you are frowning; you will not be docked any pay."

"I am not worried about that but thinking where I should go."

Shanelle was thinking to herself they had found gold.

Early Monday morning, they caught the train to Dover and the ferry to Calais. Their brand-new passports were welcomed by a French officer. The train to Paris was quite fast and they arrived in Paris late in the afternoon and were met by Clément. He ushered them into his brand-new Jaguar and they were both in awe.

"I like the style of this car and there are not many in Paris. I have booked you into a small family hotel for two nights but there will be no problem if you want to stay more. I will take you there and book you in. If you are up to it, I will take you to my establishment and introduce you to my workforce; even though I think that term is American, I still like it."

They had a beautiful room with a small balcony and a toilet, shower room and a bidet. Shanelle and Hazel were laughing at who would be the first to use it. Clément took them to his 'establishment', which was a huge shop with a back room that had a dozen seamstresses. He pointed out that they were making some dresses similar but not the same as Shanelle's creations.

"You can copy but I still have the label."

"That is a good point but you are so incredibly honest I can't believe it. I forgot to pick up the dresses you bought with you; I was distracted by having two beautiful ladies with me."

"They are in our luggage and you will get them tomorrow."

Shanelle saw the notice in the shop front with a large photo of her and Hazel. Now she was blushing. The evening meal was a delight and they were encouraged to try frog legs and they actually enjoyed them. When Clément dropped them off at the hotel, he gave them both a kiss on the cheek and said that night was the best for a long time. Hazel was giggling and Shanelle was anxious to try the bidet.

The next day, Clément explained that his father opened his first 'establishment' on Montmartre but the rents were too expensive so, when Clément took over, he moved but not far. Many of the old customers followed him. He was doing so well, he opened up two more establishments in other suburbs. He really had no need to 'move with the times' but he wanted change. His father was all for change and had told him to go to London. Now he was in league with two lovely ladies who were the future. Shanelle knew his English was excellent but sometimes he used phrases that were new to her vocabulary.

The second evening meal was better than the first; they even tried escargot and cheval. Later, it was explained it was horse meat. Shanelle had eaten it before as, just after the war, there was a horse meat shop on the Dudley Road. At the end of the evening, Clément dropped them off and gave each a peck on the cheek. On impulse, Hazel gave him a long kiss on the lips. He told them this was the best evening ever.

The next morning at the train station, Hazel gave him another long kiss on the lips.

"I will be in London very soon."

During the train journey, Hazel was trying to explain herself. Shanelle said there was no need for explanation, she understood. Their only problem was that they did not see much of Paris. On Thursday, they opened the shop to a very enthusiastic Lucy. She had numerous sketches and lots of prices. She had evaluated similar items and Carnaby Street was twice as pricy as the suburbs.

In two days, Shanelle had a phone call; Clément was saying he could not keep her dresses in the window as they were selling within minutes. He would come to collect more and maybe something else. He wanted at least another dozen dresses and he did not care what style. Now Shanelle and Lucy were very busy with the sewing machines.

Clément arrived and entered the shop. Lucy had come from the back room after hearing voices. Clément went straight to Lucy and kissed her hand. She was looking at Shanelle wide-eyed and open-mouthed. He then announced that three beautiful ladies in one shop was something new to him.

"Don't worry, he is our agent in Paris."

"I am disappointed, I have been demoted, I thought I was your partner."

"Sorry, Clément, my honesty came through when diplomacy was called for."

Clément gave her a broad smile and blew her a kiss. Lucy was still standing in shock.

"I have come to pick up some dresses but also to take one special lady to lunch. I hope you can let her go."

"If I say no, I will lose my best friend."

Everyone was laughing but Lucy was still bemused about this situation. After Hazel and Clément had gone, Shanelle explained everything to Lucy. Lucy asked why this shop attracted interesting people. Shanelle could not give a good answer.

After lunch, the couple came back in a very excited state; Shanelle was afraid to ask why.

"Thank you for the dresses and could I take that men's shirt you have in the window?"

"Of course, it has been there two days and I was waiting for the weekend when we get a lot of strange people in the area."

The shirt was in a pale pink colour with bright flowers and was waiting for the hippies to come to town. Clément put the dresses in an empty suitcase with the shirt on top. Clément was hoping the customs would take a look. Hazel asked if she could go to the airport and Shanelle was nodding, she should go. Hazel came back in a very excited state. She said she had been invited for a week and Clément would send the airline tickets. She would stay with his assistant who was an older lady who could act as her chaperone. She was not worried about a chaperone but she had never flown before. Lucy was listening to all this and was as excited as Hazel.

The next day, Shanelle received a phone call from Clément, he was very excited on the other end.

"I put that shirt in the window, my assistant was telling me no. Within five minutes, a man walked into the shop (using your term) and asked if I had it in his size. I told him it was just a sample, but if he wanted, I could get it made in England. He was very excited, but in the next hour, we had three young men come into the shop, and now, I have orders for three shirts. I will send the dimensions in the mail. All the time, my assistant is saying incredible, in French of course, 'incroyable'. The interesting thing was that the first man was about fifty; I really thought that shirt would not sell."

Shanelle was looking at Lucy's sketches and it reminded her of Mr Beasley and that brought a tear to her eye. Lucy could be her double and she had to keep her. Shanelle talked to the accountant and bullied him into agreeing to a raised wage for Lucy. Now there was a dilemma; Hazel was going for a week but Shanelle expected that soon she would be going forever. She needed to talk to some 'level heads'.

She went to Surrey to talk to her old bosses; they still owned forty per cent of the business. Shanelle was very welcome; the business was booming and the accountant only had good reports. They would like to have an interest in the business, and if Shanelle wanted another twenty percent, they were willing to sell. Shanelle explained that was not her problem.

"My partner will almost certainly get married in the near-future and go to France. I have a very good assistant and I am considering making her a junior partner, should I hire another girl or just farm out some of the work?"

"If you farm out some of the work you lose some control, whereas if you hire someone you can guide them. My wife and I think times are changing so fast with the mini all the rage in 1966, we cannot keep up. You will have a young staff who can keep you up with the times and we know you will prosper. I am just telling you to do what you think best, we will be behind you all the way."

Now Shanelle was reassured and would wait until Hazel had come to a decision. In the meantime, her estranged husband came around to borrow money. He was squatting around and Shanelle knew he had several lovers. She was tempted to tell these girls about him but she could not be bothered. He was given some money out of Shanelle's own pocket and told to never come around again. Shanelle was thinking it was hopeless to try to get a divorce.

Shanelle went with Hazel to the airport. Clément had sent tickets and the return flight was in one week. Hazel was a nervous wreck. She had dresses, three shirts in her luggage and a pair of outlandish men's shorts. Hazel had checked her passport three times and Shanelle was smiling to herself. The next day, she received a funny call from Hazel.

"Are you drunk?"

"No, I am so excited I cannot get my words in order, he has proposed to me."

"Is he there, I would like to talk to him?"

"He would like to talk to you, here he is."

"Shanelle, firstly, I want to tell you my proposal is sincere and I am in love with your friend, I would never do anything to hurt her."

"That is good news otherwise you would have to answer to me."

"With that sinister note, let me lighten the mood. I put those shorts in the widow, and so far, I have had two enquiries, one from a woman. It appears to me that everything you do turns to gold."

"Thank you, Clément, are you going to let Hazel go after one week?"

"You just put an idea in my head but I will let her return to England."

Shanelle was very excited, she could not wait for Hazel to return. She met her at the airport and Hazel excused herself; she was too excited and wanted to talk when they reached the shop. She was still catching her breath from the flight and two glasses of white wine. Now Shanelle wanted to fly.

"That week was the best of my life. We have been all over Paris to museums, nightclubs, art galleries but the best was to visit Clément's parents. I was so nervous, I had to have a sip of brandy before we were introduced. They saw I was nervous and made me sit and have a cup of tea, with milk. His mother is so beautiful and the dress she was wearing took my breath away. I was wearing a suit you made me and she and her husband were admiring my clothes. His father is also a handsome man and commented on my accent. I told him about Birmingham and I think he knew more than me. He had seen the Town Hall and the museum and he had even been to Dudley Zoo."

"Were they posh?"

"I would say very polite posh but they treated me very well."

"Big question, when is the wedding and where?"

"It will take a couple of months as they have to post the bans. I want you to make my dress and be my maid of honour. Lucy will be my bridesmaid."

"Maid of honour, you are older than me but I accept. We should take your mother, my mother and Lucy's mother or there will be no one on your side of the church."

"Should I invite my father?"

"I never knew you had a father but that is a question for your mother."

Hazel contacted her mother and found her father had died in Canada just before Hazel went to Paris. Now Hazel became depressed and Shanelle had to have a serious talk.

"I don't think you knew your father; he left you years ago. Your mother made a new life and so should you. As his child, I am sure he would want you to be happy in your future life. He can't be at your wedding but my father was not at mine although he was able. Go live your life and carry his name, let your mother enjoy your wedding."

Shanelle was not sure if anything she had said would make any difference. For once, she was asking herself whether she should have kept quiet. Apparently, it had an effect. Surprisingly, Hazel's mother and Shanelle's mother had passports; they had been to France when they were young. Lucy and her mother were encouraged to get passports.

Now Shanelle had to design a wedding dress for Hazel, a dress for herself and a bridesmaid dress for Lucy. She impressed on Lucy their dresses should not outshine the bride's dress. Lucy was in another world; she was going to Paris to be a bridesmaid!

Hazel had brought the measurements for shorts and Lucy was happy to make various designs and was adding belts in all sorts of colours. She had designs for underpants and sent them to Clément. Shanelle stressed that Lucy was doing a lot of the work and even some design changes. He was now in awe of this young girl; after the wedding, he would invite her to spend a week in Paris.

Hazel would fly to Paris but Shanelle, the mothers and Lucy would take the ferry. They all met at the train station and everyone was instantly friendly. They were all excited and Shanelle had to calm them. They were met at Paris Railway Station by a large limousine. They were all shocked including Shanelle; Lucy could not believe her eyes. In the hotel, they had three rooms and Lucy was with Shanelle. She came from the toilet and asked Shanelle about that new contraption. Shanelle was remembering her first time and told Lucy how it worked. Lucy's mom had the same problem and the other mothers told her how to use it. Now everyone was laughing.

Shanelle talked to Hazel and asked if they had intercourse. Hazel said Clément wanted to wait until they were married but she was happy to do it as soon as possible. Shanelle said Clément was a special man, he was Hazel's best thing in life and to just relax and enjoy the ride. Shanelle was thinking about how her first time had been so different.

The church was beautiful and Shanelle noticed there was a very handsome couple sitting behind her mother. The groom's side was packed. Lucy was so nervous, Shanelle had to calm her down. Shanelle took a better look, studying the lady's outfit. This couple were certainly not poor people and must be friends of Clément. The service in French with a bit of English seemed long, but after signing the register in the vestry, it seemed that they were out in the sunshine very quickly. Shanelle was wondering when the photo shoot would begin but Clément said that most of the photos would be taken at the reception as his mother had a problem with bright sunlight. Shanelle was impressed; on his big day, he was thinking of his mother.

Hazel was helped into the bridal car which was a Rolls Royce. Shanelle, Lucy and the best man sat in the second Rolls Royce. The best man's English was poor but the ladies' French was almost non-existent. Lucy could not stop smiling and Hazel was laughing much of the time, even during the service, Clément was obviously telling her what was going on. So far, this was a happy wedding and Shanelle was hoping that the reception would keep it that way.

The reception was in a large upstairs room of a rather posh restaurant. Clément introduced his mother, father and brother to Shanelle, Lucy and the mothers. Shanelle whispered that his brother looked nothing like him. He said his brother had been adopted after his parents were killed in a car crash. The line-up for the reception of the guests was the bride and groom, the groom's parents, the best man, the bridesmaids and the English mothers.

Shanelle asked Clément if this was normal.

"No, I am making it up as I go along, with Hazel's permission, of course."

Shanelle loved his sense of humour and she knew Hazel would not object to anything, she was in another world. The good-looking couple was introduced as Anastasia and Vladimir, friends of Clément. Anastasia said she would like to talk to Shanelle later. Vladimir said very little but he was smiling all the time. Lucy was just shaking hands and saying hello, she had no idea of their identities unless they spoke English and many did.

After all the guests had been received, photos of the bride's and groom's party were taken. Photos of the guests were followed by the whole party. Shanelle had seen many other photos taken and there were a lot of her. As they approached the table, Lucy was anxiously asking about all the cutlery and glasses. Shanelle told her to work from the outside in and take directions from others. Clément overheard and said a pretty bridesmaid could make any mistakes she wanted. Shanelle was also watching others as the food came. Champagne was poured and Clément asked Lucy's mother whether Lucy could have a drink. She said, 'un petit per', and he laughed and gave her a kiss on the cheek.

Shanelle told Lucy this was a five-course meal and not to fill up on the early dishes. Hazel was hardly eating anything and Shanelle noticed. She was too happy to put too much in her belly. After the food, there were speeches, most were in French but Clément gave half of his speech in English. Shanelle had declined to speak but she was regretting that decision. The tables were cleared away with such speed that Shanelle was surprised. The best man asked Shanelle for a dance and she said a waltz and he smiled. When young, she had learned the waltz and foxtrot, but most of the time, she would jive. After her first dance, which only had a few treading on toes, Vladimir asked for a dance, as she said, 'thank you,' she realised he was very handsome. She had paid more attention to his sister but now her full attention was on him. His English was excellent and his eau de cologne was the best she had smelt. She asked him about his eau de cologne expecting it would be French. He told her it was Russian and he had it shipped to France along with other things from his 'lost' country. Shanelle asked whether she could call him 'Vlad' and he was delighted.

After the dance, Lucy seemed to be the only one not dancing so Shanelle asked her whether she could jive even if the music was a bit slow. They jived and Clément's father was clapping and then young men were asking Lucy to dance. She did not miss a dance thereafter.

Anastasia came over to talk to Shanelle and sat down beside her.

"Clément has been showing me some of your dresses and I would love to wear them but they are unsuitable for my lifestyle. By the way, my friends call me 'Nastia'."

"I could never call you that, it does not sound good in English."

"Oh, yes, I see it sounds like nasty. Anyway, my brother and I will be coming to England soon, visiting an uncle in Hertfordshire. I would love to visit your establishment which I gather you call a shop."

"You are very welcome, you may find Carnaby Street and the surroundings a bit bizarre. I make dresses for young girls who are following their fashion; I rarely wear my dresses. Many are simple to make but each dress is a 'one off', I hope you understand that expression."

"Yes, I do and I understand you have to make a living."

"By the way, where do you buy your dresses?"

"Well, some are from Clément but most are from Russian tailors all over Europe. Any capital city will have a Russian émigré tailor; most of them escaped during the revolution. I regard my clothes as old fashioned but I have to keep up an image. I see my brother wants to dance so I will let you go."

Shanelle danced with Vlad and he was more talkative this time. He had seen her talking to his sister and was telling Shanelle they would visit her in London. He also told her they were related to the Russian Royal family. The second dance was much easier than the first. After dancing, Shanelle went to talk to Hazel, they had hardly had time to chat.

"We are going to a place called Thierry, a small village in the hills above Nice. We will spend tonight in Paris and then tomorrow fly to Nice. Clément has arranged a bus tour for your group to see Paris. I am floating, it is all happening so fast. By the way, I see how Vladimir looks at you, I think he is interested."

"I only met him today, anyway, I am a working girl. To change the subject, I see Lucy is enjoying herself, she will be hard to come down to earth in England. I thought that the best man would ask me for a second dance."

"He will just before you leave, apparently, he is very shy."

Shanelle went to sit with the mothers who were all enjoying themselves. They all had plenty of dances and loved this reception. Ivy winked as she said her daughter had an admirer. All the ladies laughed and said, don't let us keep you. Finally, Shanelle had a dance with the best man and he informed her that transport was ready when they wished to leave. The bride and groom had bid everyone good night and now it was time for Shanelle to gather everyone for the ride to the hotel. Vlad came over and wished them goodnight, kissing everyone's hand. Back in the hotel, Lucy was hard to shut up but she finally went to sleep. Shanelle was thinking about Vlad and his sister.

The bus tour and the trip back to England were a delight for all. Shanelle was telling herself she had to fly next time she would be coming back. In London, Shanelle was talking to Lucy's mother and asking her whether she would like to help in the shop. Lucy was such a good seamstress she wanted her sewing full-time. She found that Doreen was a single mother and had never married, but after seeing Hazel's wedding, she was envious. Doreen was only too happy to serve in the shop, she had served in other shops before. She was over the moon with the salary and she would have no problem working six days a week. Shanelle was wondering what it would have been like being a single mother with a husband who could not care less.

Ivy and Hazel's mother had promised to meet more often and this wedding had cemented a little group.

After the honeymoon, Hazel was on the phone; she was excited.

"I cannot imagine a more romantic holiday. We went to a little village in the hills where he has a stone cottage. It looked like it was built hundreds of years ago, but inside, it was very modern. The village had narrow, cobbled streets and the villagers were very friendly. Clément put on a barbeque and all the villagers bought a plate and plenty of wine. The air was so crisp and clean, and for some reason, I started to think about the fog. The sex was wonderful, I was not sure what to expect, but after a while, I was the most enthusiastic. Now I am trying to learn French as I will be in charge of one of the establishments. Please come and visit when you can, I miss you."

Now Dorothy was running the shop, Shanelle could afford to take some time in Paris. Dorothy and Lucy could live in the flat above the shop. She needed an excuse so her visit was not thought of as a holiday. Shanelle talked to Clément; she proposed to bring samples of the outlandish material she was using and some patterns. He could order what he wanted and his seamstresses could do the sewing. The only request was that he should put her label in the clothing. His reply was that he was afraid to put his label in the items (they both laughed). He said that half of his window was devoted to her clothing and he thought he was selling more of her clothes than his but they were cheaper (again, they both laughed). He was very glad Shanelle had hired Lucy's mother. He said those mothers seemed to be enjoying his wedding as much as he did.

Clément always made simple compliments that were genuine and also warm.

Shanelle was planning her flight to Paris when Anastasia and Vladimir came to the shop. Anastasia was astounded yet delighted at what she was seeing in Carnaby Street. Vlad was just shaking his head and said he wondered how men could go out in such clothes. Shanelle loved Anastasia's dress and asked where it was made.

"My tailor in London lives in Soho, I can take you to meet him if you want; Vladimir wants to go to the hotel to book the dinner and you are invited."

Vlad excused himself, kissing everyone's hand. Anastasia sat for a while looking at some of the dresses and then they went by taxi to Soho. The tailor had an upstairs flat which was his living quarters and workshop. Shanelle thought this would be too hard to find. Anastasia introduced Isaac who was a small old man with a very thick English accent. He showed Shanelle some of the dresses he was making and she showed him some of her sketches. She wanted a long dress and they could negotiate the price. Shanelle was not interested in the price, she wanted a dress made by a professional. Anastasia watched as these two interacted and only had to do a translation a couple of times; English to Russian and vice versa. Suddenly, Shanelle wanted a second dress to put in her window, and if it did not sell, she would keep it for herself. She told Isaac she would pick him up one day and take him to Carnaby Street.

Anastasia took her to the hotel and told Shanelle the dinner would be at nine p.m. Shanelle stayed in the taxi which took her to her shop. She asked Dorothy if she could do her hair, she was going to wash it first. They could close the shop early so that Dorothy was not disturbed. Dorothy had never seen Shanelle in such a 'flap'. Shanelle had made herself a suit that was very presentable and she had high-heeled shoes which she had never worn. Dorothy was very complimentary of the new look; Lucy was saying she had a new boss.

The dinner was excellent and Vladimir did a lot of talking. They were going to their uncle for a family celebration which could last over several days. They would stay with him another week and then Vladimir would come back to London. That fit in very well with Shanelle's plans, as she was going to Paris for a week.

The flight to Paris was short but enjoyable and Clément loved the assortment of samples. His head seamstress was a bit shocked by the colours and patterns. Shanelle spent most of the time with Hazel in the 'second' establishment but she did get to see plenty of Paris in the evening. Coming to the end of her stay, she was starting to think about Vlad; she was envying Hazel's married life.

Back in London, she picked up her two new dresses. The price was very reasonable and she thought Isaac should have asked for more. She decided to keep both dresses but to put one to exhibit in the shop window; she was wondering if there would be any interest. It sat there for a couple of days, and one Saturday, two older ladies came into the shop, enquiring about the dress. They admitted that they had come to see the sights of Carnaby Street but they had seen something more to their taste. Shanelle showed them some good quality cloth (she had kept some from the stock of the previous owners, which she had not used). She measured them and gave a rough price; she could not give a firm price as she had to talk to the tailor. One lady gave her a business card, they were both from Bath.

She was in a very good mood when she took the order and cloth to Isaac. She cajoled him into coming to look at her shop. He told her he rarely left Soho. As they travelled in the taxi, he was looking everywhere. When they entered the shop, he saw his dress in the window and was smiling. On seeing the other garments, he lost his grin and was shaking his head. Shanelle had anticipated his reaction and was pleased. She offered him a cup of tea which he took without milk and sugar. He watched Lucy cut and sew cloth and that bought a smile to his face. Isaac told Shanelle he had never married, and when he left Russia, he left his sweetheart behind, and because of her politics, she had been sent to a labour camp. She was almost in tears and she promised herself he would get as much business as she could provide.

Vladimir returned to London and invited her to dinner where there would be two other couples, his cousins. She put on her dress and Dorothy said it needed some jewellery. Shanelle did not have jewellery and Dorothy suggested she could lend her a pearl necklace; Lucy would go to fetch it.

The dinner was excellent and everyone spoke good English. One of the ladies commented on her attire, Shanelle had no rings or painted nails and the pearl necklace made her look natural and pure. Shanelle was not sure how to take that compliment but Vlad was agreeing with everything said and grinning from ear to ear. The two couples excused themselves as they had to go to Brighton for the night. That left Vlad and Shanelle alone. They chatted and somehow it was coming around to him asking her to go to bed. She pre-empted him by asking whether he had a condom. That stopped him in his tracks and he admitted he had never used one. Now he was speechless and she told him she would buy some for tomorrow night; she was afraid of getting pregnant.

The next day, she bought some condoms; the chemists near Carnaby Street were used to all sorts of people buying condoms. She decided to put on her second dress but still used Dorothy's pearls. They had a light meal and were off to Vlad's room. He loved this new dress better than the previous one and Shanelle watched him undress her. He was so gentle and slow, her only complaint, which she kept to herself, was that it was taking so much time. She was careful to remove the pearls herself. He undressed and she was seeing male beauty. There was plenty of foreplay and everything was taken with ease. The funny part was helping him put on a condom. She did feel this intercourse and enjoyed it, she was still comparing with the first time. They lay together and she decided to stay the night.

In the morning, she awoke early and quickly showered. She had to get to the shop early enough to change and open up before nine a.m. Vlad wanted a kiss before she left and a promise she would come in the evening. A morning taxi to Carnaby Street in an evening dress did not faze the driver. She smiled to herself as she opened the shop door; there was nothing extraordinary in this street. Each night she slept with Vlad and persuaded him to try some local restaurants; she did not have to dress in her best clothes. At the end of the week, he was going back to his uncle's place and he proposed marriage. She told him she was already married and he said a divorce could be arranged. Shanelle politely turned down his proposal and said they could remain friends. He said a man and a woman could not be friends without intimacy. She indicated that intimacy did not have to stop.

A few days later, Anastasia arrived at the shop and they went upstairs for a chat. She said her brother was heartbroken and was threatening to commit suicide.

"I hope he does not do that because I really love him. I just think our lives are so different and I do not want to give up my life."

Anastasia understood and would try to calm her brother.

A few days later, Ivy was visiting Hazel's mother and came to the shop for a chat.

"Clément has invited me and Hazel's mom to go to Paris for a week. He thought Hazel might be missing her mom. She tells me she hardly saw Hazel as I hardly see you. I wish you had a husband like him."

"Actually, I just turned down a proposal of marriage from a Russian gentleman,"

"Do you mean that handsome bloke you were dancing with at the wedding?"

"Yes, his father is duke and he is a count. I would not fit into their lifestyle."

"That is incredible! My daughter, a girl from Birmingham, does not want to be a countess, she would rather stay a dressmaker."

"I am a clothing fashion designer, a fashion designer!"

The Sailor

Dave was good at junior school and easily passed the eleven-plus to go to grammar school. His mother was a widow; his father had been killed in Germany during World War Two. She had the support of her two older brothers who were bachelors. They loved David (everyone called him Dave except his uncles) and they were very pleased that he would go to the best senior school in the area. The school uniform was expensive and so his uncles helped his mother buy the new clothes and all the equipment for sport.

The first day at his new school was a problem for Dave. His mother and his Uncle Charlie wanted to escort him to school. He persuaded them that parents were not allowed inside the school grounds and had to stop at the gate. Dave left them at the gate and quickly walked down the drive to his new school. He was oblivious to any other boys and their parents; he just wanted to get inside the school. On the drive, the boys seemed to stick to the left side and the girls to the right side.

The first day was a mixture of pleasure and pain. At the break, some older boys tried the custom of fagging, whereby older boys would hold down the first-year boy and stuff grass into their mouths. Dave was having none of this tradition and fought off several older boys. He was successful and could get back to class with no grass in his mouth. For some reason, he was in the second form, there was no first form. These older boys were in the third form.

The pleasure was to be seated next to friendly boys. One or two were happy he had fought back against the fagging. His first year was a good experience, as he made friends with boys who lived outside his area. Actually, living in Birmingham, they all lived outside his area.

After the first year, where he did well, he entered the second year in the first grade. His uncles were so proud, they gave a party. The second year passed but David started to get bored. He was always getting up in class and asking why? Every subject had Dave wanting to know more. French taught with verbs but no spoken French had him wondering whether this language would be useful. Dave was now questioning everything he was taught.

The teachers were getting a little frustrated with Dave. His end-of-term reports always said he was good but disruptive in class. He tried to explain to his mother that he always wanted to ask questions and did not get satisfactory answers. His Uncle Charlie understood his frustration and seemed to be the only one on his side. During the third year, he wanted less school and feigned illness a couple of times to go home and relax. He hated homework and did as little as possible.

During this year, his mother took up with a man who Dave immediately disliked. This man was an ex-soldier and liked order. Dave did not like order and there were a few arguments about what Dave should do around the house. At the wedding, Dave wanted to protest but Uncle Charlie dissuaded him. Life at home and at school was making Dave think about running away. He found a part-time job delivering groceries and that took him out of the house more often. The less contact he had with his stepfather the better. His stepfather was pleased that Dave was doing something useful. He did not consider education useful.

The owner of the grocery shop said he had to let Dave go as he was being bought out by a chain of groceries. That decided Dave that he would run away. He had a little money saved and he was already fifteen so he could have left school. The next problem was where to go. One of his friends at school suggested London; he could surely find work there. He could hitch a ride to London as there was plenty of traffic going that way

Dave packed his small suitcase and included his birth certificate as someone might question his age. All his school clothes were rejected except his school tie. He hated wearing a tie and cap but decided the tie could be included as it would take up little room in his case. He waited until his mother and stepfather had gone to work and then caught a bus to near Birmingham Airport. He then hitched a lift in a lorry to London. The driver let him out at Maida Vale, saying this was near to the centre of London. The driver showed Dave that there was a canal where he could relax.

Dave sat on a bench near the towpath. Maybe getting a job could be easy but where was he going to stay? As he sat with his head down, a man sat on the bench.

"What is the problem, son?"

Dave had a strong urge to tell this man his story, he did not know why.

"I have run away from home and I have nowhere to stay."

"By your accent, you are from Birmingham."

"No, sir, I am from Smethwick, pronounced Smerrick, but you are close. Actually our house is on the Birmingham/Smethwick border."

"By the way, I am Reginald and I live on one of those house boats."

"You mean, one of them barges."

"I am corrected; they are barges and probably came from Birmingham. You are in luck, I am going away for two weeks and the man who was supposed to take care of my boat has fallen sick. Would you look after my barge?"

"I would love to, sir, but I only have a little money and couldn't pay you rent."

Reginald had to laugh, "I was going to pay you but do you have any identification?"

"Yes, sir, here is my birth certificate."

"Well, you are full of surprises; I just love your honesty."

Reginald made a mental note of the details and took Dave to his home. Inside, there were two bedrooms, a kitchen and a sitting room. Dave was impressed and surprised by the space. He had seen many barges but had never been on one.

"I will be away for two weeks and you are to keep this place clean and tidy. You are welcome to anything in the fridge but do not drink my wine. Here is twenty pounds to spend on food. Do not leave this boat unlocked."

Dave was now sleeping well on the barge, and unless another boat was passing, the canal was calm. He spent very little of his twenty pounds; he was saving for what came next. Reginald arrived from his holiday. Dave was thinking he would have to move out but Reginald was pleased with Dave's work.

"I work about eight hours a day. If you are willing to keep this place clean and tidy so that I can relax when I come home, you are welcome to stay. I am a magistrate."

Suddenly, Dave's questioning clicked in. "You are not a judge but what limitations do you have as a magistrate?"

"You just asked me a question no defendant has ever asked. This could take a little time to explain."

"I am listening."

Reginald explained the law and the judicial system and where the magistrates fitted into the system. At some point, he was questioning his knowledge but Dave seemed satisfied.

"You have given me a lot of food-for-thought and now I should introduce you to some of my colleagues."

Dave was allowed to sit in on some court cases and now he was interested in the law.

"I watch the proceedings but I find there are few places to ask questions."

"You have a way of asking questions that I and my colleagues have difficulty answering. I want you to come on one of our boat trips, but first, we must get you a passport. One thing I must do is get you to contact your mother or uncle."

Reginald invited Charlie to visit and the couple hit it off straight away. Dave was very glad to see Charlie and introduced him to a high court judge. Reginald explained that Dave was a natural; he asked good questions and some of his senior colleagues were shaking their heads at some of the questions.

Dave's passport was a formality and he was off to the South of France. He had never been on a plane and had never seen a beach. On the plane, he breathed deeply as the plane took off; this was his first coffee but the stewardess was so pretty he had to thank her and drink, but it was bitter.

Landing was an eyes-closed experience. Alighting from the plane was good as it was warm, maybe even hot. Dave looked at the sky; there was not a cloud and no wind. They were taken to the harbour and Dave saw the biggest boat he had ever seen. To be fair, he not seen any boats up close to this size.

They were ushered aboard and one of the sailors said, "May I carry your bag, sir?"

"It is not heavy but maybe you know where it should go."

This was the first time he had been called 'sir' and he was a bit flustered. He already knew most of the group but they were all older men. He felt out of place as there was no one of his age. Reginald told him to just enjoy himself. He asked a sailor whether he could go to the bridge. He was told, as a paying passenger, he could talk to the captain but not get in the way when they were leaving the dock. Also, he had to be out of the way when they were docking at a new port.

Dave approached the captain and introduced himself. The captain was aware of his youngest customer and said he was welcome on the bridge but not to get in the way of his crew.

"Do you own this boat, sir?"

"No, this boat is owned by a charter company. We rent the boat to groups and they tell us their planned route. We can visit several ports in a two-week period and we basically take them where they want to go. They live on the boat and do not have to book accommodation in any port. This sea is generally quite placid and we can plan any trip to within a couple of hours except if there is a storm. Every sailor would like to avoid storms but they can happen out of the blue. Let's hope your trip is quiet weatherwise. Let me ask where you are from, your accent is not a London accent."

"I am from Smerrick on the border with Birmingham. I ran away from home and Reginald took me in and introduced me to all his friends."

"That is a coincidence; I also ran away from home to live on the sea."

Dave couldn't believe the captain was talking to him as if they knew each other. The captain gave him permission to interact with the crew and help them if necessary. The captain understood Dave was a fish-out-of-water with this group.

"I understand you are a protected one."

Dave did not understand the statement but nodded.

The captain pointed to a sailor on the deck. "He is called Alf and our oldest crew, he will show you what he does, if you are interested?"

"Yes, thank you, sir."

Dave approached Alf and explained that the captain said that he could see what he did.

"Ah, you are the protected one."

Alf's Scottish accent was so thick Dave couldn't understand what he said.

Dave said, "I will get used to your accent."

"I will get used to yours, so welcome."

Alf explained that he had lots of duties. He would help secure the ship when docking and release the ropes when they were leaving port. He would examine the engines four times a day, listening for any problems. Most of his time was spent keeping the deck and cabins clean. Some of the other crew would clean the outside of the boat. He was no longer agile enough to do that job. He was going to retire in a few weeks and go home to his wife. Besides the cleaning duties, he had to do minor handyman duties. The slight vibration would make screws loose and he always carried a couple of screwdrivers.

Dave enjoyed his time with Alf and loved polishing the brass fixtures on the bridge; Alf called it the wheelhouse but told Dave not to say that in front of the captain. All the other passengers seemed to be enjoying themselves and Dave had little contact with them.

During the first week, Dave had his sixteenth birthday and there was a cake and a party. The cook had learned from Alf that Dave liked fruit cake. This was a brandy fruit cake with thick icing and Dave thought it the best he had ever eaten.

The captain explained that each trip was different and the visiting party would tell him what they would like to see. Most groups wanted to go to the Greek Islands. This group had been on board before and had a detailed plan. Setting off from Nice, the first stop should be Naples. Then they wanted to go to Sicily, either Palermo or Messina or both. Then to one or two Greek Islands, finally to the south side of Crete, the way back to Nice was up to the captain.

Dave watched as the captain and navigator plotted their course with distances and average speed. This was fascinating and Dave wanted to ask many questions but kept quiet. He left the bridge to talk to Alf. Alf said that this group was a bit different than most groups who wanted to go straight to the Greek Islands but Sicily was worth a look. Now, there were no restrictions but many places would be out-of-bounds during the war and for some time after.

Arriving in Naples, the group left the boat and asked Dave whether he would like to join them, he declined. Alf had promised to take Dave to places the visitors would not normally visit. Alf took Dave along the dock area and pointed out the kinds of ships in the harbour. They visited the back streets and saw how the average Italian lived. This was not a tour of monuments, art galleries and museums, this was an introduction to the way ordinary people lived. This first visit to an Italian city stuck in Dave's mind, and in future, he visited many cities in the same way. He sampled some of the local street food and learned to barter.

Palermo was similar in that Alf did the down-to-earth tour. Dave did try a glass of wine which Alf called sweet, but to Dave, it was almost sour. Everyone they met was friendly and Alf had a limited Italian vocabulary. He impressed on Dave that he should learn some languages. They tried some barbequed fish but Dave preferred fish in batter like from an English fish shop. Alf laughed when Dave commented on the fish.

"Your palate will change as you grow up and visit more places,"

The trip to Messina was a short one and Dave spent most of the day on board. Alf was helping to clean the cabins and Dave was helping him. He knew most of the men in the group and had assumed they would all be as tidy as Reginald. Alf said these men were on holiday and so not to make judgments. Alf explained that there were many different groups that hired the boat. This group was one of the tidier groups, including women's groups.

From Messina to the Greek Islands was a longer trip. Alf said that on long trips the crew would take it in turns to sit near the engines and make sure there was no problem. All Dave had to do was sit for about an hour and make sure there were no strange noises. The throb of the engines was almost sending Dave to sleep when he heard a clicking sound. It did not occur for a while and then, as Dave was thinking he was dreaming, it came back. He couldn't find Alf and decided to speak to the captain. The captain sent word for the engineer to meet him in the engine room. All three met in the engine room and listened. Dave was about to apologise when the clicking sound happened again. The captain and engineer both shook Dave's hand before shutting down one of the engines. Luckily, they were close to the islands where they could dock.

They docked at an island called Poros which was quite close to Piraeus, the port of Athens. The captain explained that this island was not on a normal trip but hoped the passengers would enjoy it. He was thinking that if they needed spares, it would be wise to be close to Athens. Meanwhile, the engineer had let the engine cool and opened it up to reveal the block. As Dave watched, the engineer soon found the problem. One of the piston rings had cracked but not disintegrated. They had spares and the captain was very happy. He told Dave that he had spotted a problem that could have curtailed their voyage and cost a lot of money. Several of the passengers had enjoyed Poros, which was new to them, and they thanked the captain.

Alf had a word with the captain about taking Dave on as a replacement when he retired. The captain promised to have a word with Reginald. Dave was called to the bridge and asked if he would like to become a sailor. He had proven to be useful around the boat and he could be taken on as temporary crew until Alf retired. Dave was ecstatic; he loved this trip and hated to leave the boat to an uncertain future. Reginald was pleased and said he would let his uncle know of his new job.

As the group left the boat in Nice, they all shook Dave's hand. They wished him a good future and invited him to visit them when he was in London. Dave was both sad and happy but more of the latter. Now he had a job, a place to live and work he enjoyed. After a couple of days in Nice where Dave spent most time on the boat, they were off again on a new trip. This new group were three American couples who wanted to go along the Spanish coast, then the North African coast, ending in Alexandria. The captain had explained that, for a good trip, they would need two weeks. They had no problem with two weeks. Dave helped them embark and carried their luggage, he had never seen so much.

As they were leaving Nice, Dave was serving one of the passengers. "I like your accent."

"Thank you, sir, I like yours too."

"Where are you from?"

"I'm from Smerrick on the border with Birmingham, in the Black Country."

"I have never heard of the Black Country."

"I think it was named by Queen Victoria because of all the smoke and grime from the industries. I would like to chat more, sir, but I have some pressing duties."

As Dave moved away, Alf caught his attention. "Don't get too familiar with the passengers."

The day passed and the captain called Dave to the bridge. Dave was wondering if he had done anything wrong.

"One of the passengers has asked whether we can spare you for a couple of hours to talk about English. We are here to serve the passengers but be careful what you say."

The next day after breakfast, he sat on the deck with the passenger called Zack. "I am a Professor of English and I want to know more about your kind of English."

"Well, at school our master said that when we read Shakespeare we should say the words in our sing-song sought of way. They may make more sense that way."

"I have to try that, you just taught me something."

"I was told that some of our words come from Elizabethan English and others come from old German. I always used to ask questions about words."

"Can you give me a sentence in your dialect I might have difficulty with?"

"Yo bay, om ya?"

"Yo must be you but the rest would have me guessing.'

"It means 'you are not, are you?' Bay comes from baint, you probably know the word aint."

"Just carry on and don't let me interrupt, unless you do not like me taking notes."

"Yowm scribbling what I say and I dow give a fart. Sorry about that last word. Now, if I say he is riffy, I mean he is dirty and probably smells. The letter 'h' is often dropped but sometimes used in the wrong place. Our old mon was hon is tod an he fell in the cut. Meaning, my father was on his own and fell in the canal."

Troy's wife interrupted and told Dave she had to apologise for her husband who was supposed to be on vacation.

"No problem, I am enjoying telling some of our local twang."

"My dear, these few sentences have given me an idea for a whole new course which will pay for our vacation."

"To get the feel for our language you must visit our region and specifically go to the markets, there, you will hear various dialects."

"Give my wife a sentence."

"Tha bist in a misery as yor old mon is mutton jed. You are sad as your father is dead. I am sorry to use rhyming slang but my father did die in World War Two."

Troy's wife started to cry and Dave was very apologetic.

"My father died in World War Two and you are the first person I have met who has had the same experience,"

Dave now realised he had to be more sensitive to the passengers. This trip ended and Dave received a note with a large tip. The note said that Zack would visit the Black

Country and his father-in-law's grave. He would be teaching English differently as he now knew it was not one language. There was an address and an invitation to write letters and visit any time.

What impressed Dave with that last trip, was Alexandria; it was so different to all the other ports they entered. The dock looked like chaos and there were people everywhere. One of the deckhands advised they only walked in twos in this port and Dave was asking why. The answer was theft, assault and rape.

"Rape, what do you mean?"

"Well, if you were unlucky, they may rape you, and if you were very unlucky, a girl might accuse you of rape."

That was a sobering thought, and when ashore, Dave kept close to the other crew. The noise and smells were incredible but he couldn't understand anything that was said. That brought back Alf's advice to learn other languages. Back on board, Dave breathed a sigh of relief but he wanted to come back and see more.

The next passengers were all American ladies. Late in the morning, he went on deck to see if they needed drinks. As he approached the group, one of the ladies was naked from the waist up.

He did a quick about-turn and heard her say, "Have you never seen a naked woman?"

"To be honest, you are my first naked lady. I hope I did not embarrass you but you embarrassed me."

"I must use that first line in our magazine."

"I want to use the second line in our magazine," said one of her friends.

Dave was just standing still not quite sure what to do. "I will cover up so you can serve us drinks."

After a few seconds, he turned to face them, they were all smiles. He enquired where they were from and most of them were from New York. They were all journalists working for various women's magazines. They were all curious about his accent and he amused them with a few sentences. After that rocky start, he found them a very fun-loving group. This was a good cruise and a handsome tip at the end made it a very good trip. Dave opened a bank account in Nice, and as he had very few expenses, it contained a tidy sum.

After a few trips, the boat had to have an extensive service and Dave had a week's holiday. He could afford a return flight from Nice to London, where he visited Reginald. He took a bus to Birmingham and visited his Uncle Charlie. He also saw his mother but refused to see his stepfather.

Arriving back in Nice, he was able to visit the bank and found a reduced balance. He had never thought about money before. He realised if he wanted to visit England frequently, he had to save as much as he could. The crew gathered together and the captain spoke about their next trip. He said the passengers were very important customers and everyone should be on their best behaviour. All the crew had been in the navy except Dave. They all knew their place and warned Dave to tread carefully. Dave loved some of the stories his mates told him about their times in the navy.

This new group were just four men on the boat for one week. Dave was assigned to look after one of the passengers. He was to look after the man's every need. What Dave did not know was that this was the "big cheese' of the company that owned the boat. His name was Sebastian, and although he was French, spoke perfect English. One of his self-imposed tasks was to assess Dave, who was their youngest employee and the one with the least experience.

Dave knocked on the cabin door and Sebastian asked him to enter. "I am Dave and I am here to fulfil your needs, sir." Dave was trying his best to talk 'posh', fulfil was not a normal word he would use.

"Call me Sebastian and now tell me about your accent."

"I come from a place called Smethwick, pronounced Smerrick, maybe you have come across Chance's glass. The town is part of the Black Country and our English is not far removed from Elizabethan English. By the way, as I am in Nice, very often I am trying to improve my French as my schoolboy French is very poor." Suddenly, Alf's words came back; do not get too personal with the passengers.

"We will talk again but can you get me a bottle of cold water."

"Yes, sir, certainly, sir, I will be back in a couple of minutes."

One of the crew had recognised Sebastian so everyone knew except Dave. Along with looking after Sebastian, he had other duties and did not realise that he was being watched. At the end of the cruise, he told Sebastian that it was a pleasure to serve him and hoped they would meet again.

"We will certainly meet again."

This was a short trip, but it had only been a local cruise. After several more cruises, Dave was getting to know the Mediterranean but he did not know his next trip would be very different.

When they were in Nice, Dave was called to Sebastian's office. The receptionist was so good-looking Dave could hardly tell her he wanted to see Sebastian. Most of the female guests on the boat were much older than Dave but this young lady was about his age. He realised that he was comfortable talking to older ladies but this girl threw him.

Sebastian welcomed him and asked how his French was coming along. Then he came to the point.

"I have had a ship built in Bombay. It is going to Japan where I will sell it. I want you to sail on this ship and I will meet you in Yokohama. You will be my representative on the boat and watch everything that happens. You will be my eyes and ears, although the language will be Hindi or some local Indian language. Do not interfere with the running of the ship but talk to the captain regularly. You might ask why I picked you. Well, you are an easy-going fellow, not set in your ways as some of the navy-trained sailors are. Listen to the engines, this voyage is a long one. If you keep notes, keep them well hidden. If this crew is good, I will retain them for further voyages. I am sure you will not let me down. You will fly to Bombay and be met by my agent."

As Dave left the office, he wanted to scream thank you, but then his eyes settled on the receptionist, and in his best French, all he could say was thank you. Back on the boat, several sailors wanted to know what had happened.

One said, "Did you get the sack?"

"No, my next assignment is to fly to Bombay and then sail to Yokohama."

"You lucky bugger, I went to Yokohama after the war and loved the place."

The next hour was taken up with stories about India and Japan. All his crew mates were envious of his new adventure. Dave received lots of suggestions and warnings and all the crew were happy for him. The captain came to the meeting and announced Dave was captain material. Now, Dave was blushing and being teased.

The captain took Dave aside and said, "Sebastian likes you, and if you do a good job, you will be rewarded. Sailing in the China Sea is very different from the Med. It can get rough and there are still pirates. Make sure you keep an eye on the charts and see how the captain negotiates problems. Like the crew, I envy you."

Dave had to fly to Paris from Nice to catch a flight to Bombay. The flight to Bombay was on Indian Airways and he no longer closed his eyes at take-off or landing. The stewardesses were very good-looking and the food was spicy but delicious. He enjoyed this flight although it was a bit long. At the airport, he was met by Bruce, the agent. Bruce was from New Zealand and had an interesting accent. They went to a hotel which, luckily, was air-conditioned. Dave was feeling the heat in the taxi. After check-in at the hotel, they went to the bar. Bruce ordered a beer and was surprised when Dave ordered a red wine. Bruce sat opened-mouthed as Dave poured ice-cold water into his wine.

"I was told you were different but that takes the cake."

"I like wine, but in this climate, I have to drink more and so I must dilute my wine. By the way, I normally only drink low-grade French wine, we call plonk."

"Any French wine in Bombay, whether plonk or not, will be expensive."

Breakfast was sort of English-style but every dish seemed to be spicily hot except the cereal. Bruce took him to the dock where he boarded the new boat. The boat looked good but he decided the ropes tying it to the dock were not new. Now he was in an observant mood. He couldn't understand the crew, but after a few days, he could see they were seamen. He met the captain and was on the bridge as they departed the dock. The captain spoke excellent English and pointed out one of the crew who spoke English. This man had been in the British navy during the war. Dave went to the engine room to view the engines; they were Rolls Royce engines and had a familiar sound. Dave was interested to listen to them as they accelerated out of the harbour. The sailors in the engine room just stared at Dave but said nothing.

Very soon, they were out in the open ocean and then Dave realised this was not the calm Med. He sat with the captain and looked at the planned journey. The captain warned that their route could change, dependent on the weather. They would go around Ceylon and head for Rangoon where they would refuel. From Rangoon, they would head for Singapore. The captain liked Singapore and the president Lee Kwan Yew had an organised society that included Chinese, Malays and Indians.

From Singapore, they would travel north towards Japan. This was dangerous as there were pirates in these seas. Two of the crew were expert marksmen and the captain said they could outrun any pirate vessel. The captain was not worried about shooting at pirates. He explained a few shots would deter them. Dave realised he had never handled a gun. He talked to the crewman who spoke some English about training with a rifle. He took a rifle and the crew were all smiles. His first few shots missed the floating targets but then he understood the sway and pitch on the boat and hit serval targets. The crew were clapping and he had many handshakes.

That evening, he lay on his bunk and wondered if he could shoot at another man. There was no need as they docked in Singapore harbour. They were met by another of Sebastian's agents. This man took him to a hotel and asked if there was anything to report. Dave reported about the ropes but this crew were OK. Dave asked about pirates in their next leg. The agent admitted that the navies of various nations were trying to control piracy with limited success. Then Dave asked whether he could get a Tommy gun. The agent was taken aback but promised to see if it was possible. The next morning, a case was delivered to the ship with Dave's name as the only recipient. This was not long after the Malay insurgency and there were plenty of guns around.

As they set off from Singapore, Dave unpacked the case to reveal a Tommy gun with ammunition. Even the captain was astounded, the crew were rejoicing. This was an impressive toy and Dave was starting to have the crew on his side. He was hoping not to use the gun but he rationalised that he was protecting Sebastian's investment and his own life.

The sea was rough and Dave learned to avoid seasickness. A few small boats approached but two sailors with rifles on their shoulders were enough to make these observers sail away. As they sailed towards Japan, the sea became a little calmer and Dave was starting to enjoy the voyage. He had learned a little Hindi and was a favourite with the crew. He was relaxing on deck when two small boats approached; the crews of these boats had guns which they were showing. Dave pulled out his Tommy gun and gave them a spray across their bows. They did an about-face and headed away. The captain thought Dave should have shot at the boats; his opinion was that two sunken pirates would be a good thing. Dave said he was afraid of hitting one of the pirates.

Dave was observing everything on this long trip to Japan. He particularly spent a lot of time in the engine room. He was asked why he wanted to listen to engines. His answer was that he liked their constant series of sounds. Even the captain was bemused by Dave's enjoyment of the engines. As they came into Yokohama Harbour, they had a pilot who guided them to the dock. There were boats everywhere, but as they docked, this dock was almost deserted.

Sebastian was at the dock and he welcomed the captain and Dave. Sebastian then introduced Ito, this older Japanese gentleman, who was going to buy the boat. As they sat on the dock, Dave talked about the journey and the confrontation with pirates. Mr Ito was intrigued by Dave's use of the gun. Sebastian sat and watched Dave charm this buyer. Mr Ito was laughing when, at the hotel, restaurant Dave poured water into his wine.

Ito said to Sebastian that Dave was different and he may be the future. Ito said that Dave should stay with the boat. There would be a Japanese crew but he wanted independent feedback. Sebastian stressed that Dave was an important member of his company. Ito wanted to know more about Dave.

"I think you come from Birmingham, I have a factory there and recognise the accent."

"Very good, sir, but I come from Smerrick which is next to Birmingham."

Ito said laughingly, "I will have to buy a factory in Smerrick."

Dave was invited to Ito's house and Sebastian told him that was a great privilege, he had never been invited. Now Dave was worried he knew no Japanese but he could eat anything. A chauffeur-driven Rolls Royce picked him up and now he was nervous. On arriving, Ito introduced him to his wife. Now he was on common ground as long as she spoke English. She did speak English and that put him at ease.

Mr Ito looked on as his wife engaged his invitee in conversations about England and English. Ito's wife was a Professor of English and here was a different English speaker. She had been used to proper English and here was a young man speaking something different. Dave was in a comfortable space until a young lady joined them. Ito introduced his daughter, Itichko, and now Dave was all at sea. Itichko was very good-looking and so slim with a smile that melted Dave. Dave had to resort to talking about the weather; it was all that came to his mind. There was an explosion in his head and all he could think of was a Tommy gun.

The next day, the family were going to look at the boat. Back on board, Itichko was all he could see, she was the daughter of the owner and out of his reach. The next day, there was a meeting with Ito and Sebastian, and Dave was included. Terms were agreed and Dave was to be employed by Ito for six months to oversee the operation of the ship. There would be a Japanese crew but Dave was to report directly to Ito. Dave was very ready to accept this arrangement; all he could think of was Itichko.

As they were about to finish the meeting, in walked Itichko, she wanted to see the boat. Dave offered to show her the boat as he knew every corner of the vessel.

As the two young ones left the room, Ito was laughing, "There will be six giggling girls waiting for a look at the boat. I will see how he handles this situation."

As they left the office block, Dave was confronted by a group of giggling friends of Itichko. They were all so beautiful he had to get on the front foot.

"I speak no Japanese and I hope you can understand my English."

Itichko said, "We all speak English but might have some difficulty with the way you speak it."

Now he had a thought; talk about his dialect and the Black Country. The giggling stopped and they were all listening. The drive to the boat was very short and they all seemed to want him to speak about the Black Country. He guided them to the boat and kept on telling stories. He had a captive audience, and when Ito arrived, he had them all sitting on the deck listening to every word.

Ito shook his head and said to Sebastian, "This boy is something special. I thought they would have him confused but he has tamed them. Any man who can talk about coal to an audience of young girls and have them captivated is special."

Later, when Dave was lying in bed, he was amazed at both himself and the beauty of these girls. They were all as pretty as Itichko and he had been able to talk to the group with ease. Some of his local history lessons had come in useful. Most of his thoughts were about Itichko but he would have to concentrate on his duties so as to not let Sebastian down.

When Sebastian was leaving, Dave went to the airport with him. "Enjoy Japan, I am sure you will see more of it than I ever have. It is a fascinating country but there is a strong culture here and most are much less liberal than Ito. Don't be afraid to ask questions particularly about how you should behave in certain situations. The older generation could be much harder to please than your young ladies."

Back in the harbour, Dave said goodbye to the Indian crew. They were booked on a freighter back to Bombay. They would be passengers on a freighter, a first for them. The Indian captain was very pleased as, back in Bombay, Sebastian had another assignment. He thanked Dave for a good report and Dave told him the whole crew should be thanked for making that voyage a pleasant one. The whole crew lined up to shake Dave's hand and thank him.

Now Dave's only problem was what to do with the gun. Ito said to leave it on board as piracy was not unknown in Japanese waters. Dave next welcomed the Japanese crew. The captain and one or two of the crew spoke English but the rest only spoke Japanese. Dave had to learn some Japanese and now he had a smattering of several languages.

The captain was keen to take the boat out for a trial without passengers. Dave was expecting a short trip in the harbour but he was surprised when they went far out to sea. This captain was putting the boat through its paces. The captain even came down to the engine room to listen to the engines. Dave was very impressed and told Ito so when he saw him. He also informed Ito that the ropes were new.

The first trip was for Ito and his friends. Mrs Ito insisted that Dave had no duties and he would sit with them and talk. Itichko and a couple of her friends joined the group with only one man. Mrs Ito introduced him as a Professor of English Literature. Now Dave thought he must introduce this fellow to Elizabethan English as spoken today. Again, he had the audience spellbound as he talked about 'bay', 'mon' and 'thou'. He described the Black Country and various dialects. He was now becoming very good at answering questions. Mrs Ito was saying she had to go to England; she never realised how a language could be spoken differently in a small area. Mr Ito and his friends watched on as Dave had this group in the palm of his hands. Even one of Ito's most conservative friends said that this boy should be employed to entertain the guests. Dave was now entertaining various groups, mainly Japanese but a few Korean and Chinese groups. They were all educated but not enough to understand Dave at first introduction. Ito was doing business with all these groups and Dave was helping with all his efforts.

Dave was enjoying himself but still keeping an eye on the boat. It was now like a personal possession. He noticed that some of the fittings were coming loose with the engine vibrations and none of the crew was assigned to fix those problems. Dave saw that the crew had directions but anything outside their instructions was ignored. He reported to Ito and received an unexpected bonus.

It was now coming to the end of his contract and he would be going back to Nice. Ito threw him a party and all of Itichko's friends were there. Dave gave a speech in which he said Japan was a revelation and he would come back if he had an invitation. Ito's wife and Itichko were in tears as he said he had found a new family. Dave was using his best English but threw in a few words particularly, Sayonara.

The flight to Paris and then Nice was uneventful but all Dave could think about was Itichko. He had never told her how he loved her and now it was too late. All his mates were happy to hear his stories and the Tommy gun was a particular story they enjoyed most. Now he was back on the Med and entertaining new groups. He had to admit he enjoyed the Asian groups more.

Sebastian was buying and selling boats and the emergent economies in Asia were very good for business. Ito and his friends were making Sebastian rich. He received a cable from Ito.

"I have a rebellion in my house; my wife is going to England with or without me. My daughter is going to join her mother. My best friend tells me I must bring Dave back. Can you spare him?"

Sebastian sat back and looked at his life; he had made a lot of money but no one had ever said they needed him. Dave was something special; he could cross cultures and hold them in the palm of his hand. Actually, Sebastian was jealous of Dave's power. He called Dave to his office and asked whether Dave would like to go back to Japan and work for Ito on a long contract.

I am a runaway from Smerrick and my future is on the other side of the world, I say yes, yes, yes!

A Master's Certificate

Before joining Ito in Japan, Dave had decided he needed a master's certificate to become a captain. He had to do his exams in English and Hong Kong was the nearest place to Japan where he could take the exam. Correspondence with a college in Hong Kong showed him there was a lot to learn. He had to talk to Ito about letting him go to Hong Kong for a couple of weeks. Dave was setting off on a new adventure but now he had an object in mind.

Ito had booked a flight to Japan via Hong Kong and Dave was able to rearrange the flights so he could stay a couple of days in Hong Kong. The first thing he noticed was the smell as he descended from the plane. Tokyo was much cleaner. He had watched as they descended over the bay. The houses and some multi-storey buildings were very close. At the airport, he was able to book a hotel in Kowloon and a car to take him there. As soon as he left the airport, it reminded him of Alexandria; people everywhere. He watched as the driver negotiated pedestrians and cyclists. He had never seen so many cycles and thought he must try a taxi in Alexandria to compare the experience. The hotel was not the best but was near the markets. Dave's impression was that the markets were everywhere. His room was clean and tidy and he was able to relax as the noise outside was dulled by the double-glazed windows.

Two days in Hong Kong were exciting; he couldn't believe the street food available. Rolex watches were very cheap. Suits made to measure in twenty-four hours were tempting but not for Dave. He visited a few hotels and was ushered in by Sikhs in full uniform. He talked to one and said he was from Smethwick where there were many Sikhs. This man was contemplating leaving Hong Kong to go to Smethwick where he had relatives. Dave advised that most of his countrymen worked in dirty industries and maybe Hong Kong was better, except for the smell.

Arriving in Tokyo, he was greeted by Ito. Dave explained he stopped over in Hong Kong as most of their Chinese customers were from Hong Kong. Ito was thinking that Dave was different and his initiative set him apart from almost all Japanese. He secretly wished he was Japanese and could marry his daughter.

Ito had arranged a party in his house and there were several friends of his daughter present. Dave decided to talk about the Med and how he became a sailor. He even told them about running away from home; they were all spellbound. Mrs Ito asked why he had talked so openly. Dave said there should be no secrets between friends and he viewed Ito's family as friends. Ito rose and said that was not necessarily the Japanese way but he respected Dave's honesty.

Ito took Dave aside and said he wanted him to go to England with his wife and daughter. They would spend two weeks with no expenses spared. Dave suggested they stay in the Grand Hotel in Birmingham. Dave was excited and 'no expense spared' had stuck in his brain. Ito was happy with any arrangement made by Dave. He wanted his wife and daughter to enjoy themselves and come back safely.

Dave planned the journey with Mrs Ito. She had never been to Amsterdam, and from Amsterdam, they could fly to Birmingham. Dave had never been to Amsterdam but he wanted to see canals. He explained to Mrs Ito that his time on Reginald's boat was a happy time. Mrs Ito was now wishing he was Japanese and could marry her daughter. Sebastian suggested a good hotel in Amsterdam and was watching Dave's new life with interest.

Arriving in Amsterdam, they decided to stay for two days and the first trip they took was on a canal. Dave introduced them to the different boats, he was in rapture. They visited the Red Light district and Mrs Ito was shocked. Itichko pointed out it was not much different to Shinjuku or similar areas in Tokyo. Mrs Ito started to understand her daughter knew much more than she had thought.

The flight to Birmingham was short, and at the airport, they were picked up by a chauffeur to take them to the Grand Hotel. Dave was going to stay at the Grand Hotel; he wanted to tell the world he had made it but he had to enjoy it internally. He was trying his best English as they booked in and then he was wondering if they would have refused the booking if he spoke normally. This was Friday evening and Dave took them on a short walk around the city centre and then to a pub. Mrs Ito was intrigued by all the sounds and speech of the locals. Several times she asked Dave what was said. Dave was noticing many of the patrons were staring at Itichko and he decided to go back to the hotel.

Dave said that they would go to the Bull Ring market on Saturday; they would walk there and catch a bus to Dudley Market. At breakfast, they had muffins and Dave explained they were called pikelets and muffins were a more BBC word. They would hear some unusual words and he asked Mrs Ito to listen to the different words and accents. Mrs Ito was smiling to herself; she had only been instructed by three other men: her father, her brother and her husband. Now this young fellow had her wanting to obey.

At the market, Dave stayed close to Itichko but Mrs Ito chatted with the stallholders. The double-decker bus to Dudley was a delight for all. As they passed through Smethwick, Dave pointed out the Council house and the Blue Gates pub. Mrs Ito was just listening to the conductor. This conductor was very vocal and seemed to talk non-stop.

Dudley Market was filled with different sounds and Mrs Ito said she wanted a break to assess all the words she had heard. Dave took them to a local pub. In the pub, they went to the lounge as Dave said the bar was just for men.

As they entered, there was a group of women. Dave greeted them and asked how they were.

"Wezze just avin a rest, it is ot out there. Weel be back out at work soon. Looks lioke yove scored, as theym both bostin." Now he was hoping Mrs Ito couldn't translate that comment. After a quick drink, Dave ushered them to the bus. They were able to get the front seat on the top deck. As they passed from Dudley through Tividale on to Oldbury then Smethwick, Dave said there would be slight changes in the accent and maybe some different words. Mrs Ito said that this was an enlightening trip and one of the best days she had ever spent. All Itichko could say was, 'unbelievable.'

Dave had arranged with Mrs Ito to have his mother and uncle join them for dinner. Mrs Ito's comment was that they could fatten out the bill as Mr Ito was paying. She had a good sense of humour. The dinner was good and Mrs Ito talked extensively to Dave's mother and uncle; she was listening to their accents and words. Dave was talking to Itichko and asking whether she was not bored. Her answer was that, like her mother, she liked language and was fascinated with the sounds she was hearing, her comment was that this was better than skiing.

The next day being Sunday, they wandered around the city centre and entered a few churches. Mrs Ito was interested in the sermons and the speech of the preachers. Itichko was interested in the clothes the ladies were wearing. Dave was just interested in watching Itichko. As they would have a chauffeur-driven car on Monday, they would stick to the centre of Birmingham. Mrs Ito wanted to find some more comfortable shoes and they found a shoe shop open. Then Itichko wanted new shoes. Being a Sunday, there were not many shops open but Dave felt they must have visited them all. Dave had never been shopping with well-heeled ladies before and all he could do was tag along. He was able to get them into a pub for a cheese cob and a pint (for Dave only).

Late in the afternoon, they returned to the hotel and Dave was thinking he might need more comfortable footwear. Mrs Ito said she must update her diary and left Dave and Itichko alone. Dave was tempted to tell Itichko he loved her but the correct words would not come. Dave was sweating and asked Itichko whether she was hot but she was not. As they sat in the lounge, he asked her where she would like to go tomorrow when they had a car. Itichko answered that, so far, Dave had picked all good places and she would enjoy anything he suggested. Dave was regretting his lack of courage.

The next day, Dave decided they should go to Stratford and maybe they could get tickets for the new theatre. During the drive, Dave picked out a few sights he knew but he had never been to Stratford. They were in luck; there were good tickets for Hamlet on Friday. Now Mrs Ito was very excited. Dave was pleased as he had never seen any live performance of Shakespeare. From Stratford, they went to Warwick, and after lunch in an old pub, they visited the castle. When they signed the visitor's book, the lady standing nearby said they did not get many

Japanese visitors. Mrs Ito said that would change; they had castles in Japan but not quite like this.

Dave was planning their next day and decided they would visit the glassworks in Stourbridge. While he was at school, they had visited these works and Dave was fascinated with glass blowing. Dave warned Mrs Ito that the accents would be different but he loved the glass blowing. Itichko couldn't believe what you could do with glass. Dave watched the men and they couldn't believe Dave was with the most beautiful girl they had seen. When Mrs Ito entered the shop, the girls behind the counter couldn't believe how much she ordered to be shipped to Japan.

Mrs Ito looked at Dave and said, "My husband might find this is an expensive trip." She had a broad smile on her face.

"Well, Dave, where can you take us next?"

"I thought we might try Wales."

"It would be hard to beat today but let's go."

Dave consulted the chauffeur as he had never been to Wales. The chauffeur suggested Bewdley to Bridgenorth and then to Ludlow. They could view the ruined castle in Ludlow, and depending on the time, could have lunch. If it was early, they could cross into Wales and have a pub lunch in Llandrindod Wells. There they could listen to Welsh speakers. The chauffeur understood that Mrs Ito was interested in speech. Dave explained she was a Professor of English and previously only listened to BBC English.

"She is getting an education in the way real people speak."

"This is no ordinary Japanese lady; she has a dry sense of humour and is very open to new ideas."

The ladies loved the countryside and the towns. The ruins of Ludlow Castle were a success and Mrs Ito bought a book about the castle. She would use some of it in her lectures. The pub in Llandrindod Wells was a spoken delight. Dave said, 'lechyd da,' or, 'yaki da,' to a group as they entered, it was the only phrases he knew and thought they meant 'cheers'. At once, they were involved in a conversation and Mrs Ito was listening to these new accents. Dave asked if anyone could speak Welsh and several of the men gave a few words but then a woman arose and gave a short speech in Welsh. She explained she had welcomed visitors from the other side of the world. Mrs Ito thanked her in English and they sat down to a ploughman's lunch.

On the ride to the Elan Valley, Mrs Ito couldn't believe how friendly these people were to complete strangers. They seemed to have no inhibitions about talking openly. Dave asked whether she caught the sort of sing-song speech.

"If only I had a tape recorder; I cannot forget that woman's explanation."

Dave explained that the drinking water for Birmingham came from a dam at Rhyadar in the Elan Valley. Itichko had been silent for much of the trip, but at the dam, she started to ask questions, many of which Dave couldn't answer. Dave felt she was baiting him, and so, he turned the tables and asked about Tokyo's water supply. They both smiled as neither of them had good answers.

The ride back to the hotel was filled with Mrs Ito's observations. The scenery was beautiful but the speech of the Welsh was the highlight. Dave gave an imitation and they were all laughing. Mrs Ito said it was as good an imitation as she could remember. Arriving back at the hotel, they were all tired and retired to their rooms. At dinner, Dave said they should visit Ito's factory. He had contacted the manager, Mr Wills, and said they would be there in the morning. Mrs Ito took it as a duty and Itichko, surprisingly, was keen to see a factory.

They entered the factory which was like a big warehouse with lots of machinery. They went to the manager's office which overlooked the factory. The place was surprisingly clean. Mrs Ito wanted to wander around the factory and talk to the workmen.

Dave asked Itichko, "What shall we do?"

"I want to see what they make so let us go look."

Mr Wills had directed Mrs Ito to the oldest hand who was operating one of the new lathes Ito had bought. He then accompanied Dave and Itichko to see some of the finished parts. Dave asked whether some parts were for marine engines.

"Yes, any engine will have wear, but in my experience, marine engines often have more wear. You would not expect saltwater could affect an engine but it seems to be a factor.

"My father's boat might need some parts soon."

"Miss, we will be very happy to supply any parts he needs."

They gathered in Mr Will's office for tea. Mrs Ito and Itichko had weak tea without sugar but Dave and Mr Wills had tea with milk and sugar. Mrs Ito explained that drinking tea in Japan had a special ritual but she just liked to drink tea and enjoy the taste. She then asked Mr Wills whether he was married. He replied in the affirmative and she invited him and his wife to dinner that night. She had already invited Bill (the older man operating the lathe) and his wife to dinner at the Grand. She said the manager should not come by car as there would be plenty of beer and wine. His reply was that he did not have a car; Mrs Ito was surprised.

The dinner was a great success and Dave told the group about his impression of Japan and the Far East. Bill chimed in with stories about the war where he served in Gibraltar. Mrs Wills had been a nurse during the war and was still a nurse in a local hospital. Mrs Ito was taking this all in and smiling all the time. At the end of the dinner, the guests left with lots of best wishes. Mrs Ito said she had to write all she had heard in her diary. That left Dave and Itichko in the lounge.

This was Dave's chance. He said, "Itichko, I love you."

She replied, "I love you too but I am engaged to be married and the wedding should be this year. He is a distant cousin and this marriage was arranged many years ago."

All Dave could say was, 'oh'; he was devastated.

She said, "I am sorry and good night."

Dave could only nod and think about what could have been. As he stood up, it was as though he was drunk; he went to the bar and ordered a glass of red wine. He did not water down this glass. His dreams had been shattered. Thinking for a while, he admitted to himself that his dreams were impossible; a good-looking Japanese girl from a wealthy family could never marry him. Now he had to concentrate on work, what else could he do?

The next morning at breakfast, Mrs Ito suspected Dave had a problem.

"You are quiet, what is the problem?"

"Today we are going to Stratford but what will we do in the next week?"

"I can't suggest anything except Oxford where I have been before."

"Has Itichko been there?"

"No, that is a good observation, I also want to visit Cambridge."

All Dave could think about was Itichko; he had never kissed her, had never wrapped his arms around her. Now he had another week close to her but was not able to touch her. He had to concentrate on work but Itichko was always there. At the Stratford theatre, he sat next to Mrs Ito so as not to sit with Itichko They all enjoyed the play and there were a few tears. Mrs Ito said she would bring Ito to

Stratford and spend a week seeing Shakespeare's plays. Dave wondered whether that was a good idea.

The next week was involved with visits to Oxford, Chester and York but not Cambridge. On their final evening, the chauffeur and his wife were invited to dinner. Roy (the chauffeur) said that he had enjoyed all of their tours but the best had been to Wales where he learned to listen to the different speech. Mrs Ito was so happy with that observation.

Dave was still in a sort of trance. The love of his life was to be married to some bloke he did not know and couldn't visualise. What could he do now?

As they were leaving Birmingham Airport, Mrs Ito put the last two weeks in perspective.

"I have never listened so much. I have never talked so much and never walked so much. This holiday has been so good due to Dave. I am not sure I can do this again but I will try."

Landing in Tokyo, Ito was very excitedly greeting his wife and daughter. He shook hands with Dave and praised him for bringing his family home safely. Mrs Ito and Itichko both thanked Dave for the best holiday ever. Dave was still 'in mourning' but getting used to it.

The next few weeks had Dave on the boat and he did not see Itichko until invited to dinner. At the dinner, Mrs Ito was effusive in her compliments to Dave and all the people she had met. She now had a new course at the university encouraging students to go to England and listen to how English people speak.

One surprise for Dave was that Itichko was at the table with her soon-to-be husband. His English was quite poor but Dave was sure it would improve in the Ito family. Dave could hardly look at Itichko as he was still in love with her. He then made a decision that he had to leave Japan. After that dinner he had to decide how to approach Ito. He would ask Ito to let him go to Hong Kong to start a course to get his master's certificate.

The next day, he approached Ito to ask for a couple of weeks' leave to go to Hong Kong. He wanted to be a captain. Ito said he had asked at the right time. Ito, with a Chinese partner, a Mr Li, were buying a boat that would operate out of Hong Kong. Dave would go as Ito's representative and do a similar job that he was doing in Japan. He could take plenty of time to get his certificate.

Dave had met Mr Li on one of their trips but he did not know Ito and Mr Li were partners. As he was departing Japan, Mrs Ito came to wish him a bon voyage, Itichko was in the north of Japan visiting relatives. In a way, Dave was thankful she was not there, he was still in love. Mrs Ito was thanking Dave for all his efforts and finally gave him a hug. This was very different and it took Dave by surprise. Mrs Ito winked at Dave and said not to tell her husband. Dave was flabbergasted he had become used to Japanese custom and this was totally out of character.

Arriving in Hong Kong, he was met by Mr Li. The boat was not going to arrive for a few weeks and Mr Li would open an office in Kowloon. Dave could use some time to see how he could get his master's certificate. Dave should also plan future trips and get to know Hong Kong. Mr Li's daughter, Lily, would help Dave in the office and on board dealing with Chinese clients and passengers. Mr Li's main business was in real estate and Dave would have a flat, rent-free. It was in Kowloon close to the office and Dave soon found his way around this densely populated area. He found the college and enrolled in a maritime course. Everything was in English and soon Dave had delight in answering questions that other students found difficult. This was different from school but he soon got into question mode. When Mr Li opened the office, he met Lily. She was a good-looking girl but Dave's thoughts were still about Itichko.

The office opened before the boat arrived but Mr Li was keen to investigate the whole travel business. Dave was in his office pouring over maps to plan one, two and three-day cruises. Meanwhile, Lily was contacting airlines and shipping companies to try to set up a travel business. Dave visited the ports and talked to a lot of the captains of freighters. He was getting an idea of shipping, in and out of Hong Kong.

One day, Dave was in his office when he heard shouting coming from the outer office. He left his office to find a small man shouting at Lily. He asked Lily what was happening. She explained that this man was claiming her father had cheated him. Dave turned to the man and told him, if he had a problem with Mr Li, he should talk to him. He would not allow his assistant to be abused, and if the man would not leave the office, Dave would call the police. Dave also threatened to eject the man himself.

The man left with a few words Dave did not understand. He would have to learn some 'local' language.

He said to Lily, "If you have any problem like this in future, call me. After work, I will escort you home."

Lily still lived with her father and aunt in a rather large flat. As they walked to her flat, Dave said she should warn her father and be careful on the way to work the following day. On impulse, he asked Lily if she would like to go to dinner. Lily could pick the restaurant and Dave could eat almost anything except monkey brains and dog.

"I think those items are banned in Hong Kong, and yes, I would love to go to dinner."

Dave and Lily walked to a local family-run restaurant and ordered their meals. Dave had a little help from Lily.

As they waited for their meal, Dave asked, "Tell me your story, and if you are interested, I will tell you mine."

"You are the first man who has ever asked my story. My mother died when I was very young and I do not really remember her. My father's sister came to live with us to take care of me, as my father was trying to build his business. When I was older, they sent me to boarding school in England, in a place called Malvern."

"I know it well; I have been there at least twice."

"Initially, I hated the school until I made friends, then I enjoyed it so much I was unhappy to leave. I think it was the best time of my life so far. Arriving back in Hong Kong, I went to university and it was so aggressive. I regret not going to university in England. I worked in one of my father's factories and then this opportunity came up and I jumped at the chance to be regularly on a boat."

"Well, I left school at fifteen, I actually ran away." The meals came and Dave continued to tell Lily his story. It was a very pleasant evening and Dave suggested they do it again. Lily was very enthusiastic about that idea. Arriving home, Lily told her father about the abusive man in the office.

"I will deal with him and I am glad you and Dave are getting on well."

Lily's aunt was seeing more into this evening.

"I will like working with this man, he is the first man to ask 'my story.' Most men I know want to tell me about themselves."

Aunty's suspicions were confirmed.

As the days passed, Lily spent quite a lot of time in Dave's office. He was showing her routes for one, two and three-day trips. He was trying to see the potential times of these trips. Lily was reporting to her father and her aunty was listening and nodding. Finally, the boat arrived and Dave and Lily went to inspect it. Dave explained that, if you wanted return customers, you needed to see they were comfortable, but more importantly, was the performance of the boat and the crew. The inspection of the boat was a revelation to Lily. Dave pushed and pulled, tightened screws and looked in every nook and cranny. Dave explained that the next test was to take it out for a run.

Lily was excited and asked what they would do and where to go. Dave said they should go out into the open sea and give it full throttle. The only problem was that they would be in the engine room listening to the engines. Lily was rather hoping they would be on deck but being near Dave was compensation. Dave showed her the engine room and the bridge. He was envisioning driving this boat.

Dave's college course was going very well and he realised he had more experience than any other student in the class. He was also learning about the Cantonese language. Kowloon was soon his playground, and with Lily at his side, he was enjoying life. He was spending very little of his salary and was contemplating travelling to England or Japan, but with the boat being launched soon, he couldn't leave. His thoughts of Itichko were fading but she was often in his thoughts. He had heard she was married and so he had to put her out of his mind.

One night, Aunty asked Lily about Dave.

"He left school at fifteen and ran away from home."

Aunty had left school at twelve and she knew many friends had run away from home. As Lily told his story, Aunty came to like Dave. She kept her opinions to herself but asked whether he could make a good husband. Lily was shocked but replied she could see no better man. Then Aunty surprisingly said she saw no obstacle. Lily now had to assess her feelings and how they could work.

Mr Li and Aunty were on board for the first trip along with a few of Mr Li's associates. Dave had instructed the captain to take them slowly out of the harbour and give it everything it had got. Lily and Dave were in the engine room with a few aghast crew. Dave explained they were listening to anything in the sound of the engines. They sat close together and listened. Meanwhile, on deck, the passengers were enjoying a free ride. One of the passengers asked where Mr Li's daughter was. She was in the engine room listening to the engines. This friend immediately booked a trip for two days. Other friends were queuing up for trips. Mr Li realised this was a good business.

A Mr Wong (who was Mr Ito's friend) came to the office and asked where they could go for two days. Dave showed him maps and times of each potential journey and explained, if he wanted, Dave could plan a cruise. This man was impressed he was given a choice. Now the office was open, Lily had more customers. After a few voyages, she had requests for river trips in England and France. She was now enjoying her job. Dave found he was spending more time in the office planning more and more exotic cruises.

Dave had a letter from his uncle saying that one of his old schoolmates was coming to Hong Kong. Charlie had given him Dave's address and the address of the office. In a couple of weeks, his friend, Alex, walked into the office. He asked for Dave who came out to greet him.

"Who would think we would meet in Hong Kong? When you ran away, I thought you would be back in a couple of days and we meet here, of all places. I think I advised you to go to London."

"Yes, you did and I fell on my feet. What brings you to Hong Kong?"

"I am to be a bank manager on Hong Kong Island. The bank has sent me here for two weeks to look the place over."

"Will you stay? I would like to have an old friend close by."

"Yes, I think so, as the salary is very good. By the way, your receptionist is a stunner."

"She is my girlfriend and her father owns the company."

"Does she have a sister?"

"Sorry, no, but she knows lots of girls here. Let's go to the dock and I will show you the boat we are running."

Dave had just admitted that Lily was his girlfriend. As they were leaving, he introduced Alex to Lily and said he would be back in a couple of hours. At the dock, Alex was astounded at the size of the boat.

"We do overnight cruises and so we need to sleep up to ten passengers and feed them. Come on Saturday as we are doing a short harbour cruise. I will square it with the boss."

Mr Li was very happy that Dave's friend was to be a bank manager; possibly a good contact. Dave fixed up a dinner with Alex and he would bring Lily to the island. Dave explained to Lily that Alex had a more refined accent but they had been good friends at school.

"Remember, I lived in England for several years and not all of it was spent in Malvern."

The dinner went very well and Lily admitted she did not get to the island very often but she was offshore almost every week. Alex knew Malvern very well as he had worked in a bank in Worcester. The restaurant served English-style food and Lily was telling Dave they should come again as she missed roast beef and Yorkshire pudding. Alex said he had an interest in Chinese food and Lily said, when he came back, they would go to their favourite restaurant in Kowloon. On the way home, Lily said she had enjoyed the evening and she would look for a companion for Alex.

They first went to Dave's flat where things got amorous and then Lily said, "I will not have intercourse before marriage."

Dave was shocked, and after saying, oh! he said he would not marry before he obtained his master's certificate."

They both laughed.

Lily said, "I am getting letters from my friends in England and they are telling me these are the, 'Swinging Sixties,' and morals have become looser. That is not happening here and this is where I live."

"Well, you know more than me but I respect your attitude, so give me a kiss."

The Saturday cruise was a short one, with a tour around Hong Kong Island and then around some of the other islands. There were only a few passengers and Lily took care of them. Dave was busy pointing out some sites while telling his life story. Lily had heard it before but Alex was getting the full tour.

Lily had put marriage in Dave's brain and how was he going to approach Mr Li. Little did he realise that he had a supporter in Lily's aunt. He decided he must get his master's certificate before doing anything. Lily was now running a travel business and Dave told Mr Li they really needed a shop front and an assistant for Lily. The boat was bringing in a steady income, but if the travel shop took off, that could be very profitable. Mr Li was very pleased that Dave had his daughter enjoying her job and he had his eye on a shop in Kowloon.

Dave obtained his master's certificate and Lily was at the ceremony with her father and aunt. The dinner that evening was a feast, and although Aunty did not visit restaurants, she enjoyed not cooking the food. After the dinner when they were at home, Lily told her father she wanted to marry Dave. Mr Li was hesitant and then Aunty spoke up.

"We sent Lily to boarding school in England and she came back a very well-mannered girl, totally unsuitable for Hong Kong. She went to university and was not happy. She felt she was being bullied, but the other students were being normal Hong Kongers, push yourself forward and push everyone else back. Working for you was a relief, but when Dave came along, he involved her in decisions and made her a strong woman who enjoys her job and life. I know your objection; he is not Chinese, but you find a Chinese man better than Dave."

Both Lily and her father were shocked by the outburst. Lily had never heard her aunt talk to her father so forcefully. Mr Li said he would think about it but he wanted to concentrate on the travel shop.

Within two days, they had found a shop and an assistant for Lily was hired. 'Lily was so happy but did not tell Dave of her chat with her father'?

What was on his mind was how to approach Mr Li. He talked to Alex about the problem and Alex's advice was to go for it, and if he got the sack, he could easily find another job, now he had his master's certificate.

Lily was involved with her new shop and decided not to push Dave. Her assistant was another good-looking girl and Alex visited the shop regularly. Alex explained to Dave that most of the single girls in the bank were stunners but he couldn't get involved with employees.

Finally, Dave plucked up courage to ask for Lily's hand in marriage. Mr Li was silent for a few seconds, which seemed an eternity to Dave. He agreed and said if he had refused, he might lose a sister and a daughter.

As Dave left the office, all he could think about was his good luck. He kept telling himself, "A runaway at fifteen, marrying the boss's daughter, even my educated friend is envious."

Fog Drives Tony to Africa

Tony was sitting in front of a coal fire in his parent's house. His chest was warm but his back was cold. There was a fog outside they called a 'pea soupa' and he had just driven home from work in his old Morris Minor. The fog was so thick he was driving by instinct and had hit the curb twice. It was lucky that there was not much traffic on the road and he had few difficult intersections to negotiate. This was the late fifties and his home was in Birmingham. His parents had a two-up-two-down house and it was draughty. They had newspaper in the cracks around the windows and carpets near the doors but the cold wind seemed to get inside the house. Double-glazing was not in Tony's vocabulary, and even if it had been, his parents could not afford it. Tony wanted to go anywhere warm and away from this fog; it even turned his snot black.

Tony was employed at a chemical factory making phosphorus. He had been taken on as an apprentice fitter at fifteen when he left school. The company let him go to college one day a week. He enjoyed this time and went to night classes twice a week. His job in the factory was to go around and find leaks. He soon learned to avoid white phosphorus as it stuck to the skin, and when dry, it would spontaneously ignite. There were water baths around the factory but he was warned they were rarely emptied and had white phosphorus in them. His job had earned him an exemption from National Service.

He had learned to drive with the help of one of his cousins. He was earning enough to buy an old car when he was eighteen. This was his transport to work although he could have caught the bus and have a long walk past unsavoury chemical factories. Tony had completed his apprenticeship and continually looked for another job. He was also interested in going somewhere warmer than Birmingham. This night in the fog spurred him on to look seriously for another job. His company had a small library and the college had a notice board with jobs. In one of the magazines, he saw a job in Kenya for a fitter. It was at a chemical factory and he applied, hoping his job experience would help. His father warned him that the Mau Mau were still active and it might be dangerous. His father was an avid reader of newspapers and always reading about Africa. His interest was spurred by one of his relatives who had served in the Boar War and had survived many battles.

In his interview, Tony impressed the interviewer with his engineering experience. He got the job and his father said Tony's salary was twice what he earned driving buses. Tony resigned and had some time to read about Kenya. His school geography had never touched Africa and his first surprise was that the capital city, Nairobi, was near the equator. It was at about five thousand feet above sea level and could be cool. Tony converted twenty degrees Celsius to Fahrenheit and thought that was warm.

He was informed he would take a ship from Tilbury to Mombasa. He would then go by train to Nairobi. This was exciting news for Tony; he had never been to London and the furthest he had been from Birmingham was Blackpool. At his leaving party from his work (at a local pub), several of his workmates wanted him to write, they wanted to travel anywhere exotic. He enjoyed his trip to Tilbury and stayed in London two nights and saw all the usual sights. He wished he could have stayed longer.

The ship was a freighter and he had a comfortable cabin with his own toilet and shower. At home, they had a tin bath but he certainly preferred his shower. The only problem was that there was little to do. There was a small library with some interesting books but he was not a great reader. Entering and leaving ports was interesting and the Suez Canal was a highlight of the voyage. He looked around the engine room but found it too hot. He was glad he did not have to fix any of the equipment in that hot house. The bridge was interesting but he only spent short periods there as he felt he was in the way. The crew was friendly but he could not wait to disembark.

As the ship approached Mombasa, Tony was getting excited; he was bored with the ship. As he disembarked, he noticed the heat and humidity. On deck, there was always a sea breeze but the still air in the port had him sweating profusely. He was met at the dock by the company agent. He was a small bald-headed fellow who

Tony assessed as being sixty; it turned out he was only fifty. Tony was booked into a local hotel for one night before catching the train to Nairobi.

Charley, the agent, suggested Tony have a shower and then meet him in the hotel bar. He asked if Tony had any shorts and some light clothing. Tony did not have much luggage and it did not contain shorts. He did have sandals which he had only used once in Blackpool. The shower was refreshing but he was soon sweating again and the ceiling fans only had a minimal effect. In the bar, Charley was drinking a beer followed by a whisky. Tony had a cold beer and it was refreshing. Charley said the bar bill would go on Tony's account which would be paid by the company. After two beers, Tony was getting hungry so they went to the restaurant to have lunch. Charley was a talkative fellow and seemed to be telling Tony his life history through the meal.

Charley was agent for several companies and was directing goods and employees through the docks. He had been in Mombasa for several years. His wife had left him after a couple of years; she could not stand the heat and humidity. He had a live-in maid who took care of him and his desires. Tony was a bit shocked at these revelations but realised he probably would not see Charley after the next day. Charley said that he should use the mosquito net at night and whisky would keep the mosquitoes away. Tony took the first piece of advice but ignored the second. Charley warned that he should not leave the hotel in the evening. There were plenty of pick pockets and prostitutes around. He would be picked up after breakfast and put on a train. Charley said they may not meet again so the best of luck and enjoy the evening meal.

Tony was shaking his head as Charley departed. He must have had five beers and three whiskies, at lunchtime! Now Tony was alone and deciding what to do, when he thought he would lie down for a while. He awoke at five p.m. and it got dark at about six-thirty and so he saw nothing of Mombasa. He went to the bar and had a cold beer; it was refreshing and he was enjoying this beer. In the restaurant, there were some dishes new to Tony so he thought he should stick to something he knew. He picked roast pork with apple sauce, roast potatoes and peas. The meal was delicious and the pork crackling was the best he had ever tasted. It would be a long time before he had that meal again.

Breakfast was also good; it was bacon and eggs with toast and marmalade, and there was no black pudding. He had his bags packed and was sitting in the lounge when an African lady walked up to him and asked if he was Tony. This was obviously Charley's maid and she was not bad looking. He was escorted to the car and taken to the train station. The lady said nothing and Tony did not know what to say. She handed him his train ticket and she was gone. Tony stood for a second or two and asked himself what happened. He boarded the train and found he was in First Class; Charley certainly knew how to spend company money.

This was a pleasant train ride with fantastic scenery and many wild animals. He had the window open to get the breeze, but as they climbed into Nairobi, the breeze started to get cool. Suddenly, he felt cold and shut the window. He was thinking he had left Birmingham to get away from the cold and here he was shivering. The journey from the Mediterranean and Mombasa had acclimatized him to a warmer climate.

He was met at the station by a young Kenyan in a suit and tie. His English was very good and he explained the factory was on the outskirts of Nairobi and they would be going to meet the manager. There was a car with a driver, Tony, and the young Kenyan sat in the back seat. This fellow said his name was Oliver and was the assistant manager. Tony thought it was a funny name for a Kenyan but he was now concentrating on the road, after a few near-misses his concentration increased. Oliver noticed and said this was normal in Nairobi and would get better as the traffic became less. Oliver was correct, and as they approached the factory, there was less vehicular traffic but a lot of human traffic.

Arriving at the factory, Tony was escorted to the manager's office. The manager was Scottish and seemed a bit confused as to what Tony would do. Oliver excused the manager as he was in a review of the factory. Oliver took Tony to the flat where he would live. He told Tony to be careful as the Mau Mau was active in the area. He would have a car and a driver and warned not to go out at night on his own. This was not quite what Tony wanted to hear.

The flat was furnished and the fridge had plenty of food. The stove was connected to a gas bottle so he could do his own cooking. The only problem was that his mother did all the cooking at home. He could fry eggs, make toast and make tea but little else. Oliver said he would find a cook and that was a relief for Tony. The bed was comfortable and he had a good sleep on his first night.

The next morning, he was picked up by the driver who dropped him off at the office block. He found his office and decided to take a walk around the plant. He saw lots of leaks with steam coming from flanges. Now he wanted a plan of the factory so he could fix some leaks. He went to the manager's office and was fobbed off by instructions to talk to the assistant manager. Tony was disappointed with the manager so he found Oliver. He asked for a plan of the factory and forced Oliver to walk around the factory pointing out faults. Tony was amused at Oliver walking around the factory in a collar and tie.

"Unless I have a plan, I cannot decide how to isolate these faults. What valves can I turn off to be safe and not stop production? By the way, is there a maintenance crew?"

"I am not sure, I will try to get the plans from the manager; leave it with me."

After one day, Tony was frustrated but in need of some lighter clothes. He asked the driver where he could buy shorts and tee shirts. The driver took him to a local store which had some gaudy tee shirts. He bought a couple of the less gaudy shirts and then they went to a tailor to make a couple of pairs of shorts. After the tailor took his measurements, Tony was told to come back tomorrow. The tailor seemed rather pleased and Tony thought this was the most efficient place of work he had seen. He realised it was hot and he was sweating so the driver took him to a shack selling beer. The cold beer took his mind off work problems and he started to look around and enjoy the sights. Except for the factory, this was rural Kenya with horse, cattle and human-drawn carts. Every cart seemed to be loaded to capacity and they all moved slowly. This was all new to Tony and he stayed for a second beer to take in the ambiance.

It took a few days for Oliver to produce the plans and then they sat down to mark out the locations of faults. Tony had a crew of two workers who had no idea what they were doing but they were good at loosening nuts and bolts. Tony soon found out that many of the valves were in poor shape so he put in an order for new valves. This stirred the manager who wanted to know why they needed to spend money on new equipment. Tony tried to explain that, although they were working, they were very old and could fail at any time. He picked out one valve and said failure would shut down the factory. That stirred the manager into action. Parts were not readily available and had to be ordered from England. Tony thought of Charley; he was going to make money.

Parts took an age to come from England and Tony settled into sitting around most of the time. He enjoyed his lunchtime beer at the local bar and he became popular with the owners. His shorts were a perfect fit and he wore them constantly. His problem was that he was bored in the evening. His cook was an older lady and cooked good meals and he had no problem with food or the news, but he missed company. He talked to the driver and said he wanted to go to Nairobi. The driver said he could book a hotel for a weekend. The driver was not keen on staying in Nairobi but would pick Tony up when he was ready. Tony thought that a good idea; his driver was one of the smarter Kenyans he had met.

He booked a hotel and had a good room and lunch was splendid. He sat at the bar and had two beers but no one spoke to him and he was too shy to introduce himself. At the desk, he found there was a restaurant called the Carnivore and they had entertainment in the evening. He took a taxi to the restaurant and was confronted with a menu like nothing he had ever seen. There was wild game on the menu including crocodile, boar and ostrich. He decided to try an ostrich sandwich and loved it. After a couple of beers, the Kenyan beer was very good, he decided to go to the nightclub. The ladies outside were pleading with him to take them inside. He was later to learn prostitutes were not allowed. Inside, he enjoyed the music but found all the females were taken and so he had to sit, admire and drink. That weekend was OK but did not relieve his loneliness.

The manager invited him to dinner but his wife was very 'stuck up' and Tony did not enjoy one minute. Oliver invited him and he met very educated Kenyans. They were awaiting independence from British rule but were not unhappy with the status quo. They regarded the Mau Mau as terrorists and wished the British Army would annihilate them. They were Kikuyu but these Mau Mau Kikuyu were regarded as communists and stood for ideals they did not have. Tony was introduced to Oliver's sister and she was the most beautiful girl he had seen. Oliver noticed his interest and told Tony his sister was technically married to a relative from the age of twelve. This was another disappointment for Tony.

One weekend in Nairobi, he decided to go to the Nairobi Club. The driver took him there and waited for Tony to reappear. Tony had a beer and sat on the veranda watching some members playing lawn bowls. He had played bowls with his father but that was crown green bowls, this was flat green bowls. There were three men playing; two white men and one local. This young man came to Tony and asked him if he would play. Tony said he had no bowls and was used to a different green. A set of bowls was produced and his sandals were OK, but if he bowled regularly, he would need flat sole shoes. Tony tried a roll-up and soon understood the bias of the bowls. Tony was to play with Ali and they soon won the game. Tony and Ali went to the bar. Tony learned that Ali was a doctor, and at the bar, they met an older doctor. Tony was enjoying this company. They were telling him the problem with the Masai. They were nomads but when a child was ill they would bring him or her to the hospital. The child was treated but then the tribe had moved on and the child had to wait in the hospital till their parents returned. This was news to Tony and he was enjoying listening to things he had never heard before.

Every time Tony came to Nairobi, he went to the Nairobi Club. He took out temporary membership and bought some flat-sole shoes and a set of bowls. This was the only time and place he enjoyed. After ten months, he contacted the company and requested a transfer. He was bored with his life in Kenya. He had trained two local workers in how the plant worked and how to identify problems and how to fix them. They were unhappy to see him leave. Oliver had made a friend and was unhappy to see Tony leave. Tony was offered a similar job in a factory near Johannesburg.

His new job was similar to the last but this was a bigger factory. He was introduced to his secretary, Elanora (call me El). She was a pretty but rather large girl. She winked and told him she had a boyfriend. Tony said, 'lucky man', this was the first conversation he had with a young girl for a long while. He asked why he needed a secretary. She explained there were regular reports and letters to the management and she could always make him tea. Tony liked this girl; she had a good sense of humour. El told him if he had arrived a few months earlier he could have become her boyfriend. Tony had never experienced a young girl talk like this to him so he smiled, not knowing what to say.

Now he told El he was going to walk around the factory and would she accompany him to take notes, she looked at him and said,

"Wow, you are different; don't you want to meet the manager first?"

"No, I want to know things he may have missed."

El had to change her shoes and off they set. The workers were surprised at a manager and his secretary taking notes. Tony noticed the absence of white faces but that did not go into El's notes. Tony asked El to direct him to the manager's office and promised to be back soon. The manager was a white South African and had been warned that the new fellow had been around the plant.

"What did you see on your tour?"

"I am glad to say, not too many problems. A few leaks here and there but not bad for a large plant."

"I like your honesty. My interest is to keep this plant working at full capacity and I rely on you and my management team to keep those goals."

"If that is the case, you must take my advice when I tell you of a problem and a potential solution."

The manager was smiling to himself; this employee was different and spoke his mind. At the next management meeting, Tony observed there was not one black face. He chatted with El and found her ancestors were English but her boyfriend was Afrikaans. He confided in her he was rather shy when it came to women although he could talk to her like a sister. She was amused by that phrase as she did not have a brother but had always wanted one. She determined that she would help him have female company; she rather liked Tony.

Tony found his maintenance crew had much more knowledge than the crew in Kenya. He could teach them little but could only watch them fix problems. His only expertise was to identify problems or potential problems. His reports to El were very simple; everything was OK or in hand. She advised him that she needed more detail. At one point, he was wondering whether she could go out and report and let him do the typing; the only problem was that he could not type.

El asked him whether he would go on a date with her flatmate. He had never been on a blind date and was hoping the flatmate was a little bit slimmer than El. El's boyfriend came to pick her up and he was huge. He had to stoop when he walked through the door. When Tony shook his hand, it was twice the size of Tony's.

"This is Johannes, I call him Jo and you can do the same. He does not do much talking and I do most of the talking."

Johannes nodded his head and Tony said he understood.

The driver was not too keen on being out at night but Tony reminded him he was getting overtime. As Tony walked into the restaurant, he saw El and Jo, and opposite, was a slim blonde girl with her back to him. Suddenly, he was excited. As he came to the table, El introduced him to Dorothea, call her Dot. She stood up and shook Tony's hand. He was lost for words but could say hello. El took over the talking and Tony was relieved he did not know what to say. After the first course of the meal, he found his voice and started to talk. Dot was very quiet and Jo almost said nothing besides, 'Ja'. Dot was looking at him when he spoke but he was afraid she was not keen on him. In a way, it was torture because he was infatuated with this girl.

The next day in the office, he told El that her flatmate was beautiful but she was not keen on him.

"You are totally wrong; she likes you but she had to concentrate to understand your accent. She has led a sheltered life and she had never come across your dialect."

"Wow, I never thought of that, maybe that is one of the problems I have had in Africa. How come you understand me?"

"Often I pretend I do but I am getting used to the way you speak. I think 'bloke' means man and 'wench' means girl but what is 'knackered'?"

"Did I say 'knackered'?"

"Yes, but I did not put it in the report as I did not know what it meant. I think you were talking about a piece of equipment."

"It means 'tired' and I meant 'old and past its use-by date'. Wow, I will have to think about what I say; please ask if you do not understand any of my phrases. I'll have to use the bit between my ears."

They both had a laugh at that last phrase; Tony was enjoying talking to El and would tell her some new words when he thought of them.

A second date was organised and Tony was practising talking with a BBC-type accent. It was not easy but he was also trying to drop some words that were more colloquial English. He could hardly remember what he had said at the first meeting but he hoped he would not be repeating himself. Tony actually liked Dorothea rather than Dot and would call her by her real name. He decided he might tell about his voyage to Mombasa and a little about Kenya.

At the second meeting, Tony thought Dot looked more beautiful than before. He would have to remember to call her Dorothea. El did most of the talking and Jo just nodded, then she realised that Tony wanted to talk to Dot. Tony apologised for their last meeting. Dot said it was OK but could he speak a little slower; she was intrigued with what he had to say but she had a problem with some words. Tony thought he had been a twit (idiot) last time but would try better this time as she was worth it.

This time, when they parted, he gave her a peck on the cheek and she gave him one back. He had talked about the voyage to Kenya, which everyone enjoyed; both El and Dot were asking questions and Jo was his quiet self. He had fixed up another date and now he had to find somewhere to go. He decided to take time off from work and tour the city. The driver said there was a large African city called Soweto but he was not keen to park the car there as he might lose a couple of wheels. Most of the time they spent driving around the central business district and Tony observed several restaurants. He could not see a Carnivore but there were several Indian and Chinese restaurants. He was planning to ask Dorothea what she liked.

When he picked up his date, he asked what kind of food she liked. She said anything so he suggested Chinese. She had never eaten Chinese food but was keen to try anything. This was a good date; Dorothea did a lot more talking. She was not South African, she was from Rhodesia. Tony had never recognised the difference in accent between El and Dorothea. Her parents were tobacco farmers and she had been sent to school in South Africa. She now worked for a bank manager as a secretary. She had met El at typing school and they had shared a flat ever since. Tony was the first Englishman she had met and she loved his stories. At the end of this date, Tony had a very long kiss; he was floating.

Work was easy; he did not have to get his hands dirty but he loved helping his crew fix a leak. El told him he was a different kind of manager and was popular with the workers. She was always helping him fill in reports; he thought most of them were a waste of time but they were a necessary part of his job. He also thought most meetings were a waste of time.

El told him she was taking Friday off as she was going to meet Jo's parents in Pretoria. She hinted Dot would be on her own during the weekend. That was good news to Tony; he would love to spend a weekend with Dot. He contacted Dot and she said on Friday night she would cook some food and they could listen to some records she had bought. Of course, Tony could only say, YES!

The apartments where Dot lived had a barbecue in the backyard and Tony was going to be treated to barbecued steaks and sausages. Dot also cooked potatoes on the barbecue, along with slices of green capsicums. She had some sauces including very hot pepper sauces. Tony enjoyed the food and was thinking he had met the perfect partner. They sat and listened to some of the records she had bought. She liked rock 'n' roll and had Bill Haley and Jerry Lee Lewis records. One of the new groups was called the Beatles and another was called the Rolling Stones. She asked Tony whether he knew these musicians. His reply was that, although England was a relatively small country, it was very well populated and the Beatles were from Liverpool and the Stones were from the London area. He was sure there were bands from Birmingham and would write to his parents to get news of bands from his area.

Dot asked whether Tony could jive.

"Well, I have jived but that was a long time ago and I will be rusty."

"What is rusty?"

"I suppose, in this case, it means out of condition. With time, iron parts can become rusty and not as good as new shiny parts. I guess we use phrases but do not know their exact meaning."

"I think I understand. My father uses funny phrases sometimes; he is originally from England, Warwickshire."

"We call it Warickshire and I think parts of Birmingham are still in Warickshire. I would love to meet him."

"You will if we stay together."

Tony could not believe his ears, that was almost a proposal. Now he had to concentrate on his dancing.

"There is only one problem, we cannot have intercourse before marriage."

Tony's head was spinning. He could not believe what he was hearing; he had only known Dot for a few weeks. Now she made him think about marriage. On his drive home, he was assessing the situation. Tonight was only the second night they had kissed but it was long and passionate. She was beautiful, a good cook, a good dancer, intelligent; what more could he want? Saturday and Sunday were such a pleasure and it went so fast. They had talked about a multitude of subjects, had been passionate without going too far. Tony thought this must be the best time he had had in Africa. On reflection, this was the best time anywhere.

On Monday morning, he met El in the office; he wanted to talk to her about the weekend but had to listen to what she had to say. She had met Jo's family and had enjoyed the brothers and sisters but sensed Jo's parents did not like her. Jo told her they were not important and had proposed marriage. She was going to accept his proposal and hoped she would get Jo's parents to like her.

Tony told her about his weekend and said he was thinking of marrying Dot but he was worried about her parents.

"Go for it, man, you won't find better. By the way, I want you to be Jo's best man."

"Surely that is Jo's choice."

"He likes you because I like you.'

El was being her straightforward self. Now there would be one wedding for practice and then, possibly, a second. Everything was passing so fast. Tony asked El whether he could talk to Jo in private. El looked at him with a frown.

"You are not trying to talk him out of marrying me."

"No, of course not, I want to know how he feels, I treat you as the best female friend I have ever had. I just love your honesty and I would never betray you."

Tony and Jo met at a bar and Jo became talkative. He explained that El did all the talking as, in mixed company, he was shy of other women. Tony asked how he talked to his sisters. He laughed and said they always talked to him and he rarely had anything to say. Jo had moved to Johannesburg for work but also to get away from his parents. As he was so large, they always wanted him to do all the heavy jobs. He had met El at a nightclub but all he did was listen to her. At first, he could not understand everything she said but he loved the way she said it. She talked differently to any woman he had met; Tony could relate to that.

Tony told El she had a man who loved her and she should grab him before someone else did. El gave him a kiss and said he was telling her everything she was thinking. Now Tony had a chance to talk to El about his situation.

"Dot is an interesting girl who I met at typing school. She was quiet and shy; she was also a bit homesick. I took her under my wing and showed her around town. She was not used to the nightlife coming from a rural home. At one of the night clubs, I met Jo; he was completely out of place, as he also came from a rural home. Now I had two people out of their comfort zone. I just took over and we all became friends. Dot was looking for a man and I thought of you. You are so different, I thought you might appeal to her."

El never pulled any punches but Tony was so happy she had introduced him to Dot. The only problem for Tony was that it was all going so fast. He loved Dot but wanted some time to think. He was going to be best man at a wedding and he wanted to know more about Jo. Tony would meet Jo in a bar once a week and they would just talk with a few beers. Tony found that Jo worked for a printing company; he would put the trays of prints in the printing machines. It was easy and the trays were not heavy for him. He wanted a more challenging job but could not find one. He was afraid El was too smart for him and wanted to better himself. Tony invited him to tour the chemical factory on one of his days off work.

Jo was astonished at all the pipes and valves. Tony pointed out one large valve and said if he turned that valve off, he could shut down the whole plant. As they went back to Tony's office, Jo told him that was the best tour he had ever had. Then he thought and said that was the only tour he had ever experienced. They were both laughing as they entered the office. El wanted to know the joke. Tony said to Jo he should tell her later. Now Jo was roaring with laughter. El was frowning but said she would prise it out of him. One evening, Jo brought along some maps of England; Tony was a bit surprised but pointed out Birmingham and London. He said that living in the middle of the country it was a long way to go to the seaside. Jo had never seen the sea. Tony filled in with a little bit of history he remembered and Jo was astonished at the dates. He told Tony he had to go to see a castle and beaches. Tony advised him to have a cheap honeymoon and save up for a better honeymoon in England. He also told him to go in summer as it would colder than Johannesburg but not too cold and foggy. Then Tony had to explain fog. Jo was loving these talks and would ask El about going to England.

El and Dot were planning the wedding and liked having Tony and Jo out of the way.

Tony and Dot were kissing and cuddling but nothing more. Tony was thinking he was too young to be a father. Dot was planning a journey to see her parents after El's wedding. Her parents lived near Bulawayo which was four hundred miles as the crow flies but over four hundred-and-fifty miles by road. Some parts of the road were not very good so they would have to stay overnight somewhere. Her problem was to have one room or two in a hotel.

Two days before the wedding, El's parents came from Cape Town. Her father was from England, Cornwall. Her mother was fourth generation South African and as outspoken as El. Tony enjoyed them both. Tony sensed El's mother was not keen on marriage to an Afrikaner. Tony explained Jo was not a political animal, he was just a gentle giant who could not be blamed for his birth. El's father told him that was well put and that maybe a gentle giant could handle his daughter. For that remark, he received a punch in the arm from his wife.

Dot was a bridesmaid and Tony the best man. Tony thought Dot outshone the bride, made up with her hair done, she was so beautiful. Tony was starting to wonder if he was good enough for her. Tony met Jo's brothers and sisters. The meeting with Jo's parents was more formal. Tony got the impression they were not happy with the wedding and were only there because this was their eldest son.

The wedding was in the Dutch Reformed Church but they had asked for the minimal service. The pastor was delighted to have this couple in his church and Jo's parents were told to accept this new-style wedding. Tony was thinking this was a nice touch. The reception started with a prayer and a hope for a long and happy marriage.

Tony's speech as best man was well received. He explained that Johannes and he were good friends. He said when he first met Johannes he looked at this giant with very large hands, but he found this was a gentle giant. At first, Johannes was quiet, but when they went to the pub alone, he was a different person. They had discussed work, geography and history. This man was a perfect match for his wife.

"I am his best man because I regard him as my best friend in Africa. I have advised him to take his beautiful wife to England when he can afford it."

The most enthusiastic clappers were Jo's brothers and sisters. His eldest sister said Tony had probably heard more words from her brother than the rest of the family. Even his parents were smiling. El's father said Tony had just given him an idea for a wedding present. He would pay for them to go to England and visit some of his relatives in Cornwall. Tony said to wait for the summer as he regarded winter in England to be the reason he was in Africa. Both of El's parents laughed at that last remark.

The bride took over the duty of the groom's speech, with his permission, of course. She thanked Tony as her boss, her friend, and particularly, as the friend of her husband. She gave a very good speech appreciated by all. Then it was time to dance and Tony and Dot could practice their moves. All of Jo's siblings wanted to learn to jive and so there was a lot of instruction going on. It did not spoil Tony's pleasure as there were a few slow dances where he could get close to Dot.

Dot was planning the trip to see her parents and introduce the man she planned to marry. Tony was a bit worried as these were rich people; Dot had gone to finishing school. All he knew about her parents was their names, John and Victoria, and they were farmers. Tony was going to borrow an old Land Rover from the company as Dot told him much of the road could be rough. They would not be in a hurry and could take two days. Tony had not driven since leaving England but had not lost the knack. He explained 'knack' to Dot along with a lot of his sayings. The mechanics had checked out the car and said not to drive too far and fast without a rest. Tony was popular with all the black workers; they laughed when he spoke but would watch him intently when he was helping his crew.

Dot and Tony would take turns driving. Dot said Tony should start the journey on good roads and she would take over when the road got rough. After a couple of hours, Dot took over driving. Tony was a bit apprehensive but Dot was a good driver if a little lead-footed. The road became little more than a track in some places. Where there was tarmac, the lorries all seemed to want to occupy the centre lane. Tony saw many wrecks by the side of the road. They had travelled about two hundred-and-fifty miles when they decided to stop. They booked into a small hotel that only had one room available with a double bed. Dot had put on a gold ring and so they booked in as husband and wife. That solved one of Dot's problems but bedtime would be the next problem.

They had dinner of barbecued steak and chips; these were different chips than the ones in England but he loved them. At bed-time, Dot said she would wear pyjamas and Tony should do the same. Kissing and cuddling were OK but no more.

"You mean no funny business."

Tony was not going to translate that phrase, he was in torment. They were both tired and slept very well.

Breakfast was cereal and then eggs and boerewors (sausages) and strong coffee. They were given biltong (dried meat) to chew on the road. Tony asked Dot to drive for a while as he had eaten too much breakfast. As they crossed into Rhodesia, there was no problem. Dot just showed her driver's license, and as soon as Tony answered a question, they were waved through with a laugh. As they were approaching Bulawayo, the road improved and Tony took over driving. Dot was enjoying chewing on the biltong but Tony was still digesting his breakfast.

As they were getting near to Bulawayo, Dot took over the driving as the farm was several miles outside the city. Tony could see the delight in Dot as they were travelling through the countryside. Finally, they turned onto a long dirt road and Dot was laughing.

"I'm going to tell Daddy he has to fix this road if he wants me to visit again."

As they approached the farm, Tony realised this one-storey house was huge. Now he was getting worried about meeting Dot's parents. The Land Rover accelerated and came to a screeching halt. Dot jumped out and threw her arms around her parents. Tony was still sitting in the car wondering whether he should interrupt the greetings. Dot rushed over to his door and apologised for neglecting him. He shook hands with Victoria first and then John.

"You are from the Midlands."

"Yes, I am from Birmingham."

"I have been here so long I could not pick the accent; I have not heard it for a long time. I am originally from near Kenilworth but I have lived here many years."

Tony thought Victoria was cool towards him, and at the dinner table, she asked many questions. John sat back listening to the interrogation. A couple of times, Dot came to his defence and told her mother she had married an Englishman. That rebuke calmed Victoria and now they enjoyed dinner. John said tomorrow he would show Tony the farm. Tony had a good night's sleep and decided not to eat too much breakfast. John took him on a tour of the farm and confided that he wanted to get Tony alone.

"When I came here to work on the farm, I met Victoria, the boss's daughter. Her grandfather had purchased this farm and decided to grow tobacco. We have had some good years but I am getting worried about the political situation. Do you want to marry my daughter?"

Tony was surprised by the sudden change in direction of the conversation.

"Yes, I want to marry your daughter; she is beautiful, has what I call spirit and is a good cook. I forgot she is a good dancer and likes my kind of music."

"What do you do for a living?"

"Well, when I left school, I became an apprenticed fitter in a chemical factory. After my apprenticeship, I decided to look for a job abroad, not because I disliked my job, but because I hated the weather."

"I moved here because of the weather, go on."

"I went to Kenya and enjoyed my job but I was confined by the Mau Mau and got bored."

"You just made a good point; I think we might have the same problem here in Rhodesia, go on."

"After a year I was lonely and applied for a transfer and came here. I am now the manager of a crew who fixes problems in the factory. They are much better than the crew in Kenya and probably do a good job without me managing them."

"I love your honesty, as I thought you would tell me you had some exalted position and tell me of your importance. Now I will show you the farm."

Tony met many workers and they were all smiling. John explained the workings of the farm. They had a few dairy cattle that produced milk for all the workers. The eggs produced by the chickens were shared by the workers. There was a vegetable plot and excess produce was given to the workers. John explained that contented workers were good workers. What worried him was that they were being told they could have it all.

Tony enjoyed his tour and was so pleased he had met John. John told Tony he would handle Victoria. Obviously, John was on his side. Dot said her mother was living in the past. Tony took that as there had been an argument. He told Dot that her father was on his side. She said her father was a realist and her mother a dreamer. They spent a couple of days on the farm and Tony sensed a slight change in Victoria in his favour.

On the return journey, Dot was making plans for the wedding. Tony explained they might need a second wedding in England for his parents. Dot loved the idea of two weddings and two honeymoons. The journey felt shorter and they stayed in the same hotel, without 'funny business'.

A few weeks passed and El and Jo came back from England. He was a different man, he even talked when Dot was present. At the pub, Tony could not stop him from talking. They had gone to Cornwall to meet and stay with relatives. He had learned to understand the way they spoke. He could not forget the greenery and fields surrounded by bushes. A trip to an old mine site had him thinking of another world. He was a country bloke and was looking at everything with those eyes. He was fascinated with the rivers and the sea. He had been to Plymouth and could not believe the size of the ships. In London, he was amazed at the bridge that opened. What excited him most were the double-decker buses that were everywhere. The biggest castle he had ever seen was a bit of a disappointment as they could not get in because the queues were so long. He wanted to go back but how could he get a job?

Tony talked to El about her experience. She loved every minute but the best was the change in Jo; it was as though he had been liberated.

"Because of his size, everyone gave him some space except in the pub. He would go to the pub and they were crowding around him, they were listening to everything he said. My relatives loved him, and when one of my relatives took him out on a boat, he seemed to be in a trance. He wants to go live in England but how?"

"Dot and I think he should send letters to a newspaper in Cornwall telling them of his experience in Cornwall. He should also learn as much as he can about printing. You ought to learn shorthand and you can help him with English. You should also apply for a British passport."

El came and gave him a kiss and said he was a better thinker than a manager. Tony was wondering about that comment, but after all, it was from El.

Dot was involved in planning the wedding when momentous news came. Ian Smith had declared Rhodesia independent. Tony and Dot were not sure what that meant but her father said nothing would stop them from getting to the wedding. World opinion was against this declaration and there was bound to be economic consequences. Dot said that stops a honeymoon in Rhodesia. Tony thought this was a good time for Dot to apply for a British passport.

Tony asked Jo whether he would be best man. Tony told him to imagine he was in the pub and just tell them a little about Tony and Dot. Jo had written a couple of letters to a newspaper in Cornwall and they wanted more. El was editing these letters but she told Tony she was doing less with fewer corrections. Jo was comparing rural Cornwall with rural South Africa and already had a following of readers who were writing to the editor.

In one article, he had said he would like to see more of England. This produced ten invitations to stay in all parts of England. A paper in Bristol had reproduced his letters.

"You've made my husband famous and I can't stop him talking. My father is very pleased I am applying for a British passport and even my mother agrees."

"Jo needed to find something he could do, now we have to find him a job. By the way, has he sent any letters to South African papers?"

"You are an ideas man, now I have two in my life, why didn't you come here earlier?"

John and Victoria found they could cross the Rhodesia / South African border. They had suggested they stay in a hotel but Tony had told them to stay at his flat. It had two bedrooms and the men could have a groom's party while the ladies could go to Dot's flat. Tony was very interested in talking to John and maybe he would have some idea about how they could find Jo a job.

Two days before the wedding, John and Victoria arrived. They all met at El and Dot's flat and they were introduced to El and Jo. Everyone was in a happy mood and Jo said a few words in front of Victoria. Tony had the driver take the men to his flat. The driver was very happy he was on double time. Later, he would take Jo back home and pick up Victoria.

Tony had beer, whisky and brandy available but John said he preferred beer. Tony was keen to talk about Ian Smith and get John's opinion.

"It is early days yet but I foresee lots of problems. My agents tell me that some countries could boycott tobacco;

not good news for our farm. Then my workers have been telling me there are groups forming who want black rule. Some of these groups are arming. I have a good rapport with my workers but they are being told they can have it all; the farm, that is. I think we should sell. The farm belongs to Victoria, her grandfather made the farm then her father ran it, and finally, it passed to Victoria."

Jo piped up, "I could never see my parents selling their farm."

"We have enough money to buy a small holding in England without selling the farm, but if we were not here, it would collapse. Of course, if you produced a grandchild and moved to England it could be a different story."

"Hang on, John, we are not married yet." Jo was roaring with laughter. Jo started telling John about his letters to newspapers in England. He was telling them the difference in farms in the two countries. He had offers to come to England and stay.

"You could apply for a farm manager's job. The only problem is, it takes days to get newspapers here and then your replies would take days. It is worth a try but you could write in your letters that you would love to manage a farm in England and use some of your South African methods. You would get used to and know all the animals. You would name them and get them used to your presence. It might work as, what I hear from England, is that the sixties is the time of peace and love."

Tony was thinking that was a long shot. There was plenty more conversation, plenty of beer consumed, then the driver came to ask if he could take Jo home. Jo was shaking John's hand vigorously and Tony told him to stop, he did not want a wounded father-in-law. When Jo had left, John said he was the best Afrikaner he had ever met.

"I don't know what happened to Jo but he had an audience for his stories down the pub in Cornwall and has come out of his shell. His wife is my secretary and I could not wish to know a friendlier couple. She used to dominate him but now I feel they are both on a par." Victoria arrived all excited; she loved the wedding dress and all the preparations for the wedding. El had such a loving personality and she would make a wonderful bridesmaid. She had not met the other bridesmaid who was Jo's eldest sister but Dot had picked her so she must be OK.

The next morning, Victoria wanted to go as soon as possible to see Dot. John said he would like to visit the chemical plant. He remembered some of the old factories in Coventry but he was a country boy. Tony was thinking he could not have a better father-in-law. Jo already had a letter to go to the English newspapers and El was telling him to calm down. El was telling Tony she thought Jo had not slept last night, he was so excited.

The wedding was at a Church of England church. Tony's crew sat at the back of the church and he welcomed each one. Jo was more nervous than Tony and Tony was telling him to calm down. Victoria was sitting alone and Tony thought her beautiful; probably the source of Dot's beauty. Tony would love to have his parents present but he was planning to have a second wedding when they went to

England. Dot, her father and the bridesmaids entered the church and Tony could not resist a peek. He wanted to keep looking but Victoria nodded no. When Dot stood beside him, he suddenly noticed she was several inches shorter than him. He had danced with her, walked with her and driven with her but this was the first time he had noticed the height discrepancy.

After the wedding, they went to the back room of a very good restaurant and had a private function. Jo's speech was short but full of praise for Tony and Dot. John said a few words saying he liked his new son-in-law. Elize, Jo's sister, wanted to say a few words. She thanked Dot for inviting her to be a bridesmaid. She would take this dress back to the farm and show it off whenever she could. Thanks to Dot, Tony and El, she had a new brother who seemed to be popular in England; she would have to look at some maps. That elicited lots of laughter from those present including Jo. Elize talked extensively to Victoria, they were both country girls.

Tony and Dot left for a short honeymoon in Pretoria. John and Victoria would stay at Tony's flat until the honeymoon was over.

On the drive to Pretoria, Dot told Tony that tonight he could do what he wanted. Tony was asking himself what he wanted. He thought it was a pity that she had told him at the start of the journey not at the end. They checked into the hotel but it was early in the afternoon. Dot had the solution; they should make love, have dinner and make love again. Tony could not disagree but it was all so cut and dried.

As they undressed, Tony realised he had married a real beauty. Dot gave him a condom and told him she did not want to get pregnant yet. She also said she was a virgin and he admitted he was the same. There had been some chances in Kenya but he had wanted the first time to be with someone special. This was the time, and after a bit of fumbling, Tony was breathing heavily and Dot was moaning. After the climax, almost simultaneously, they lay back in each other's arms and fell asleep. Dinner was nothing special but the second time was heaven.

The few days in Pretoria were a wonderful time; they did very little except enjoy each other's company. Arriving back in Johannesburg, they were greeted by a happy Victoria and John who said they had enjoyed a second honeymoon. Tony had visions he had to keep secret, even from Dot. El was full of praise for Tony setting her husband in motion. Tony told her the ideas were John's and it was a long shot. Elize had taken Jo's letters back to her parents and now the whole family was writing suggestions.

Life settled back into a routine and Tony did not need a cook, he had married one. The plant was running well and Tony started to think about jobs in England. Then a bombshell; Jo was offered a job to run a farm owned by an English rock star. This man had read Jo's letter and loved getting to know the animals. He had a small farm near Birmingham and he could not run it himself. There was a farmhouse and plenty of money to spend on improvements; the salary was so big, Jo had to try three times to convert it to Rand. El had her British passport, and when she told Tony, she had to cry on his shoulder. El's parents were ecstatic and told her they would visit England at the first opportunity.

John's advice had worked, much to Tony's surprise. Now Jo was nervous and Tony told him his boss was just an ordinary bloke who could play a guitar.

"I can't play any instrument."

"You don't have to, all you need is to manage a farm; by the way, do you know any songs."

"I can't sing, they even chucked me out of the church choir."

Jo and El packed up to leave and Tony had a problem to find a secretary. Tony decided to invite Elize; she was doing typing for a local bank manager and so knew how to type letters. El was delighted her sister-in-law would take her position and was hugging and kissing Tony. She told Tony she was nervous about moving, but Jo was so positive she had to take his enthusiasm.

El and Jo were met at Heathrow by a limousine and driven to the farm near Kidderminster. Jo's boss was waiting with a film crew. When Jo alighted from their transport, he dwarfed his boss.

"My god, I am employing a giant, by the way, my real name is Roy although my stage name is different. Wow, this is your wife. I am envious that you could marry such a beautiful lady. My farm is going to become a beautiful place with you two here."

Jo was at a loss for words but El butted in and asked whether he knew the Beatles.

"I do and we will invite them over for a meal if you can cook."

"Give me a barbecue and good meat and we shall see."

"I love your accents. I only hope my cows can understand you."

That bought lots of laughter even from the film crew.

Jo said he would meet them all and talk to them and they would understand him. Roy stood next to Jo and said, you inspire me to compose a song. Jo apologised and said he could not sing. Everyone was laughing and Roy said he had just met an uninhibited man.

El's letters to Dot were all about these strange people. She was now employed as a secretary to the band. They just did life differently; she knew they all smoked marijuana. Jo was talking to the cattle and chickens and had noticed more milk and eggs. Roy could not get enough of Jo; they had been invited to several concerts. She was still waiting to see the Beatles and the Rolling Stones.

Jo and Roy sat down several times to talk about the farm. Roy asked about Afrikaner music. Jo was telling him mostly they sang hymns but there was also the local black music which was full of rhythms. Jo would get him some records so he could hear this music.

Meanwhile, Dot and Tony were enjoying married life, Tony was continually looking for jobs in England. The news from Jo had him more interested in going home. News from John and Victoria was not too bad, things were changing slowly. Then Dot said she was pregnant, now Tony was in a panic. He wanted the child born in England. He had no problem with the local hospitals but he wanted his child born in England. Victoria was with them within two days of hearing the news. John was left to run the farm; Tony was disappointed. Dot was very keen to have the baby in England and Victoria agreed.

Tony was planning to go to England, when a job offer in a refinery came through. He was relieved he did not have to leave Dot alone. John had spoken to Tony and said to take any job, all he had to do is talk Victoria into selling the farm. Even if Victoria would not agree, they still had enough money to buy Dot and Tony a home. Tony thanked John and said, with a decent job, he could get a mortgage and buy a house.

Meanwhile, El had invited her parents to visit, she was also pregnant. There was plenty of room in the farmhouse and she had advised Roy that any parties should not have drugs. Roy was just shaking his head in astonishment; this couple was straightforward, they did not pull punches. Ted and Elaine, El's parents, arrived at Heathrow to be greeted by El and Jo in a limousine.

Ted was impressed and asked if they had hired this vehicle.

"No, I just told our boss we needed a nice car to pick up my parents and we would need one next week to go to Cornwall."

Arriving at the farm, Jo introduced them to the cows. He called out a name and a cow came to meet him. He patted her on the forehead and then called out a different name and another cow came to him. Ted was very impressed and El told him that Jo could do that with the chickens. He was now training the pigs they had bought. Roy came to visit the farm to meet El's parents. He told Ted he had hired Jo and El and they had done wonders with the farm; it could soon make a profit. The good news for El was that there would be no parties soon as the band was off to America. He told El they could call one of the pigs, Roy.

"No, that would be disrespectful to our boss."

Roy roared with laughter and said, "You are priceless."

Ted and Elaine enjoyed their stay on the farm. El took them out in an old Land Rover; she had recently passed her test. Ted loved the pubs by the River Severn, he said it was something he really missed. El did not drink but her mother started to enjoy a shandy. Jo apologised for not going to Cornwall; he had to look after the animals. Cornwall was the place he wanted to revisit but he had found a local pub he enjoyed. He was still writing letters to the newspaper in Cornwall. El told her parents that when they visited the local pub she lost Jo, he was in another world with people surrounding him also in another world.

Ted decided they would stay another couple of weeks; he was interested to buy a property and Elaine wanted to be close to a future grandchild. A couple of the band members came to talk to El about their contracts and El introduced them to her father. He was a financial consultant for a big company in Cape Town. He looked through their contracts and said they were so one-sided they could be challenged in the courts and they should get a lawyer. The band members asked him what they owed and he said nothing. He was only giving them friendly advice and he had no license in England. The next day, a case of whisky arrived, addressed to Ted.

Dot was so excited she was going to England; Tony warned her it might not be too warm in the summer and winter could be cold. There were fewer fogs (lately called smogs) since the Clean Air Act but he was hoping Portsmouth would be spared his pet hate. John was excited about their move to England and was telling Victoria to take a trip and have a look. Dot was very keen to have a second wedding before they settled down near Portsmouth.

Tony realised his parents knew little about Dot or the situation in South Africa or Rhodesia. This was the time to write lots of letters and send plenty of photos. Tony's mother was excited to see more photos of her daughter-in-law. Tony had sent wedding photos but everyone looks good in wedding photos. She was also delighted with the news of a grandchild and second wedding. His father did not say much except Tony looked brown and he had married a 'bostin wench with a gorgeous kissa' (face).

Dot and Tony were met at Heathrow by El with the limousine. Jo could not come as a calf was being born. Dot detected a change in El's accent; that had evaded Tony.

"We are meeting so many people, and every time we go down the pub, I have to do as much talking as Jo. These people are so friendly and they soak up everything I say about Africa."

Dot was impressed with the roads and the green countryside. At the farm, they were met by a happy Jo, there had been no problem with the birth. Dot and El were both thinking of birth. Suddenly, El started to cry.

"Don't worry about me, I am so glad we are all together, this pregnancy has made me very sentimental. I have had a bit of morning sickness but I am often thinking of the past."

Dot said she had not really had morning sickness yet but she also had mood swings. This was news for Jo and Tony; they started to think about what their wives were going through. The first night they spent in the farmhouse, and on the second night, they had to go to the pub. El drove as she would not drink. Dot had a shandy and the men had several beers. Dot was very impressed with the pub; it had oak beams and was built in the 1700s. The landlord was very welcoming and told Tony his friend, Jo, was so popular he always had a crowd of happy drinkers. Jo was so tall everyone could hear and watch him speak.

On the third night, Tony opened the door to a long-haired man who introduced himself as Roy. El quickly took over and introduced Roy to Tony who was from Birmingham. Roy told her he was off to America with the band, she told him the farm was making money and she would have the accounts when he returned.

In America, Roy was interviewed by a New York journalist.

"In this business, everyone is trying to rip you off and take your money. Back home, I have a farm and my manager and his wife are trying to make me money. If they make me one quid I will value that more than all the money I make on this trip."

This was reported in the British press and El bought several newspapers so she could take cuttings to send to her parents and Jo's parents. Tony hired a car to go to Portsmouth to look for a flat and see about his new job. He found a flat to rent and came back to a happy Dot. She was getting to know all the animals and Jo was telling her she had the gift. Tony took her to meet his parents; they lived in a very small house and this was inner city Birmingham. Dot loved her parents-in-law, but when alone with Tony, she asked why they did not live in a better place.

"My parents have lived in that house since they were married and that is where my brother and I were born. They know all their neighbours and half the street. I think one day they will move but my aunt, mom's elder sister, lives close and they are as thick as thieves. By the way, I have talked to my younger brother, who lives in London.

Next weekend, we will visit him and stay overnight. We will go by train as I do not know my way around London and we could get lost."

Dot had never been on a train and was excited to see London. El took them to the station in Kidderminster and they would change trains in Birmingham. Dot loved the rhythm of the train and she saw a lot of the suburbs of Birmingham including the industrial areas of Birmingham. Tony told her of the bombing during the war and she was fascinated. The trip from Birmingham to London was mainly through green countryside until they reached the outskirts of London. Euston was a large station and Dot wanted to stand and take in the view of the biggest building she had ever been inside. Tony realised what seemed normal to him had to be looked at with different eyes.

Tony's brother was called William and he was a management consultant. His office was just outside what was called the City of London. Dot was amazed at the narrow streets and the difficulty the taxi had to get to the office. In the office, they were given a coffee as William was busy with a client. This was the first time Dot had seen computers. These were fairly primitive computers but Dot was fascinated, and when one printed out a letter, she shrieked with delight.

William greeted Dot and winked at Tony; he said they would go to a local pub and have one beer and then go to a restaurant on the way home. He had to pop into the pub to be seen with a beautiful lady in his entourage speaking with an interesting accent; it could be good for business.

Dot had not eaten proper Indian food but she liked hot dishes. William ordered too much food, and at the end of the meal, William asked for a 'doggy bag'. Dot could not believe what she was seeing.

The next day, William took them to see all the sights and then dropped them at Euston. He said, as they would be living in Portsmouth, it was a short ride to London and they were welcome to stay anytime. William gave Dot a hug and kiss; he told her his brother had found a diamond. Tony reminded him about the wedding and William said he would not miss it.

Back at the farm, El asked Dot what was her most prominent memory. Dot said it was the 'doggy bag' as it was so unexpected. Tony told Jo that, this time, his brother had to be best man. Jo said he was happy and relieved. Elize had been invited to the wedding and El was going to pay for the flight. She wanted to see her sister-in-law and show her how they lived. Victoria was coming but John would stay on the farm.

Elize and Victoria came on the same plane and had the limousine treatment. Tony was in Portsmouth finding the place he would rent and learning about his new job. All the ladies had a happy reunion and the driver had Champagne provided by Roy. The two ladies were very tired when they reached the farm but had to meet all the animals. Elize had to tell Jo he should relax his hugs as they were crushing her. In the next few days, El was driving them around the countryside and introducing them to the pub. Elize was a hit and had a crowd as big as her brother. Victoria was amazed at how friendly people were. In one of her communications with John, she said if they bought a farm they had to grow strawberries. She had been to a farm where you could pick your own. She probably ate more than was weighed. She tried to offer the farmer more money but he said they had calculated for 'losses'. They had walked along a railway line and the fence was covered in blackberries, which she picked and ate.

John was very pleased with that news as Victoria was having serious thoughts about selling the tobacco farm. He got in touch with Tony and told him to encourage Victoria to look at farms for sale. Tony came to the farm at the weekend to be joined by Roy and the band. Elize and Victoria were astonished at this bunch of scruffy men who were so polite and generous. Roy asked Victoria what she had seen and liked in England and she told him about the strawberries and blackberries. The next day, three pounds of strawberries and a pound of blackberries were delivered, addressed to Victoria. El introduced the band to Elize and reminded them she was Jo's sister. Roy had to go outside to have a good laugh. Elize had brought some records which she gave to Roy and he was so happy. He took the band to the recording studio attached to the farmhouse to listen to the music.

When the band was leaving, Roy came and thanked Elize.

"We listened to all those records and it was music we had never heard before."

"I think they are a bit rough as these are local records that will probably never get out of South Africa."

"Now I have them, you have given me a priceless gift."

"You can blame it on Jo, he told me what to buy."

Roy just shook his head, these people were so genuine.

The wedding was held at the farm with a local vicar presiding. Elize had no problem with her bridesmaid dress but El and Dot had to modify their dresses for obvious reasons. Victoria met Tony's parents and William; she was very impressed with William. It was a fine day and everyone was happy. Tony took Victoria and Dot on a drive around the Midlands and Herefordshire and they always seemed to be looking in real estate adverts for farm sales. Victoria soon cottoned on but went along with Tony's ploy. Victoria visited their flat near Portsmouth and quietly told Tony she had money in England to help buy a house. She told him not to tell John. Tony thanked her and said he had a deposit and could easily get a mortgage with his job. Again, there was a lot of looking at real estate adverts and these showed that farms were more expensive than in the Midlands.

Elize stayed for a while and seemed to be taken with a local farmer. He promised to visit Johannesburg in the near-future.

Time passed, and in the space of a couple of months, two baby boys were born. El's father had resigned from his position and bought a house in Bewdley. He had a license to operate as a financial advisor and had members of the band as immediate clients. Other musicians contacted Ted and he had more work than he could handle. He had to take on a secretary and an assistant but still had some time to enjoy the pubs and visit his relatives in Cornwall.

Victoria visited and loved her grandson. She wired back to John to sell the farm. Tony was very pleased and thought she should see London if she could drag herself away from her daughter and grandson. He phoned his brother and asked if he would book Victoria into a good hotel and have someone show her London. William was only too happy as, when Dot visited his local pub, he had acquired some new customers. He would take time off work to show her the sights. The visit to the pub near his office was a hit, with several patrons wanting to know about Rhodesia. When Victoria returned to Portsmouth, she was full of praise for William and said she had to buy a computer. Her biggest surprise was the 'doggy bag'; she was impressed by not wasting food. Dot had not told her mother about the bag and said that was also her biggest surprise.

A large international tobacco company was interested in the farm, and although Victoria was reluctant to sell, John was over the moon. John was happy to get decent salaries for his workers. They were unhappy to see their managers leave but happy with their wages. The big company brought in a manager and John and Victoria showed him the ropes and then they were off to England.

They sold much of their furniture but still had a container-load of possessions. Victoria had tears when they departed but she was keen to see her grandson; John had not yet seen his grandson.

Arriving in Portsmouth, John and Victoria were greeted by a chubby little boy who seemed to love Victoria but was wary of John. Tony took John to see the refinery while the ladies enjoyed playing with the baby. They discussed finances, and again, John offered to buy them a house. Tony explained he was already buying a house in the country and he had a decent mortgage, but if there was a problem, he would ask John for a loan. John was very pleased with that response.

John and Victoria caught up with their container on Roy's farm. They met Elaine and Ted and went to their house. Ted told John it was the best thing he ever did coming back to England. Fairly quickly, John and Victoria found a farm to buy not far from John's birthplace. The house-warming at the new farm was a joyous affair, with everyone living within easy driving distance, even Portsmouth was not far. Roy sent a present, a pig, who he demanded be called Roy.

Elize's farmer friend had visited South Africa and a wedding was in the offing.

Sam the Sweeper

I was working in a small laboratory on the edge of Smethwick and Birmingham. This was a lab involved mainly with stress testing of materials. I was hoping to get into the chemistry lab but was being moved around to get to know the operations of the labs. Actually, I was bored and looking for another job more to my liking. While I was taking measurements of the elongation of heated metal rods, I came across Sam. He was the cleaner, sweeping up the lab and keeping things tidy and safe. I had plenty of time and I gravitated to this likeable fellow. He was a middle-aged man with a small pot belly, but although short of stature, he was obviously well-built. He had a very cheery personality and would often whistle while he swept the floor. We talked regularly as I was not too occupied with my duties. Sam was an interesting character and loved to chat; he had a sort of sing-song voice. Initially, he told stories about his life before the war but the interesting stuff came when he started to talk about the war (World War Two).

Sam's dad died during World War One and he was brought up by his mother. She taught him many things including how to play chess. His mother was an intelligent lady with a good secretarial job. They were not poor but life was a struggle. It was a happy time until his mother took up with a man Sam disliked. They were married, and although Sam could have left home, he had nowhere to go.

Sam was drafted into the army in 1939 and was glad to get away from his stepfather. Somehow, Sam landed up in the intelligence corps. They gave him an ill-fitting uniform and told him to report to the sergeant major on parade. The sergeant looked at him, shook his head and said he must have been drawn out of a hat. Sam could not understand why they had picked him; he had no language skills and only a basic education. Of course, he was only a lowly private making tea for the officers and carrying papers from desk to desk. His unit was located in a very large house surrounded by a barbed wire fence. Sam was not allowed to leave this compound. This house was obviously part of a country estate and Sam did not know exactly where it was. He had not taken any notice when he was driven to his new home.

His major duty was to make tea and deliver it to the officers. His other duty was to deliver memos to the officers. These memos had lots of information about proposed operations and signals from units in the conflict. Sam was seeing all sorts of proposed operations but was not supposed to be looking at them in detail. His tea deliveries gave him plenty of spare time to look at plans he should not have seen. He scanned many documents, calling it Sam's speed reading. Often, he would be chuckling to himself as he read some of the documents.

One of his mates asked him why he was always laughing. He told him he was observing all that was going on and it was like haphazard chess. Of course, his friend did not know chess or understand Sam's joke.

Most of the officers rarely said anything to Sam but one officer would chat. This officer was getting information from Egypt so Sam looked at some atlases in the library. He was surprised how big Egypt was and more surprised with the size of the Sudan to the south. The other surprise was most of the population lived along the Nile and there was a lot of desert. His chatty officer saw him looking at maps of Egypt and realised Sam had been glancing at his memos.

One day, this officer asked Sam for his opinion on some operation. Sam was surprised but looked over the plans. He thought about the operation for a minute and said, don't do it, get out, it is too risky. Sam had been thinking of chess where you needed several plans ahead. The officer laughed and admitted that was his opinion but the higher brass would overrule him. Sam now took an even greater interest in the operation and he was correct, the operation he had looked at was a failure. Sam's friend, Major John, now started to talk to Sam about lots of operations that, technically, Sam should not have known the information about.

Sam was living a good life; he was not fighting and life in the barracks was easy as he was just an office boy. Most of the privates in his barracks had no interest in what was going on; they were just enjoying an easy life and loving the mess. He had a comfortable bed and good food; what more could he want.

One Friday, Major John informed Sam that he was going to Cairo and Sam was to go as his batman. They were leaving the next day and Sam would get no leave. Sam should have his entire gear ready at seven a.m. and to leave no personal belongings as he would not be back. Sam had various thoughts, but mainly, there goes the good life and now for a bit of adventure.

Sam had never been out of England, let alone more than twenty miles from Birmingham. Cairo, what would it be like? was Sam's first thought and then, second, where is the front line? Getting to Cairo in a war was not even in his thoughts. His mates in the bunk house brought him down to earth. He was going by ship into the Mediterranean, passing Gibraltar and there was no shortage of German ships in the Med. Sam started to think that this posting was not looking so good. There was nothing he could do, and then it occurred to him, he could not swim. On Saturday morning, he reported with his gear and was told to get in a lorry heading for Portsmouth. He did not see Major John who obviously had better transport.

Arriving at the dock, he was directed to a destroyer. The ship was large, but he was to find out, not very comfortable. As a batman, Sam had a bunk on lower decks and then realised he was claustrophobic. He tried to spend as much time as he could with Major John, who had a cabin with a porthole. Major John gave him a book on Arabic phrases and would say words in Arabic so Sam could listen to the sounds. Sam was laughing at some of the phrases like, *may I have a cup of tea please* or *where is the urinal*? Sam had a good memory and could imitate sounds.

Thankfully, the voyage was smooth and they reached Cairo without a shot being fired. Landing in Cairo was an experience. It was hot, and although the army was disciplined, everything else was chaos.

Major John was laughing when Sam asked, "What can I do?"

"Nothing, let it all happen, the army will sort it out."

Sam just followed Major John and they were directed to a waiting vehicle. He was lost, he did not know what to do but Major John told him to sit in the back as no British soldier should walk in Cairo. The ride through the streets of Cairo was harrowing as there appeared to be no traffic rules. The Jeep approached a huge building and John said they would be staying there a while and apologised that his batman would be housed in the servants' quarters. Sam just stared at the building which, to him, looked like a palace; where were the servants' quarters?

A man in a turban and a flowing white gown showed Sam to his quarters. Sam was delighted he had a room to himself; the room was sparsely furnished but the bed was OK and there was a shower room with a toilet. He later found that this amenity was shared by six other rooms, but still, he was in a room on his own. There was a mosquito net over the bed and he had to ask Major John about this strange 'thing'. Major John had been in Egypt before the war and that was one of the reasons he was to be stationed in Cairo. He advised Sam to learn a bit more basic Arabic as it would come in useful.

The next few months were a happy time for Sam; Major John did not really need a batman and there was plenty of time for Sam to learn Arabic and move around Cairo. He was a British soldier walking the streets. The phrase book that John had given him was not very useful in the souk but some words such as *amshi* (go away, or words to that effect, were useful). Sam was never sure of the meaning until he learned more colloquial Arabic. He wandered around the souk but bought nothing. He was always aware of John's advice to beware of pickpockets. He talked to lots of stall holders and learned more information than he was giving. To him, it became a game. As he wandered around Cairo, he realised that he could not read the signs. With the help of one of the servants, he started to read and write Arabic. He bought newspapers and magazines and found he had a bit of a gift for learning Arabic. He would often talk to Major John in Arabic and the other officers would frown.

Major John would call on Sam's advice about operations and Sam was learning about the fighting. He was praying that he would not see any. As for the operations, Sam was not too interested in success but more interested in reducing casualties. Major John told Sam he wished the generals had the same attitude. One day, they were pouring over a map, when in walked a general. Sam stiffened and saluted, he wanted to get out, this was uncomfortable.

The general said, "Relax, soldier, I want some advice." Sam was speechless but John prodded him into a reply.

"Well, sir, I think this forward position may be indefensible and I would prefer we retreat to a more stable position. In the meantime, try to get some of our soldiers behind their lines. The retreat is only temporary and we can attack from a better position. I think it is better to attack from a strong position rather than to try to defend a weak one."

"Thank you, soldier, you can leave us now."

Sam was thinking that he was now bound for the front line, as he had told a General to retreat. From the maps he knew where the front line was and it was a fairly short journey.

John had the good news, "You are no longer a batman and you will now liaise with some of the local troops and you are promoted to corporal, a jump of two steps. I told the general you had some natural ability and he agreed. Concentrate on learning Arabic; you will be dealing with Egyptians, Libyans and Sudanese."

Sam now entered a new world; he was a corporal advising all sorts of Arab officers about war and he had no first-hand experience of fighting. The Egyptians wanted to kill Turks, the Libyans wanted to kill Italians and the Sudanese seemed more concerned about winning and surviving. Sam liked the Sudanese and found they were friendly and calm, definitely not as excitable as the Egyptians and the Libyans. One or two of the Egyptian and Libyan officers started to complain about dealing with an ordinary soldier.

Sam gathered them together and said, "I represent the British army and I answer to a major and then to a general, we will all get along better if we forget rank." Sam was telling them to forget rank and using rank to get his point across. After this speech, interactions were smoother.

One Sudanese officer became his friend and they had lots of discussions about the Sudan and Africa. Sam started to realise that the colonisation of Africa had good and bad points. His political views started to put him at odds with his superiors in the British Army. Several officers started to question why a corporal had so much influence; many of them had little or no Arabic and could not relate to the Arab forces. They were under the misapprehension that their Arab allies were getting in the way. Unfortunately, Major John had been transferred to Italy and Sam had no protector. After a while, he was transferred to Jerusalem and sort of sidelined with no specific duties.

He now started to regularly walk around the city. In his wanderings, he came in contact with some Jews and started to learn Hebrew and have some short conversations in Yiddish. He was amazed at his language skills but could imitate sounds and remember vocabulary. He could see potential problems between the Arabs and the Jews. It seemed to be the newly-arrived Jews that were causing the problem. Many Jewish families had lived for several generations in Jerusalem. Sam knew some of these families and he had broken bread with them. He was also learning the dialect of the local Arabs; he had a foot in both camps.

The war was ending and Sam became one of the occupying forces in Palestine. He was still in the Intelligence Corps and privy to many reports of a potential division of Palestine to give the Jews a homeland. Many of the British officers seemed pro-Jewish and very few had little sympathy for the Arabs. In his walks in the city, he started to meet many more Jews than before and learned a bit about Jewish organisations. The formation of the Haganah had Sam worried and then he learnt of the more violent Irgun. British soldiers and police started to be injured and killed. To Sam, it was mainly the ordinary soldiers and police, not the officers, who were being targeted. He decided that he had to speak out, and at one of the meetings, he suggested that the leaders of the Haganah, and particularly the Irgun, should be 'locked up'. In the audience, there was little support and he realised that he was not going to last long in Jerusalem. He had not used the word 'terrorist' but one of the officers advised that locating these terrorists could be dangerous as they were protected by people around them. Sam's reply was that people protecting terrorists were also terrorists.

The meeting ended abruptly and one of the officers came to Sam and sympathised with his cause, but almost to a man, the audience had been against him. Sam frankly told the officer that, when high-ranking officers were killed, the army would take note. Within one week, Sam had orders to return to the UK where he would be demobbed. He visited a few of his friends, both Jewish and Arab, and said it was time for him to go home.

He loved the journey to Cairo but had no time to wish Egypt farewell. The voyage home was fairly long as the ship visited Italy, France and Gibraltar. On landing at Portsmouth, he heard about the explosion in the King David Hotel. He had been in that hotel many times and realised it would be full of top brass. There was no one to tell 'I told you so'.

After he was demobbed, he tried to find a decent job but there seemed to be obstacles at every turn. He had his new ill-fitting suit and was not really welcomed at home. Sam had a lot of knowledge but no one was interested in his Arabic or Middle East experience. He started to think he had been 'blackballed' and so he found a menial job not needing references. He had several jobs and, in 1960 he was sweeping out a large lab and whistling as he worked. In his mind, he was planning how to beat the enemy, with his broom.

In the lab, we were a bunch of young lab assistants ranging in age from about eighteen to twenty-four and enjoying Sam's stories but not believing a word of them. The group agreed to try a few tricks to catch him out but we gave up when he always seemed to have a good answer. Once Sam had started a story, it seemed that you were 'locked in' until the end. Our group all agreed that he told a good story but it was mainly fantasy.

Our scepticism and doubt were to take a jolt. One day, one of the workers tripped and his fall produced a large gash on his arm. This wound would need stitches, and after being patched up by the first aid officer, the manager took Sam and the injured man to the Birmingham Accident Hospital. Sam was instructed to take the man home after release from the hospital.

As they waited for a doctor, Sam called the nurse as his fellow worker was feeling faint; he had lost a fair amount of blood. The nurse put on an oxygen mask, and as she did so, in walked an African doctor. The doctor spoke to the nurse, and immediately, Sam sat upright, he had been half asleep lounging in his chair, now he heard a sound from the past.

Sam looked at the doctor and said, "Sudani?"

"How do you know?"

"Your look and your accent told me you are not Egyptian or Libyan but Sudanese. I hope I am correct as it is a long time since I heard your accent."

All the time, the worker was waiting for his stitches. The nurse gave him an anaesthetic, and while it took effect, Sam engaged the doctor in an Arabic conversation. The doctor was amazed at Sam's language and his knowledge of Cairo and the Sudan. After stitching the patient, the doctor advised that they should wait about an hour before leaving the hospital. The doctor also wanted to meet Sam again to discuss Khartoum. Sam admitted that he had never been to Khartoum but knew a lot about the city. He had talked to Sudanese officers and ordinary

Sudanese troops. He knew a lot about the confluence of the Nile and the good growing soil along the three rivers. The ordinary soldiers had told him about the souk in Omdurman. The doctor said Sam had made him homesick, and if he closed his eyes, he could see his home. Sam had made a new friend from a place he wished to visit.

On returning to work, Sam was in an elated mood, he had just met a Sudanese who would be his friend. Many of us were happy for him as we wondered if he had any friends. The weeks went by and he was the happiest we had ever seen him. He had been to the doctor's flat and met his wife. He had eaten Arab food and enjoyed Egyptian music and learnt a lot about the Independence of Sudan in 1956. He had decided to save and visit Khartoum and that was all he could talk about, no more war stories. We were sceptical whether he would ever get to Khartoum. He told me the doctor came from an influential family from Khartoum and he had a place to stay if ever he got there. I was wishing him luck but wondered whether there were more interesting places to go for a holiday; Paris and Rome, came to mind.

One day, two very well-dressed black gentlemen came to the lab asking for Mr Sam. He was found and they went with him to an unoccupied office. We could all see them having an animated discussion. There were many theories about what was going on but none of our theories was correct. The three men emerged from the office and there were handshakes and hugs all around. We were all trying to watch but trying to hide our nosiness. After the men had left, Sam picked up his broom and started to sweep, he was teasing us.

Finally, someone asked, "What was that all about?"

"My past has caught up with me. Those gentlemen were from the Sudanese Embassy offering me a job in Khartoum. They will pay my way and I can fly out at my convenience. I will be provided with accommodation and a good salary; I have fallen on my feet."

We were all stunned and no one was game to ask any more questions. The next day, Sam gave in his notice and everyone, including the manager, was asking whether he was making a wise decision. His answer was that he had planned to go to Khartoum, and if it did not work out, he would have a free holiday. There were plenty of questions about the job but he either could not, or would not, give any details. We gave him a good sendoff at the Railway pub across the street from the lab and it seemed that the whole lab, including the dinner ladies, was there. Sam thanked the dinner ladies for giving him the best curries he had tasted since Egypt. He thanked us all for coming and gave a short poignant speech that we did not quite understand.

"Make good friends wherever you can, only very good friends will always come to your aid and you should go to theirs."

Sam landed on his feet. Arriving in Khartoum, he was greeted by a smiling old friend. He passed through the VIP lounge of Khartoum Airport without any immigration or customs checks. He was taken to a house that would be his residence which came with a cook, cleaner and gardener; all paid for. Sam was told to keep his employment quiet and not to mingle too much with other expatriates unless they were of interest. He could join the Sudan Club but not to spend too much time drinking there. Otherwise, he was going to enjoy life in Khartoum, which he did.

I left the lab, and later, I went to work for a chemical company. My new job was more interesting and I forgot about Sam. His name never came to my mind until many years later. I had just acquired a job at the University of Khartoum, arriving in Khartoum in 1980. I had sort of remembered that Sam had gone to Khartoum but it did not pass my mind that I might meet him. It was a couple of years later when I found some information about him. I was the Secretary of the Sudan Club and the manager was looking through some old files in the old card system. These old cards had names, addresses and employment details from 1956 when the Club was formed. Almost all the old members had left Sudan or had died. The manager wanted to tidy up the records. Looking through these very interesting cards, I came across Sam. It took me a time to remember my time in the lab but Sam came quickly into my memory. This little bloke had gone to Khartoum many years before.

There was Sam's name, no address, and his employer was the Sudanese Government and the rest of the card was blank. Now I was intrigued, was he still in Khartoum and where did he live? I found one of our oldest members and asked about Sam. The member remembered him as a quiet man (maybe not my Sam) who came to the club infrequently and was always talking to the staff in Arabic (sounds like Sam). This member seemed to think that Sam had retired a couple of years ago and gone back to the UK. Checking the membership, I found that he was not a member after 1978. The head barman knew Sam well and quietly told me he might have worked for the Sudan Security Service. He remembered that, of all the members, Sam was the best Arabic speaker in the club and that included some of the staff. When he came to the club, he did not mingle with many of the members. He had a couple of beers, talked to some of the staff and was gone. He had not seen him for a couple of years but would like to talk to him again.

I was regretting having missed Sam but I did find out more from one of the British embassy employees. Sam came to Khartoum in 1960, his friend was high up in the Security Service. The embassy had kept tabs on Sam and had watched him closely. His sympathy for the Arabs was well-known. Sam's army record, particularly in Jerusalem, was known. His advice to arrest the leaders of Jewish organisations was highlighted in his file. One of the high-ups in the Sudanese Secret Service was the young Sudanese Officer Sam had befriended in Cairo. Sudan in 1960 was in political turmoil and internal security was a priority. Several changes of regime had seemed to leave the security apparatus intact and culls in other parts of the system had not affected this branch. No one knew Sam's role in the service but to survive eighteen years he must have been doing a good job. Sam had obviously served a purpose more important than sweeping a lab.

With all that information, I was enjoying Sam beating all the odds. I now understood the phrase, 'only very good friends will always come to your aid.'

Sam certainly had three good friends: Major John, the Sudanese doctor and the young Sudanese intelligence officer.

Printed in the USA
CPSIA information can be obtained
at www.ICGtesting.com
LVHW050448180823
755275LV00001BA/77